CANDLELIGHT
Supreme

"VERONIQUE, WHAT'S THE MATTER WITH YOU?" PHILIPPE DEMANDED.

How could she admit she was jealous when nothing the slightest bit intimate had passed between them tonight? And how could she *be* jealous, anyway? Philippe was her neighbor, a man she might be doing business with—nothing more.

"Dammit, Veronique, look at me!" She stopped then and turned to him. "I don't know what's gotten into that gorgeous blond head of yours, but I want you to know I consider your behavior utterly unacceptable. Possibly in America it's considered good manners for a guest to walk out on her host without so much as a parting word, but here in France it's an insult!"

"Fine!" Roni snapped back hotly. "Then you would do well not to be my host again in the future!"

CANDLELIGHT SUPREMES

WINDS OF
A SECRET
DESIRE

Deborah Sherwood

A CANDLELIGHT SUPREME

Published by
Dell Publishing Co., Inc.
1 Dag Hammarskjold Plaza
New York, New York 10017

Dell ® TM 681510, Dell Publishing Co., Inc.

Candlelight Supreme is a trademark
of Dell Publishing Co., Inc.

Candlelight Ecstasy Romance®, 1,203,540, is a registered trademark of Dell Publishing Co., Inc., New York, New York.

ISBN: 0-440-19548-9

Printed in the United States of America

October 1986

10 9 8 7 6 5 4 3 2 1

WFH

To Our Readers:

We are pleased and excited by your overwhelmingly positive response to our Candlelight Supremes. Unlike all the other series, the Supremes are filled with more passion, adventure, and intrigue, and are obviously the stories you like best.

In months to come we will continue to publish books by many of your favorite authors as well as the very finest work from new authors of romantic fiction. As always, we are striving to present unique, absorbing love stories —the very best love has to offer.

Breathtaking and unforgettable, Supremes follow in the great romantic tradition you've come to expect *only* from Candlelight Romances.

Your suggestions and comments are always welcome. Please let us hear from you.

Sincerely,

The Editors
Candlelight Romances
1 Dag Hammarskjold Plaza
New York, New York 10017

WINDS OF
A SECRET
DESIRE

CHAPTER ONE

The guard at the heavy iron security gate shook his head as the sleek silver Ferrari shot past him and streaked up the long winding drive leading to the château. The master, he was thinking, was too impatient for his own good. One day he'd lose control of that fine car of his. And of what use would his fortune or his good looks be if he were dead?

But Philippe St. Pierre's hands were sure on the wheel as he maneuvered the car around the sharp curves of the tree-lined drive. His coal black eyes never left the road. Only the taut, grim set of his mouth indicated there was more on his mind than merely getting home in a hurry. He swung the car around the final curve and slammed to a stop in front of the pale gray stone mansion in which St. Pierres had lived for nearly a hundred years. Striding quickly up the front steps on lean, muscular legs, Philippe gave a curt nod to the uniformed maid who had opened the door and marched down the long portrait-lined hallway to the library.

A fire burned cozily in the great brick hearth, since the thick stone walls of the château caused the winter chill to linger even into May. Claude St. Pierre, Philippe's semi-invalid father, was seated in his leather-upholstered wheelchair, a blanket wrapped around his thin, useless legs. The older man looked up from his book as his son crossed the room wordlessly and made for the ornately carved oak bar.

"More trouble?" he asked, watching Philippe slosh some brandy into one of the fine crystal glasses. He didn't like the look in his son's eyes nor the grim set of the strong St. Pierre jaw.

"Damn!" Philippe tossed back the full shot of brandy and planted the glass firmly on the bar. "When is this thing going to *end?*"

"They've got another formula, then?" The older man's voice was controlled, but it was obvious that the heat of fury was rising inside him.

"Not just 'another.' They've got L'Raison. Five years' work down the drain."

"L'Raison. My God." Claude sank back in his chair as if the news had sapped him of all his energy.

Philippe removed a small perfume bottle from the pocket of his gray tweed jacket. It was slim lined—no larger in diameter than an ordinary pencil—and the clear glass was flecked with gold, which caused it to sparkle when hit by the light from Claude's reading lamp. "It's perfect. An exact replica. Except, of course, the glass is of much poorer quality."

He tossed the bottle to his father, who looked at it with weary, pain-filled eyes. "It's in the stores?" the older man asked.

"It will be, within a week. By the time our product gets there, the public will have had their fill of

10

L'Raison. Especially this synthetic garbage!" Philippe sank into the chair opposite his father and sat staring, albeit unseeing, at the dancing flames in the fireplace.

"Have you talked to Jeanne?"

"Of course I've talked to Jeanne. She's as bewildered as we are." He paused. "I'm bringing her here."

"Here?" Claude gave his son a surprised look.

"I'm putting her to work in the factory. The leak has to be coming from here."

"But she's run checks on everyone. All our employees are above suspicion."

"Obviously, not all. There's been a mistake somewhere." He was quiet for a moment, his body slumped in abject despair.

"Stock show any sign of weakening?" asked his father.

Philippe sighed. "Not yet, but I'm going to have a hell of a lot of explaining to do tomorrow." Then, remembering the other thing he had to tell his father, he rose and pulled a letter from the inside pocket of his jacket. "While we're on the subject of disasters, this came today."

Claude took the letter and studied it for a moment. It was handwritten in correct but stilted French. "François's granddaughter," he murmured.

"The last thing I need right now. She's apparently not satisfied with the offer we made her. She's coming to check on the property personally."

"Well, you can hardly blame her for that. She wants to see what she's selling."

"Father, she's staying the whole summer! As if I didn't have enough to deal with."

The older man smiled. "Maybe she'll be pretty." Claude St. Pierre knew well his son's penchant for beautiful women. After all, Philippe was a chip off the old block. And what was wrong with it, anyway? A pretty woman could take a man's mind off his problems for a little while. And right now there were plenty of problems in the lives of the St. Pierre men.

Philippe snorted. "She's a schoolteacher from New Orleans. Undoubtedly some prim old maid who wouldn't know what to do with a man if she had one."

"Well, I imagine you could teach her," Claude replied dryly. Then, more seriously, "I'm sure you'll make the deal in the end. An American woman will have no use for a small plot of land in a provincial place like Grasse."

"I hope you're right. Look, I'm going to get to work. Anything I can do for you before I go?"

"No, thank you, son. I'm perfectly fine. Although . . ."

"Yes?" Philippe took a step toward his father.

"You might pour me a little of that brandy you just downed so enthusiastically."

"Yes, of course. I'm sorry."

Philippe poured out the brandy and handed it to his father. Then he left the library and climbed the massive double staircase to the second floor. His bad spirits were not improved by the sight that met his eyes as he entered his bedroom. A woman was stretched atop the blue brocade bedspread that covered his king-size bed. She was dressed in a chic black jumpsuit, which clung seductively to her well-rounded hips and long, shapely legs. The daringly low V neckline offered a tantalizing glimpse of her firm white breasts, and her tawny hair fell in disarray around her expertly made-up heart-shaped face.

"Ah, Philippe," she cooed as he came through the door, her green eyes surveying him from beneath long black lashes, "you must've gotten an early start this morning."

Philippe narrowed his dark eyes. "No one told me you were here."

His voice was slightly accusing, but the woman merely shot him a pert, mischievous smile. "That's because I wanted to surprise you. The new little maid, Louise, she's not above a little bribe."

Philippe did not smile back. "What are you doing in Grasse? I thought you were in Paris."

"How could you think that, when we're going to Nice this afternoon!" Again the display of charming innocence. "You didn't think I'd change my mind, did you?"

"You're mistaken, Marie-Catherine. *We're* not going to Nice."

She sat up on the bed and eyed him reproachfully. "But of course we are, darling! Your annual stockholders meeting is there tomorrow. Surely, you're not going to miss it!"

"I have no intention of missing it. Which is why

I'm going to Nice alone. It's a business trip, not a social romp."

"Well, you know what they say: 'All work and no play . . .'" She stretched a lovely white arm toward him. "Come here, darling, and I'll show you what I mean."

Philippe did not move. "Marie-Catherine, you've come at the worst possible time. I have a million things on my mind right now. Why don't you be a good girl and go back to Paris, and I'll phone you when I'm free."

"Oh, Philippe"—Marie-Catherine's mouth drew itself into a pretty pout—"you're always busy these days. I never see you anymore."

He softened somewhat. After all, it wasn't Marie-Catherine's fault that his company was in jeopardy. "I know, dear," he admitted, "and I'm sorry. It's just that the business . . . Well, there's been a lot to attend to."

"Poor darling." The young beauty swung her slender legs around and rose from the bed. Moving lithely as a young panther, she went to Philippe and put her arms around his neck, nestling her body close to his. "You look absolutely exhausted. I know just the cure for you." She lifted her face to his, and Philippe instinctively encircled her with his arms and kissed her warm, inviting lips. "Oh, darling," she murmured when his mouth freed hers, "it's been so long. I've missed you so much." Again, their lips met and she pulled him even closer, planting one beautifully manicured hand on the back of his neck.

This time, however, Philippe's response was

14

more restrained. He carefully disengaged himself, putting his hands on Marie-Catherine's shoulders and gently pushing her back so that their bodies were no longer in such disconcerting contact.

"Marie-Catherine, you're making this awfully difficult." He smiled at her then, but it was a disapproving smile, a smile one would use toward a charming but wayward child. "I just told you: I have work to do."

"Oh, pooh. You know very well the business won't collapse because you're away from it for a few days. What are all those employees of yours for, anyway?"

"Employees are paid to do as they're told, and I'm the one who must give the orders."

"Then order them to tend the flowers and stay out of trouble for the rest of the week. I'll wait for you in your car."

Philippe frowned at her, his irritation returning. "You know it's not that simple. You've been around St. Pierre long enough to realize that perfume making is a precise and difficult business. And right now—"

"Oh, all right!" Marie-Catherine stamped a foot in her impatience. "Go do what you have to do. But since you *must* be in Nice tomorrow, there's no reason why we can't go there together tonight." She looked up at him from beneath her thick dark lashes, her expression changing to one of total seduction. "I promise to let you get enough sleep to enable you to be alert at your meeting." Her voice was low, full of unspoken promise.

Philippe sighed. Marie-Catherine in action was

something to be reckoned with. She was obviously not going to give up, and he supposed there was no harm in taking her to Nice. "It's a deal," he finally agreed.

She flew into his arms and gave him an enthusiastic kiss. "Hurry, then, darling, and get your work done so we can leave."

"I'm afraid my work's going to take most of the afternoon. You'll have to find some way to amuse yourself."

"Most of the afternoon? But Philippe—"

"Enough, now," he cut in firmly. "I promise we'll be in Nice in time for dinner."

Marie-Catherine opened her mouth to protest, but realizing she'd gained as much ground as she was likely to get, she said only, "Whatever you say. May we eat at L'Esquinade?"

"Wherever you'd like."

"Lovely, darling. You go do your work, and I'll . . . amuse myself." She flashed him a sparkling smile.

Philippe ruffled her tousled hair as he moved past her and went into his dressing room to change.

Roni Stephens stood on the balcony leading from her room at the Hôtel Plaza and gazed down at the incredibly blue waters of the Mediterranean. She took a deep breath, savoring the feel of the cool, fresh sea air on her face, reveling in the delicious smell of the nearby gardens, which assailed her senses with intoxicating splendor. Imagine being in Nice! When this time yesterday she'd been in

New Orleans, being driven to the airport by her best friend, Darleen Edwards. She'd actually been *afraid* to make this trip; she had even suggested to Darleen that it might be best if she turned the car around and took her back to her little apartment on Carrollton Avenue.

"You chicken!" Darleen had exclaimed, continuing steadfastly toward the airport. "This could be the adventure of your life! Think of Nice! The French Riviera! The restaurants and clubs—and the casino! It's *only* the most romantic city on earth."

"And I'll be there exactly one night," Roni had reminded her, wondering how a city could be romantic when one was traveling alone. "I leave for Grasse the next day." Roni and Darleen had both read about Grasse in a travel guide. Although only a short distance from Nice, the provincial town was nothing like the glamorous Riviera resort. It boasted one luxury hotel, two or three decent restaurants, and no casino whatsoever.

"Yes, but Philippe St. Pierre will be in Grasse!" As always, Darleen was finding still another thing to be excited about. "Think of *him!*"

"Why should I think of him?" Roni had scoffed. "I've never set eyes on the man. In fact, I'd probably be better off if I just let my attorney do business with him by mail."

"And miss the opportunity of meeting him? You're out of your mind!" Darleen had looked away from the road long enough to throw Roni an incredulous stare.

But Roni had not shared her friend's enthusiasm

17

for her great "opportunity." Philippe St. Pierre, heir to the fabulous St. Pierre perfume fortune, was one of the most written-about men in the world. Reputedly devastatingly handsome and a bachelor to boot, he was forever being mentioned in newspaper gossip columns and seemed to make a career of lounging around all the glamor spots of the world, leaving hordes of love-struck actresses and socialites in his wake.

Roni had known rich playboys before. In fact, she'd been married to one, the memory of whom still left her with a dull ache in the area around her heart. Gil Tarleton was the scion of a wealthy Denver mining family, and he was as handsome and charming in his way as Philippe St. Pierre was said to be in his. Gil was blond and cherub-faced instead of dark and intense, wholesomely American instead of gallantly French, but Roni was willing to bet he could match Philippe indulgence for indulgence, conquest for conquest. Since Gil's thrilling entrance and heartbreaking exit from her life, Roni had steered clear of any man who showed the slightest indication of being a bon vivant, so much so, she had occasionally admitted to herself, that she had ruled out every attractive man she met.

"Too bad you're not coming with me," she said to Darleen as her friend pulled up in front of the terminal where a porter was waiting to help her with her bags. "*You* could take a crack at Philippe St. Pierre."

"Oh, how I wish I could! But *my* job doesn't allow for three-month vacations."

18

Roni had boarded the plane, promising to send back lots of letters to Darleen describing not only her daily activities but also her observations regarding the perfume magnate.

But right now Philippe St. Pierre was the last thing on Roni's mind. Just being here filled her with a sense of joy she hadn't experienced in years. From the moment she'd set foot in France, when she'd changed planes in Paris, she'd felt a sense of belonging, the feeling that she was home after years of wandering through the maze of her mixed-up life. But of course that was foolish, she told herself sternly. She'd never even been to France before. The fact that her mother was born here had nothing to do with *her*. She was American born and bred, and although her first tentative attempts at speaking French had met with flattering success, there was no reason on earth why she should feel so completely in accord with this utterly foreign country.

She supposed it must be in her blood somehow; perhaps her grandfather had known that, when he'd made her heiress to the Du Priex land in Grasse. *Heiress!* How delicious that word sounded! Roni knew the land wasn't much—not even a full acre—but the fact that the grandfather she'd never met had bestowed his most treasured possession on her made her feel honored and deeply touched.

She did have occasional twinges of guilt about her plan to sell the property, however. Had her grandfather considered this possibility when he'd named her in his will? He may have expected her to hang on to it and pass it down to her own heirs one day. But Roni wasn't sure there would be any heirs; her one experience with love and marriage had been so miserable that she honestly doubted whether she'd ever be able to commit to a man again. And hanging on to a piece of land thousands of miles from her home seemed too impractical to seriously contemplate, in any case. Her position as art instructor at the exclusive Lockhart School for Girls hardly afforded the luxury of frequent trips to France, trips that would certainly be required of a French landowner. Guilty twinges notwithstanding, she had decided to come to France for one prolonged visit, spend the summer in her grandfather's cottage, and then turn it over to the neighboring St. Pierre perfumery. The plan would not only give her the opportunity to have a unique vacation, but it would also give her a true perspective of the land. Although the St. Pierre offer seemed very generous, she had no real idea what she was selling. So she'd written to the notorious M. St. Pierre and explained in what she hoped was grammatically correct French that she would prefer to discuss his offer after having spent a little time on the property.

Although she was eager to see the land that was bursting with wild flowers and dependably productive fruit trees and the picturesque little cottage her mother had so often described to her, she was glad now that she had decided to stop first in Nice. What she'd seen of the delightful little Riviera city enchanted her—indeed, she could hardly wait to explore the shops and crazily winding streets.

She would have only today since the St. Pierre

stockholders meeting would take up most of to-morrow. Roni laughed aloud when she thought of *that*. Her grandfather had not only made her heir-ess to his property; he'd also left her his shares of St. Pierre stock. It wasn't a great deal, but even her modest holdings entitled her to be present at the stockholders meeting; and as it coincided with her arrival, she had decided to attend. The stock was something she intended to hang on to.

Feeling happy and thoroughly content with her-self, she went back into her room and opened the larger of her suitcases. No sense in doing much unpacking here when I'll be leaving tomorrow, she told herself as she probed under the pile of summer sportswear she had almost exclusively packed. She finally found the powder blue cotton sundress and saw it had endured the rigors of travel with only a minimum of wrinkles. She changed out of her trav-eling clothes quickly, taking only another moment to run a comb through her silky blond hair, which fell just past her almost bare shoulders. In her haste to explore Nice, she only just remembered to grab her room key before tearing out the door.

The concierge at the front desk gave her a friendly smile as she entered the hotel lobby.

"Ah, Mademoiselle Stephens . . . Is there any way in which I may assist you?"

"Perhaps," Roni answered, trying to make her French sound easy and natural. "You could point me in the right direction. I want to do some sight-seeing."

"Sight-seeing! Of course!" The Frenchman nodded eagerly. "There is a great deal to see in our city."

"Yes, and I'm afraid I don't know where to start. I have a limited amount of time."

"Then perhaps a guided tour is the answer." He pulled a sheaf of colorful travel brochures from beneath his desk and spread them, fanlike, before her. "We have several very nice city tours. And a nightclub tour in the evening, which includes a visit to the casino."

"Sounds exciting," Roni replied as she picked up first one brochure and then another. "But I think I should plan today's activities before I think about tonight." In each brochure Nice was depicted as the glamorous playground of the jet set. Full-color photos showed beautiful suntanned women and equally beautiful men lolling on the beach in minuscule bathing suits, elegantly dressed diners in candlelit restaurants, couples in chic sports attire walking hand in hand down a boutique-lined street. "Now I'm even more confused," she confessed with a smile. "They all look so intriguing I don't know which one to take."

If the concierge said something in return, she didn't hear it, for at that moment, another brochure caught her eye. *Immerse yourself in France's most luxurious product,* the copy read. *Visit St. Pierre Industries and see perfume history in the making.* The photograph on the cover page showed miles of rolling hills completely covered with lavender flowers. The glorious color against a cloudless china blue sky was breathtaking, and once again Roni had that inexplicable feeling that the scene was a part of her soul.

"You would like to take the perfume tour?" the concierge asked, seeing her expression. "It is quite wonderful, I assure you. The town of Grasse, where the factory stands, has the distinction of growing the flowers for most of the *parfumeries* in France."

"Yes, I know," Roni murmured as she flipped open the brochure and perused the photos of perfume in the making. This was the company in which she was a stockholder—one of the owners, in a manner of speaking! Her grandfather's home —*her* home now—was situated just next door to the St. Pierre lands, but she wouldn't be arriving there until tomorrow, after the stockholders meeting. How satisfying it would be to attend the meeting with firsthand knowledge of the St. Pierre factory! Nice was only a short drive from Grasse, so she could explore it at another time. "Yes, I think I would like this one," she told the still hovering Frenchman. "Can you sell me a ticket?"

"But of course, mademoiselle. And your timing is perfect. The bus will leave in just fifteen minutes."

Roni was not nearly as knowledgeable about French currency as she was about the language, but she managed to produce the proper number of francs and centimes, and after making a quick retreat to her room to snatch up her sketch pad and pastels, she made her way to the waiting tour bus. Her seat companion for the twenty-six-mile drive to Grasse was a German woman of approximately

23

her own age; but although they exchanged greetings, they did not share a common language, and any real conversation was impossible. So Roni occupied herself by looking out the window, watching the glorious French countryside roll by and listening to the multilingual guide's intermittent spiels.

About half an hour outside Nice the road began to climb. "We are now entering," the guide, an earnest young man of perhaps twenty-two, announced, "the famous foothills of the French Alps, sometimes known as the Maritime Alps. The Alps," he went on, "reach their highest elevation in France, the highest peak being Mont Blanc at fifteen thousand seven hundred seventy-one feet. We, of course, will not be traveling nearly that far. Grasse, our destination, is nestled in the foothills where its fertile soil is protected from the dampness of the sea air."

As the minibus continued its journey the countryside became a riot of exotic vegetation; orange, eucalyptus, lemon, and pink laurel perfumed the air, whereas palms and cacti lent a tropical atmosphere to the scenery. And then, as they crested a hill, the passengers' eyes were dazzled by a blaze of color. On either side, as far as one could see, flowers—bright red with just the merest hint of orange—bloomed. From her position in the bus Roni could not see the bushes on which they grew nor the rows in which they were planted; she was aware only of the certainty that she was entering some sort of earthly paradise.

Paradise. Without warning, a sudden wave of

depression washed over her, filling her with a miserable sinking feeling. *Paradise*. Why did *that* word have to come to mind? Why the one word she had so often wished to eradicate from her memory?

Paradise Island. That was lush and exotic, too, and her first glimpse of it had set her senses spinning because she was seeing it with Gil. Their quiet-but-oh-so-beautiful wedding at her Aunt Gwen's house. The plane ride to Nassau, holding hands and drinking champagne all the way. Their arrival at the Paradise Island Hotel and the luxurious honeymoon suite, which was filled with flowers and promises of candlelit dinners to come . . . The memories hurtled through her mind, each rendering its own special brand of pain and . . . unchecked bitterness. Paradise was a lie, she thought dully. Paradise was supposed to be a tranquil place, a place of beauty, harmony, and thrilling, passionate love. Not . . . She clenched her hands and swallowed back the lump in her throat. Not the way her honeymoon had turned out.

With a determined effort, she forced herself to concentrate on the guide, who had again commenced to speak. "The flowers you see," he was saying, "are tea roses, only one variety of the more than two thousand tons of flowers grown in this area. The tea roses, together with the jasmine and lavender, which bloom in July, will one day be blended into some of the perfumes manufactured by the thirty companies located in and around Grasse."

Including, Roni knew, St. Pierre perfume. The

knowledge that a part of her family had long been associated with this fabulous industry enabled her to regain her interest and determination to learn as much as possible about both the area and the art of perfume making. Here was an adventure more heady than any she could have dreamed of, an adventure that could surely help to dim, if not erase completely, the bitter, unhappy months that preceded it.

"I *will* enjoy myself," she muttered to herself firmly. She would take this experience and make the most of it. She was twenty-six years old, in perfect health, and spending the summer in France and would not let one bad experience haunt her for the rest of her life. But she tried not to think of the fact that she'd made that vow before—and so far, had been unable to keep it.

She was aware of the bus entering huge wrought-iron gates and a guard directing it on, right through the flower fields themselves.

"This is the St. Pierre land," the guide announced to his passengers. "I know you will want to take photographs before we go on to the factory, so we are going to stop here for fifteen minutes. You may wander around as you like, but you must not leave the footpaths nor touch nor pick the flowers."

The bus pulled to a stop and the group rushed out, eager to capture all the splendor on film. Roni had not brought a camera, only a sketch pad, and she silently berated herself since she could not possibly capture the vibrancy of the colors with her pastels. Still, they were all she had, and she bundled them up and hurried from the bus, determined to at least capture the awesomeness of this seemingly unending world of flowers.

She followed one of the footpaths leading upward, pleased that none of the others in the group had chosen this direction. Sketching to her was something so personal she could not bear to attempt it when others were nearby. She had no idea how far she walked before she came to a halt; she knew only that the sight grew lovelier and lovelier as she climbed, the light hitting the tea roses in such a way that they seemed to fuse into a red orange flame. She drew quickly and deftly, choosing the brightest colors from the red orange group to depict the flowers. There were so many of them that clarity in definition was impossible, so she blended them together using different shades of color until her sketch had the feeling of a Monet painting. She was pleasantly aware of the warm sun on her bare shoulders as she worked, of the fact that her hair was being slightly disarranged by a gentle breeze. She could have stayed in this place all day, breathing the intoxicating air, feasting her eyes on this artist's dream of a landscape.

She suddenly remembered that she didn't *have* all day. She looked at her watch and was alarmed to see that some twenty-five minutes had passed since she'd left the bus. With a cry of dismay, she quickly packed up her materials and hurried down the footpath, careful to skirt the rose bushes so that the thorns would not catch at her billowing dress. As she feared, the bus was gone—nowhere to be seen. She knew it had undoubtedly gone on to the factory, but she had no idea where or how far away the factory was. However, the road was there to follow, and there was nothing to do but walk it until she could find either the factory or someone who could give her directions.

She had walked for five minutes or so when she came upon a crossroads. To the right, the tea roses still covered the hills, but to the left she spotted a series of dome-shaped structures that seemed to be made of plexiglass. Although the structures were not nearly large enough to be the St. Pierre perfume factory, there might be someone there who could help her find her way; so she traipsed the short distance and finally entered what was clearly a hothouse. A damp wave of heat washed over her immediately, and her nostrils were assailed with the thick, sweet smell of the flowers. Several men dressed in overalls were working in various areas, inspecting the blooms, pruning the stems, testing the soil.

As she moved on inside, the man nearest her looked up and addressed her angrily. "What are you doing here? Who told you you could come in?"

"I . . . no one." Unprepared for this open hostility, Roni scarcely knew what to say. "You see, I was on the tour—"

"The tour does not stop here. We allow no visitors in this part of the estate." The man's face was an angry scowl. His voice was raised to such a high pitch that the other workers had looked up to see what the trouble was.

"I'm sorry," Roni replied earnestly. "It's just that I'm lost. I got off the bus to—"

"May I be of assistance?" Roni's nervous explanation was interrupted by a second man, a man whose voice was far more reasonable and whose attitude seemed a great deal more accommodating.

She turned to the newcomer and was startled to find herself looking up at a man so striking she forgot for a moment what all the yelling was about. This arresting-looking stranger was tall—much taller than Roni's willowy five feet eight—and was regarding her with the most intense dark eyes she'd ever seen. He looked to be in his midthirties, and he was extraordinarily handsome. But it was not the bold, chiseled features, the jet black, slightly unruly mop of hair, nor the full, sensuous mouth that caused Roni to stare. The man had a certain magnetism about him, an energy that crackled with such frank masculinity Roni felt a little shock begin to travel up her spine. Although he, too, had been working among the flowers, the strong, assured carriage of his broad shoulders and his clear air of authority set him instantly apart from the other workers. "It's all right, Maurice," he told the man who had confronted Roni. "I'll see to this matter."

The workman shrugged and returned his attention to the flowers as the man now in charge took Roni's elbow and gently but firmly ushered her to a spot with a little more privacy. The touch of his hand on her bare skin actually caused her to shiver. "Now," he said, releasing her but standing so near she could feel the heat of his body, "what seems to be the trouble?"

Roni took a deep breath and willed her voice to refrain from quivering when she answered. What on earth was the matter with her, anyway? The effect this total stranger was having on her was absurd! Perhaps, she thought without much conviction, it had to do with being caught in a place where she was so clearly trespassing. "I'm afraid I did something rather foolish," she admitted with an uncertain smile. "I wandered away from the bus to sketch the flowers, and I let it go off without me."

"You're a tourist, then?" the man asked.

Roni realized for the first time that his manner of speaking was quite cultivated. He was clearly well educated as well as attractive. She nodded at him. "I took the bus in Nice. If you could just point out the way to the factory . . ." Her voice drifted off, and she found herself wishing that the eyes that burned into hers weren't quite so black, that his attitude wasn't quite so imposing. She was all too aware of the warm olive complexion of his smooth skin, of the thick black eyebrows that knitted together in a reflective frown, of the faint scar that could be seen trailing down his right temple, ending just above the right cheekbone.

"You're American." He spoke the words matter-of-factly, as if there were no doubt in his mind.

"Yes. I suppose it's obvious from the way I speak." Roni hoped she was at least using the French words correctly; at the moment most of her knowledge of the language seemed to be flying right out of her head.

"On the contrary, you speak our language very well. With only a slight accent."

The compliment gave her slightly more confidence. "Thank you. Both my parents were fluent in it."

"I knew you were American by the way you burst in here. European women respect signs reading Private."

Roni's cheeks flamed. She had been taken in by his attractiveness, and now he was insulting her! Clearly, she thought, furious with herself, it was just one more example of her poor judgment of men. "I didn't see any such sign, and anyway, I need help," she retorted, feeling much more in control of herself. She met his accusing look defiantly. "If you'll be kind enough to point out the way to the factory, I won't trouble you any further." She turned and took a step toward the plexiglass door.

"I thought you were interested in the flowers?"

Was the question meant to mock her? Roni turned back to face him, unsure now of anything. The expression on his face seemed sincere. Perhaps his remark about American women had been made in jest. "I'm very interested. They're . . . exquisite."

"You said you were sketching them. May I see?" The man's glance went to the sketch pad under her arm.

"Oh, I'm afraid it won't interest you much. I only had pastels with me, and—"

"Please. May I see?"

Not knowing what else to do, Roni handed him the pad and waited uncomfortably while he stared at her work, his full mouth pursed thoughtfully, his lustrous dark hair falling waywardly over his high, momentarily furrowed forehead.

"It's very good," he said finally. "Very good, indeed."

"Thank you."

"Perhaps you might like to see some more exotic flowers. Something that might be a little more unusual."

"I'd love to. Only—" Roni broke off, wondering whether this man had the authority to escort her into other areas. He didn't look as if he could be intimidated by anyone, but nevertheless, she didn't want to embarrass herself again.

"Come this way."

He held out a hand, and after only the briefest hesitation, Roni took it with her own. She was all too aware of the warmth and strength of his grasp as he led her through the first of the greenhouses and into a second, this one abloom with a mind-boggling array of precious orchids. The deepness of the colors and the soft, velvetlike texture of the petals succeeded, for the moment at least, in distracting her from the tingling feeling that was inexplicably creeping through her body.

"They're very rare," the man told her, clearly pleased by the look of wonder that shone on her face. "They are what makes St. Pierre the finest perfume in the world. It's all right," he added, seeing her hand reach instinctively toward one of the blooms and then suddenly pull back. "You may touch them."

Gingerly, Roni stroked the luscious petal. Her fingers were butterfly light as she handled the bloom as if it were a piece of delicate porcelain. When she looked up at her guide her eyes were soft, almost misty. "I've never seen anything so beautiful," she murmured.

The man looked at her for a long moment. "Nor," he whispered, so quietly that Roni wasn't positive she was hearing him correctly, "have I."

The look on his face caused her to flush. Her breath suddenly quickened. She thought for an instant that he was going to bend toward her and kiss her. She felt herself straining toward him, wanting to feel the touch of those full, sensuous-looking lips.

But the man didn't kiss her. He simply looked at her for another moment, then shifted his weight and raised his arm in order to look at his watch. "I'm sorry. I'm keeping you from your tour," he apologized.

The spell was broken, and with the sudden return to reality, Roni regained the earlier feeling of annoyance with herself. How could she even think of kissing a complete stranger? Didn't she have any better control over herself than that? Granted, the man was charismatic, magnetic even, but that was hardly a reason for wanting to fall into his arms. Obviously there was a chemistry at work here that she didn't understand, and the best way to deal with it was to get out. Fast. "Yes, I'm sure the guide is furious with me," she said quickly. "If you could just point the way to the factory—"

"I can do better than that. I can drive you there."

"Oh, no, please. I've detained you long enough. I'm sure you want to get back to your work."

"Actually," he replied with a slow, easy smile, "I'm through for the day. I must prepare for a short trip."

"But if—"

"Come with me. It's just a short distance to the factory."

Again he took her hand and led her out of the hothouse. The fresh air was a welcome relief from the heavy scent of the flowers, and Roni inhaled it heartily, her head already feeling clearer, her feeling of intoxication quickly receding.

"You prefer the outdoors?" the Frenchman asked, observing her.

"The hothouse seemed a little . . . close. I don't know how you can stay in there all the time."

He shrugged. "I'm not there *all* the time. Come. Have a seat." He gestured to a motorized gardener's cart. Then, before Roni could react, he lifted her up as if she had no weight at all and placed her in the seat next to the driver's. "Sorry I can't offer more elegant transportation. I left my chariot at home today."

Roni laughed, relieved that the physical tension between them seemed to have abated. "Just make sure you drive carefully," she retorted.

"I always drive carefully. Especially when I'm chauffeuring a beautiful woman."

Thinking it was best to let that remark pass, she turned her attention to the flower-covered hills. "Do you ever get accustomed to all this beauty?" she asked.

"Not really. The flowers change with the seasons, so as soon as one becomes accustomed to, say, tea roses, he wakes up one morning to find jasmine in bloom."

"I envy you. I've never seen anything like this place."

The man's voice seemed to tighten. "Even beauty can have its ugly side."

The cart rumbled to a halt alongside a long, low white-washed building. This, obviously, was the St. Pierre factory.

"I can't tell you how appreciative I am," Roni said, wondering why she should be so disappointed at the shortness of the ride. "I hope I haven't been too much trouble."

"Not at all. It was my pleasure." He got out of the cart and hurried around to help her down. His strong, tanned hands seemed to hold her just a moment longer than necessary.

Again she felt that clutching in her stomach. They stood facing each other, so close that Roni could smell the tangy scent of his after-shave. She wondered fleetingly if it were St. Pierre.

Before either of them could say or do anything else, the front door of the factory building opened and the young tour guide came out. He was clearly agitated and, upon seeing Roni, rushed toward her with a great show of theatrics.

"Mademoiselle! I was coming to look for you! I have just realized you were missing from my tour. How could you wander off like that? I am responsible for everyone in my group."

"I'm sorry. I was sketching and missed the bus."

"If you hadn't turned up, my boss would be very angry with me. I am supposed to keep count at all times."

"It's my fault," Roni's escort broke in. "I'm afraid I detained the lady. There's no need to worry about getting in trouble. No one will have to know."

The guide looked at the other man as if seeing him for the first time. *"You* detained her?" he asked in surprise.

"Yes, and I take full responsibility. You may return to your group confident in the fact that you have done your duty."

The guide looked relieved. *"Mais oui.* I will return. I suggest the lady come, too, if she wants to see perfume in the making." He turned on his heel and hurried back inside.

Roni turned back to her companion, laughing. "Well," she said, "I suppose I'd better do as he says and try to be a model tourist from now on."

"Yes, I suppose you should." The Frenchman took her hand and lifted it to his lips. *"Enchanté,* mademoiselle."

His warm breath on her hand came as a shock. It was so intimate, almost like a prelude to making love. Once again, Roni felt the incredible physical tension between them, but this time she forced herself to break the spell. Deliberately, she pulled her hand away and turned toward the factory. I must be crazy, she told herself, allowing myself to be so affected by a man I don't even know. I'm the one who's sworn off devastatingly handsome men!

She felt the dark eyes on her back as she swung open the factory door and stepped inside. All right, that's enough, she decided sternly. The adventure's over now. It's time to get back to the business of learning about perfume. She hurried to the group standing in front of what looked like hundreds of panes of glass piled on top of one another like dominoes.

"The glass is coated with a highly purified fat," the guide was saying as an old woman deftly stuffed flower petals into the cubbyholes. "The freshly picked flowers are packed between these fat layers and allowed to remain there for a period of about twenty-four hours. The wilted flowers are then removed and replaced by a fresh batch, with the fat always remaining on the glass plates. The process continues during the entire period of the flower harvest. At the end of the harvest, the fat has absorbed almost all the fragranted substance emitted by the flowers and, therefore, is quite saturated with it. The fragrant fat, which is called pomade, is removed from the glass plates with a spatula, and the flower oil is extracted from it with alcohol."

It was all very fascinating, and Roni tried hard to absorb all she was being told. But on the bus returning to Nice the only thing she could remember about St. Pierre Industries was a tall, deeply tanned man with coal black eyes.

CHAPTER TWO

The heavy silver fork clattered onto Marie-Catherine's nearly empty plate. She reached for her wine goblet and took a healthy swallow. "We should have gone to the Négresco. This place is like a tomb." Her green eyes clouded irritably.

Philippe shrugged and offered a small smile. "L'Esquinade was your idea."

"Yes, but I hardly expected it to be so *dull.* Apparently, our crowd has abandoned it."

"Perhaps 'our crowd' is staying in tonight." Philippe signaled to the red-coated waiter, who hurried to the table and poured out the last of the rich ruby-colored cabernet.

"That's ridiculous, darling. We always see someone we know here in Nice." Her eyes brightened and she straightened her shoulders. "The casino! That's where everyone is."

"At this hour?"

"Well, maybe it's a little early. But by the time we finish our wine and—"

"Hold it." Philippe raised a hand to silence her. "We're not going to the casino."

"But of course we are, darling." Marie-Catherine was all smiles now. She shifted in her chair and unconsciously smoothed the thick mass of tawny hair that tumbled to her silken shoulders. "What's Nice without a visit to the casino?"

Philippe looked at her appraisingly. It was amazing how Marie-Catherine could change from a pouting child to a sensuous, seductive woman in a matter of seconds. A pity, he thought dryly, that her wiles were so useless tonight. "I'm sorry," he told her firmly. "I've got to get some sleep tonight."

She blew him a kiss. "There'll be plenty of night left, *cher ami.* Just a couple of turns at chemin de fer—"

"Marie-Catherine, didn't you hear what I just said?"

"But, darling"—her voice was light, cajoling—"surely you can wait another hour."

"And if you run into friends at the tables? I know you, Marie-Catherine. You're a very social animal."

She gave him a hurt look. "I promise to be a good girl and return to the hotel at the very moment you decide to go." Her eyes were wide, innocent.

"Good," Philippe said as if that settled it. "We'll go back now."

"After the casino."

"We are not going to the casino."

"Philippe, really! Sometimes you are impossible! It won't kill you to indulge me a little."

Indulge her a *little!* Philippe chuckled inwardly at that. Marie-Catherine was the kind of woman who expected men to become her devoted slaves.

And as one of France's top models, she was used to having a fuss made over her. But he had told her in Grasse that this was not a pleasure trip, and he had no intention of letting her think she could twist him around her little finger. True, a visit to the casino wouldn't be so terrible, but he'd had a rotten day and all he needed to put a cap on it was a beating at the tables. Furthermore, he was in no mood for noise and crowds. "We'll go next time and stay all night if you wish."

The green eyes hardened. "I intend to go now."

"Don't test me, Marie-Catherine. I'm in no mood for games." The waiter brought the check and Philippe threw some bills on the tray. "I'm going straight back to the hotel."

Marie-Catherine stood up. She tossed her head defiantly. "Oh, so *you're* going to the hotel? Well, I'm not!"

Philippe also rose and fixed her with a cool look. "No? Fine. As you please." He turned in the direction of the door.

"I'm not kidding, Philippe. If you won't take me to the casino, I'll go there by myself."

Philippe made a sardonic little bow. "I wish you a good evening."

"It's not as if I'll spend the night alone. I know a lot of people in Nice."

"As I said, you're a very social animal." He stood aside to let her pass in front of him. Her high skinny heels clicked on the terra-cotta floor. Her hips swung provocatively beneath the white knit miniskirt. Her face, animated by her flashing eyes, was extraordinarily beautiful.

"I won't forget this, Philippe."

Philippe said nothing, and she stalked to the street and climbed into a waiting taxi. She did not look at him again as the taxi moved away. Philippe sighed and turned in the direction of the hotel. He wondered why he wasn't sorrier to see her go. A great many men would gladly give up a few hours' sleep for a woman like Marie-Catherine. Perhaps one day he himself would grow to feel that way. It was a match worthy of notice—that was certain. The glamorous model and the dashing perfume heir had been the favorite subject of the gossip columnists from the first moment they had appeared together in public, at a benefit for the Paris Opera six months ago. Since then their dates had been carefully chronicled, and Philippe had heard that people supposedly "in the know" were placing odds on the chances of their marrying.

Marriage. The suggestion produced a thoughtful frown. He supposed one of these days he should do some serious thinking on the subject. Being considered one of France's most eligible bachelors was interesting, but one could hardly make a career of it. And yet . . .

Nicole. Always it was Nicole who came to mind when he struggled with the idea of taking a wife. Small, dark-haired Nicole with those huge luminous eyes that had gazed at him with a permanent look of adoration. Nicole with her tinkling child's laugh and her small delicate body, as graceful as a dancer's. He could remember everything about her —how she looked, how she moved, how she sounded when she spoke—although she'd been gone for seven years now. Perhaps, he often thought, he remembered too much. It was time to put her out of his mind. God knew he had enough other things to think about right now.

The theft of the St. Pierre perfume formulas and packaging had reached crisis proportions: two counterfeit products were in the stores already, and a third would soon hit the market. Although the counterfeit products were far inferior to the real thing, the public was beginning to pass up the genuine article in favor of the cheaper versions. Philippe dreaded the presentation of the financial report at tomorrow's meeting. The company was doing everything it could to get to the source of the counterfeiting, but so far, even the top-notch detective he'd hired hadn't turned up any names. He ran a hand through his dark hair. If this continued, the future of St. Pierre Industries was in doubt.

He reached the hotel and walked into the cool, quiet lobby. Perhaps he'd go to the bar and have a brandy before going up to bed. His thoughts during his walk from the restaurant had been disturbing. He was almost sorry now he hadn't gone on to the casino. At least it would have been a diversion.

Roni saw him the minute she entered the hotel. He was standing in the lobby, talking to the night concierge. The sight of him made her literally stop short, and a warm flush of pleasure crept rapidly over her body. He was wearing superbly tailored white linen trousers and a white silk tunic top with a deep V neckline through which she could see the top of his deeply tanned chest and several tufts of dark, curling hair. A heavy gold chain on which was mounted a large gold coin dropped from his strong, muscular neck, and she caught a flash of gold at his right wrist as well. A far cry from the simply garbed workman she'd encountered earlier today! And yet he seemed as comfortable in these clothes as he had in his gardening smock. And even more striking, she thought as she admired his strong, chiseled profile and the erect, almost arrogant carriage of his shoulders.

He apparently felt her eyes on him because he suddenly looked up and turned his head in her direction. The dark eyes narrowed as they met her gaze, and then, to her delight, they opened again and the full lips parted in a wide, warm smile.

"Why, hello!" He moved toward her, walking with long easy strides, his hard, muscular thighs outlined as they strained against the fabric of his pants. "What a nice surprise!"

"Yes. Isn't it?" Roni felt suddenly tongue-tied. This man, this complete *stranger,* had been invading her thoughts all evening, but the last thing she expected was to find him standing in the lobby of her hotel. The situation was disconcerting, to say the least.

"You are staying at the Plaza?" he asked, looking at her from beneath long black lashes.

"Yes. Just for tonight. And you?"

"The same." They stared at each other. Roni felt herself begin to blush. Of all the coincidences!

"Your husband. He is waiting for you in your room?"

"Oh, no! I mean . . ." She fought to regain her poise. "I'm not with anyone. I'm traveling alone."

He opened his eyes slightly, as if surprised. "Such a beautiful woman should not be alone in France. Perhaps you will permit me to buy you a drink."

Roni bit her lip. Should she? Although she had met the man earlier today, he was still, technically speaking, a stranger. Perhaps she should use a little caution. She was in a vulnerable position, being in this strange country, so far away from home. And the man definitely had a disturbing effect on her. And yet, he was looking at her in such a friendly way. Surely a drink couldn't hurt. Not if they were in a public bar.

"I promise not to make you drunk," Philippe said as if he could read her thoughts. "Just one drink and then we'll say good night."

"All right. I'd like that." She smiled at him and allowed him to take her arm as he escorted her to the dark hotel bar. Although the room was sparsely populated, he led her to a secluded corner table, pulled out a chair for her, and held it until she was seated. His manners were certainly impeccable.

"What is your pleasure?" he asked as the waiter approached.

"I don't know. A . . . Dubonnet, I guess."

"Dubonnet for the lady; Courvoisier for myself." The waiter nodded and left. The man turned back to Roni. "Forgive me. This is awkward. I don't even know your name."

"Roni. It's a nickname, really, but everyone calls me that."

"Roni." He said the name as if he were testing it, savoring the feel of it on his tongue. "I am Philippe."

Roni gave him a surprised look. *Philippe.* Could this man possibly be . . . ? No, of course not. She chided herself for thinking such a thing, even for an instant. Philippe St. Pierre would not have been working in his own hothouse this afternoon—and he certainly wouldn't be in Nice alone tonight!

He caught her puzzled expression and asked lightly, "What's wrong? Don't you like the name?"

Roni laughed self-consciously. "Of course I do. I was just thinking . . ." She broke off and shook her head. "It's not exactly an uncommon name in France, is it?"

He smiled. "Alas, no. But if you would prefer, I could call myself Alphonse or Gustave."

"Oh, no. Philippe's a lovely name. Let's just stick to that."

"Bon." He shifted in his chair and leaned toward her. "You are really traveling alone? Are you in France on business?"

"Partially. I'm fortunate in that I'm combining business with a summer vacation."

He sighed and leaned back. "You American women. You never fail to amaze me."

She stiffened slightly. She detected the same condescension she'd heard in his voice earlier today. "Why do you say that?" she asked him. The waiter set their drinks before them. She picked up her glass and took a small sip.

"Merely because you are always so much in control. Business combined with pleasure. It is so neat, so convenient, so very American."

"I take it that you don't think much of us, then?"

"On the contrary. I admire you greatly. Indeed, I find you fascinating."

Roni wasn't sure whether he was being serious or simply masking his true feelings. She decided to change the subject. "Do you live here in Nice?" she ventured.

"Oh, no. I, too, am here on business. My home is in Grasse."

"Have you worked at the St. Pierre factory long?"

He drank slowly, deliberately. "You might say I've worked there all my life."

Like my grandfather, Roni thought. She was on the verge of telling him about her family; perhaps he had even known some of the Du Priexs. But then she would have to explain why she was here —to admit that she was going to be spending the summer in Grasse—and at the moment, that didn't seem very wise. She liked this man; indeed, she was very attracted to him. Which could, she suspected, present a problem. The man's magnetism, the chemistry she felt between them, was so strong she wasn't sure she trusted herself to spend a great deal of time with him. He was the kind of man who could be dangerous to her peace of mind. Anyway, she reminded herself, other than his first name and the fact that he worked for St. Pierre, she knew nothing about the guy. He might be married and have six kids! In any case, she had a feeling it could be awkward if he knew she was going to be living so close to him all summer. "What do you do there?" she asked instead. "Besides rescue damsels in distress, I mean?"

He shrugged. "A little of this, a little of that. You might say a little of everything."

"You know a great deal about perfume making, then."

He nodded. "A great deal. Do you like St. Pierre perfume?"

She smiled. "Oh, yes! That is, I used to like it very much. My mother never wore anything else."

He frowned. "But you favor another scent."

"Well, I wouldn't say I favor anything else, exactly. It's just that St. Pierre perfumes are so expensive. It seems so extravagant—"

"But of course it's extravagant! That's what perfume should be. A luxury to make a woman shimmer with delight. To feel special . . . glorious!"

His response was so full of passion that Roni almost laughed aloud. "You're certainly a good ambassador for the product," she teased. "One would think you owned the company!" Again, the idea that he might actually *be* Philippe St. Pierre flashed across her mind—and again she rejected it. The man was simply a loyal employee.

Philippe sat back and lifted his glass. "I'm sorry. I suppose I've been brainwashed." He looked at her still-almost-full glass. "You've hardly touched your drink. Don't you like it?"

"It's not that. I just don't feel like having anything."

"You're uncomfortable with me? Would you like to go to your room?"

"Oh, no! Please don't think that. I'm enjoying your company very much. I guess I just don't like bars much."

He turned to signal the waiter. "Then by all means, let's leave."

"I'm sorry. I hope you don't think I'm rude."

"Not at all." The waiter was serving a round of drinks to another table, so Philippe put some money on the table. "What do you say to a short walk?"

"Yes, I'd like that. The air here is so fresh. I can't seem to get enough of it."

"Have you seen the hotel gardens?" He rose and helped her from her chair. "They are world famous."

"I intended to look at them in the morning. I didn't get a chance today."

"Good. We will go now. I will act as your personal escort." He led her back into the lobby and down a long corridor. His hand was resting lightly on her arm, just above her elbow, but she was as aware of his touch as if he were embracing her.

"You seem very knowledgeable about the hotel," she said, trying to make her voice sound even and nonchalant. "Do you stay here often?"

"Often enough." He held the outside door open for her. "There are many good hotels in Nice, but the Plaza has an old-world charm that appeals to me."

Roni nodded. "I know what you mean. I prefer older buildings, too." She was going to ask him to tell her a little of the Plaza's history, but as she stepped outside she was suddenly rendered totally speechless. The full Mediterranean moon was casting a silvery glow on the most beautiful gardens she had ever seen in her life. Roses of all colors drenched in moonlight climbed over trellises to form a wall of flowers. Mums, carnations, snapdragons, and delphinium burst from the soil in a plethora of scarlet, lavender, and pure white. The air was fragrant with the mingled blossoms, yet it smelled faintly of the sea as well.

"It's lovely, like a cathedral," Roni breathed. It seemed to her that the gardens had an unearthly quality to them, as if she had wandered into an enchanted place. "I don't know why, but I feel like whispering."

Philippe nodded. "The gardens are beautiful in daylight, but at night, they seem to have a life of their own."

"I wish I could capture it on my sketch pad. I'm afraid it would be impossible, though."

"No one's been able to capture it yet, either on paper or film. It's the kind of thing one must capture in his or her heart. It must be felt rather than seen."

Roni looked at him, impressed. What a lovely thing to have said! The man was a poet as well as a potently handsome male. She closed her eyes and took a deep breath, smelling the exotic air. She was so peaceful at this moment, so perfectly content. And then she felt Philippe's lips on hers.

Her first impulse was to pull back, the action was so sudden, so completely unexpected. But his lips felt so cool and gentle that somehow it seemed right that he should kiss her here in this magical place. She relaxed and gave herself up to the moment, savoring the sweetness, the purity of his kiss. But then it changed. It was as if her acquiescence had ignited a fire in him. All at once his mouth pressed hers in an urgent, far more passionate way. His hands, which had been resting lightly on her shoulders, pulled her to him and pinned her against his body; and then as one hand pressed hard against her back the other found its way to her hair, catching the silky strands in strong fingers that clutched and unclutched like the fingers of a drowning man.

For only the briefest instant did Roni struggle against him. But he was so strong, so determined that she realized it was useless. Besides, the feeling that was invading her body made struggle impossible. She found her arms reaching upward, encircling his neck; her hands moved across his back, feeling the rippling muscles of his shoulders under the cool silk of his shirt. She swayed to him, strained against him, her lips parting eagerly to allow entry to his probing tongue. She felt herself swept away in the passion of the moment, mindless, unafraid, unaware of anything except the hot fire rushing through her and the incredible excitement of this stranger's embrace. When at last they broke apart, when he pulled his mouth from hers, she felt her knees weaken, her breath shorten, and a fervent desire to move back to him and lose herself again in the delicious warmth of his body . . .

He didn't pull her back to him. He merely stood looking into her beautiful blue eyes with a rather puzzled expression on his face, as if he were as surprised as she by the flood of ecstasy released by their intimate contact.

"I'm sorry," he murmured. "I didn't mean to . . . take advantage of the moment. But you were so appealing standing there . . ." His voice drifted off, as if he were helpless to explain the depth of the moment.

"It's all right. You don't have to apologize." She stared at the ground, suddenly embarrassed. She felt his hand on her elbow.

"Come. I'll see you to your room." Her eyes darted upward, searching his face. Was he suggesting . . . ?

"To your door only," he amended, reading her confusion. "Reluctantly, I must admit. After all, I am only a man."

He smiled then, a little ironically, she thought, and gently steered her back toward the hotel. Neither of them spoke as they rode the lift to the fourth floor and walked the short distance to her room. She fished her key from her purse, aware that her hand was shaking so badly she was in danger of dropping it. He took it from her without comment and turned it in the lock, stepping back to hold open the door.

She looked at him with an uncertain smile. "Thank you for the drink . . . and the walk."

He nodded. "My pleasure." They stared at each

other for a long moment before he spoke again. "I hope you enjoy your stay in France."

"Thank you. I'm sure I will."

Again that heavy silence. Should she tell him she wasn't leaving the area? That she would be living in Grasse all summer long? Although the idea was appealing, she still held back. He hadn't asked her where she was going; obviously, despite their kiss, he considered their encounter just that —a brief encounter. And if she did tell him—what then? Wouldn't she be letting herself in for exactly the kind of painful experience she was so determined to avoid? Now that he had kissed her, she knew he was capable of tearing down the defenses she had so carefully built up. Better not to tempt fate. And if she should run into him later, well, she would simply have to use more control.

"Good night, Mademoiselle Roni."

"Good night . . . Philippe."

She stepped across the threshold and he released the door. Before she realized it, it had closed behind him, and all that was left was the lingering scent of him. She stood for a moment without moving, her eyes closed, giving herself up to the memory of being in his arms. And then the moment passed and she roused herself and walked to the window to let in the cool air. The sight of the moonlight dancing on the water filled her with a sad longing. Her reaction to the handsome Frenchman was partially the result of the circumstances —a strange, beautiful country; a perfumed, moonlit night; a tall, dark stranger who fitted every girl's

52

childhood fantasies. But the stirrings she had felt within her proved something else, something she had tried to deny for almost two years: she was a woman who needed love.

CHAPTER THREE

The atmosphere in the Grand Ballroom of the Beach Regency was charged with tension and anticipation. Most of the St. Pierre stockholders were men, although a few well-dressed and carefully coiffured women were present in the buzzing, milling crowd.

Last night's unexpected feelings and disturbing reflections on her heretofore carefully hidden needs were forgotten, and a sense of excitement surged through Roni as she pushed her way into the room, her alert ear picking up scattered bits of conversation about "high market shares," "price inflexibility," and "advantageous cost structures." Everyone here had an interest in St. Pierre Industries, the company her mother's family had helped to build! Once again, she felt that swelling of pride in having Du Priex blood in her veins; modest though the family was, they had certainly played an instrumental part in the making of the fabled perfumes.

She had to admit, however, that her pride was not totally responsible for her eagerness this morning. It was at this meeting that she would be seeing Philippe St. Pierre for the first time, and although she thoroughly disapproved of what she knew about his personal life, she was looking forward to observing him presiding over his perfume empire. This stockholders meeting would give her the chance to study him and form a firsthand opinion before launching headlong into the business discussion concerning her property. Furthermore, she laughed inwardly, she would have plenty of time here to memorize every detail of his looks for Darleen. Roni rummaged through her purse for the small notepad she always kept there. Perhaps she could even manage a miniature sketch of him.

A man far too old to be the famous playboy strode to the podium on the stage at the far end of the room and tapped the microphone with the tip of a fingernail. "Will everyone be seated, please?" he commanded briskly. "We're ready to begin."

The aisles were flooded with people heading for the best seats, the first row having been set aside for officers and board members. Roni found herself being carried along by the sea of bodies until she finally managed to squeeze into a row in the middle of the room and plunked herself down between a fat man chewing on a fat cigar and a slim, bespectacled fellow who had already drawn a lined yellow pad from his briefcase and was busily making hurried notes. The man with the glasses paid no attention to her. But the man with the cigar nodded slightly, and she thought she caught a look of curiosity in his heavily lidded brown eyes. Now the man at the microphone was asking the crowd to be quiet, and after making the request several times, he finally established order.

"Good morning, ladies and gentlemen. I am Raoul Moreau, executive vice president of St. Pierre Industries." There was a smattering of scattered applause. "I want to thank all of you for coming today. I know some of you have traveled from relatively great distances, and I know how *dull* it must be for you to find yourselves in Nice." This was greeted by laughter. "I'm afraid," the man added, "our meeting's going to take up most of our day, but I promise to get you out of here in plenty of time to make a killing at the casino." Again the laughter. Now the man became more serious. "Actually, the person who should be here welcoming you is Philippe St. Pierre, but I'm afraid that's not possible." At this, a rumble of alarm ran through the crowd. Raoul Moreau held up his hand to reestablish order. "It's nothing to worry about—I didn't mean to frighten you. M. St. Pierre is very well, but he's been called back to Grasse rather unexpectedly. However, he has promised me he will return just as soon as his business there is concluded, and he should arrive in time for the afternoon session. So if any of you have questions for M. St. Pierre, you may save them until then."

With a twinge of disappointment, Roni slipped her notepad back into her purse. If the business that had called Philippe St. Pierre to Grasse was so urgent it had taken him away from the start of the stockholders meeting, it was entirely possible that he might not return at all.

All in all, she thought the morning session rather boring. Various men took the podium and

56

spoke at length about assets and liabilities, and projections for the coming year and quoted a great many figures that meant nothing to Roni. Now and then a member of the audience would request the floor and comment or question the speaker. Unable to concentrate, Roni retrieved her notepad and amused herself by drawing caricature sketches of the speakers. Once the bespectacled man next to her glanced over and saw what she was doing and gave her a sour look. She was relieved when the lunch break was called.

A buffet meal had been set up in the adjoining room, and everyone in attendance was invited to partake. Roni felt out of place among the obviously successful French businessmen and women who discussed the quality of the French wine being offered as knowledgeably as they had ingested the information about St. Pierre Industries. She nibbled at a delicious *quiche aux champignons* and sipped at the refreshing mineral water she had chosen in place of the wine. When she had finished she wandered back into the Grand Ballroom.

The afternoon session turned out to be more interesting, and she actually began to feel a sense of involvement when the senior vice president of marketing took the podium and began to describe the advertising campaign that would launch L'Raison, the company's newest scent. The lights were dimmed as he lowered a screen on which were projected slides of the new ads. A woman with incredible green eyes and tousled red gold hair—the female seen in all the St. Pierre ads—slouched provocatively against the side of a cream-colored

Rolls Royce. She was wearing a form-fitting black strapless evening gown, a fabulous chinchilla coat thrown casually over her shoulders. A glittering diamond and emerald pendant encircled her long, elegant neck. "L'Raison—*Oui?*" the copy at the bottom read. You didn't doubt that the woman was drenched in it.

Roni frowned as the lights came back up and the spectators politely applauded the presentation. "So you see," the marketing man concluded proudly, "we have once again established the exclusive quality of St. Pierre perfume."

"Excuse me. May I say something?" Without even knowing she was going to do it, Roni was suddenly on her feet, waving a hand in the air. The man at the podium looked over at her in surprise. "Stockholders *are* entitled to comment, are they not?" Roni asked in a loud, clear voice.

"Why, yes. Certainly." The man managed a smile. Some two hundred heads turned to look at Roni.

"The ads are beautiful," she began, red-faced now and thinking perhaps she shouldn't have given in to her sudden impulse. "And they do make L'Raison seem exclusive. But why is that necessary?"

"I beg your pardon, mademoiselle?" The man was frowning now and straining toward her as if he hadn't heard her correctly.

"I just don't understand what the point of all that exclusivity is. Why shouldn't St. Pierre perfume be for everyone?"

"Well, of course it is for everyone," the man replied. "Everyone who can afford it, that is. But the product is known for its snob appeal."

"But why should that be? If you have something that smells good, why should you have to be a snob to wear it?" She was aware of the rumble of laughter that filtered through the ballroom. She knew she should simply sit down. Obviously, no one shared her opinion, and she owned such a small amount of stock that her views couldn't possibly matter anyhow.

Still, the man in charge was trying to be patient. "Do you have a better suggestion, mademoiselle?" he asked.

Roni steeled herself. She had started this discussion. She would be more of a laughingstock if she didn't at least try to get her point across. "I just think the ads should appeal to everyone," she said stolidly. "The idea that L'Raison is only for women who wear fur coats and diamond necklaces is intimidating. Why not depict a more average woman, someone with a fresher, more wholesome look? I'm not an expert on advertising, but I bet it would increase your sales."

The man at the podium was staring at her now in frank irritation. Roni's stomach lurched as she realized she'd definitely gone too far. No one had mentioned anything about lagging sales. Who was she to challenge the methods of an already successful company?

"May I ask the name of the lady who has been so kind as to give us the benefit of her advice?"

The voice, coming from slightly behind her, cut through the room like a sliver of ice. Worse yet, the deep tone, tinged with open sarcasm, was alarmingly familiar. A sick feeling invading her already unstable stomach, Roni turned around. Her suspicion was all too correct. She was facing the man who had held her in his arms last night!

"Your name, mademoiselle?" he repeated as she struggled to catch her breath and regain her sense of balance.

She opened her mouth to speak, then promptly closed it again. Who was *he* to ask a question like that? She straightened her shoulders and met his angry glare. "I think you know the answer to that," she told him boldly. "It seems I'm the one at a disadvantage."

"Monsieur St. Pierre," the man at the podium said, appraising the situation nervously, "if you would like me to—"

"No, Jules," the man Roni now knew was the head of St. Pierre Industries replied tersely, "I will deal with the lady." He turned back to Roni. "I assume you know, mademoiselle, this is a meeting of stockholders. It is closed to the public."

Roni clenched her fists and swallowed hard. True, she hadn't given him her full name last night, but he was implying that she was some sort of incompetent who had wandered in here by mistake. Or . . . did he think she had come here especially to see *him?* The latter thought made her burning face feel even hotter. "I know where I am," she retorted. "I have a perfect right to be here. I am a St. Pierre stockholder."

"Perhaps you should tell us all your name," the

man at the podium suggested. "For the minutes, of course."

Roni lifted her head and looked straight at Philippe. "My name is Veronica Stephens."

She saw the anger in his eyes turn into surprise, then into something she could not decipher. His handsome features arranged themselves into a guarded look, as if he didn't know quite what to say next. After only a moment's hesitation, however, he appeared to take hold of the situation, and his sensuous mouth curled into a derisive smile.

"It's nice to meet you, Ms. Stephens," he said sarcastically. "Do go on with your criticism of us."

Although totally mortified at this point, Roni did not flinch under his demeaning gaze. Just get out of this as gracefully as you can and sit down, she commanded herself. Don't embarrass yourself any further. "I'm finished," she announced. Then in a small voice, she added, "It wasn't criticism—simply a suggestion."

Their eyes locked for a long moment, hers hurt and bewildered, his dark and penetrating. Then Philippe nodded curtly and walked to the stage, and his appearance at the podium was greeted with hearty applause.

Roni stared at him, the shock washing over her in waves. It was incredible. Twice last night she'd come close to asking him if he was the perfume magnate, but she'd dismissed the idea as impossible. Why hadn't he told her? He'd let her believe he was a common workman! Her mind was so full of thoughts it was a moment before she realized she was still standing. Aghast, she plopped down into her seat, feeling her face burning with humiliation. Philippe was speaking to the group now, acting as if the incident with Roni had never happened.

"I'm sorry to have been so late." He smiled, dazzling even the men with his aristocratic good looks and easy, confident attitude. "I'm sure my excellent officers have given you all the facts and figures of our business year. I hope you are all satisfied with the direction St. Pierre Industries is taking."

Again the room resounded with applause. He's so incredibly attractive, Roni was thinking, watching him, mesmerized. She gazed at the strong brown hands resting lightly on the podium. Last night those hands had held her, pressed her against that powerful, taut body. His lips had burned into hers, setting her so aflame that the very memory of it made her squirm. But the remembered desire for him was tempered now with a pain that went deep inside her. He had been playing with her, toying with her, measuring his will against hers. She was obviously nothing special to him. Philippe St. Pierre had enough women in his life to last a lifetime. Fury rose in her once again. Not only toward Philippe but toward herself as well. What had come over her to allow her to become interested in a stranger in the first place? Right on, Roni, she told herself bitterly. You go to Europe and get duped by the first good-looking man you see. No wonder you keep messing up your love life. You haven't even learned from past mistakes.

Philippe glanced at Roni occasionally as he delivered his speech. The looks he gave her were in direct contrast to the light easy manner in which he was addressing the crowd. She forced herself to meet his dark eyes evenly, to hold her head up proudly. Why, she demanded of her fluttering heart, should *she* feel guilty of anything? Still, she could not begin to concentrate on what he was saying. It was a well-presented speech—she was aware of that—and he had the complete attention of his audience. But her mind would not settle down enough to follow the rapid French. All she could hear was that same rich voice saying in far more hushed tones, "But you were so appealing standing there."

After what seemed like an interminable length of time the room exploded with applause. It was over; she could make her escape at last. But before she could move from her seat, a hand shot up and a woman who identified herself as a reporter for a newspaper syndicate requested the floor.

"A question, Monsieur St. Pierre," she said when she had been duly recognized. "Why have you mentioned none of the trouble besieging St. Pierre Industries just now? Isn't it true that your perfumes are being counterfeited and sold in stores far below your own price?"

A surprised rumble went through the audience, and Roni saw a flicker of something close to fear in Philippe's black eyes. But as suddenly as it appeared, it was banished. "I'm sorry I can't deal with your question in detail," he answered evenly, "but I'm not at liberty to discuss the situation at this time. I can only say the problem is being dealt with, and I will make an announcement soon that should satisfy everyone." With that, the meeting was adjourned.

It was several minutes before Roni could work her way out of the ballroom. Most of the crowd seemed reluctant to leave; many were blocking the aisles as they discussed particulars of the meeting with their fellow investors. But at last she reached the door and was in the anteroom when she felt the hard grip on her shoulder.

"I want to talk to you."

Philippe's fingers were pressing into her shoulder; she could almost feel them on her skin beneath the jacket of her navy linen suit. "I have to go. I'm leaving Nice." She met his eyes evenly, and the low-pitched anger in her voice matched his own.

"We have to talk. If you're heading for Grasse, I can give you a lift."

"I have a car outside." She was aware that they were the center of a fairly large group of people, all of whom were trying to get Philippe's attention.

"Then I'll walk you to your car." He gripped her upper arm firmly and led her through the crowd, nodding to various people and begging them to excuse him for a few short minutes.

Not having much choice, Roni allowed herself to be swept down the corridor and through the lobby. But she was becoming more furious by the minute. How dare he take possession of her like this? Outside they were able to feel a little freer, and Philippe loosened his grip and merely guided her to the parking lot where her rented Renault was waiting. "You can stop pushing now," she said when they reached the car. "This is where I get off."

Philippe looked at her and his heavy black eyebrows knitted together in a scowl. "Why did you lie to me? What were you hoping to gain last night?"

"Me?" Roni opened her eyes in new indignation. "Monsieur St. Pierre, you were the one playing the little game."

"Oh? And just how do you figure that?"

"Letting me believe you were a workman at St. Pierre." She mimicked him effectively. " 'I do a little of this and a little of that.' What a joke!"

"It's true. I've worked in every aspect of perfume making during the course of my life. From tending the flowers to blending the fragrances. My father insisted on it."

"Still, you had no right—"

"You talk to *me* about rights?" he interrupted. Why didn't you tell me who *you* were? The old maid schoolteacher from New Orleans planning to summer in my own hometown!"

Roni smiled tightly. "For your information, I am a divorced schoolteacher." Pleased at Philippe's expression of surprise, Roni went on. "I didn't tell you because I thought it might be awkward if you knew I was going to be in Grasse all summer. I didn't know but what you had a wife and six kids."

"Now you're calling me an unfaithful husband." His voice was hard, but there was a glint of amusement in his eyes.

"I'll thank you not to make fun of me." She reached for the handle of the car door.

Philippe snatched at her hand and held it in an almost painful grip. "Just one more question before you go. Did you think that by seducing me you could raise the price for your grandfather's property?"

Fury raged inside her. She'd have slapped him if he hadn't been holding her free hand so firmly. "You can forget about my grandfather's property!" she hissed at him. "I intend to look for another buyer!" Using all her strength, she managed to wrest her hand free and open the door of the car. She got inside and started the engine, slamming the door with the window still rolled up. Philippe stepped back and glared at her. She felt so drained she wasn't sure she was capable of driving, but she mustered up the strength to shift into reverse and eased the car out of its parking place. As she drove from the lot she was aware that Philippe had not moved. She felt his eyes on her long after the hotel was out of sight.

CHAPTER FOUR

She was far calmer by the time she reached Grasse. Looking at the road map and concentrating on maneuvering the curves of the mountainous road from Nice had taken all her attention—there was no time to think of that insufferable Philippe St. Pierre. As she drove through the picturesque little town she strained to remember the direction the tour bus had taken to the St. Pierre estate and was relieved when she spotted the wrought-iron gates through which she had passed just yesterday. Now, of course, she drove on past the estate, searching for the small turn at the end that would lead her to her destination. She was sure she would recognize it when she saw it; her mother had described the entry to the Du Priex cottage innumerable times.

Sure enough, the small road running alongside the end of the St. Pierre property took her up a small hill lined with olive trees, through which she caught her first glimpse of the neat little wood and stone structure that looked like something out of a fairy tale. Dusk was setting in and Roni's heart pounded as the stories of her mother's childhood seemed to come to life before her very eyes. Although old François had been dead three months now, the property was exceedingly well maintained —the grass neatly mowed, the front steps and porch swept clean. Ivy crept up the stone front of the house. The open shutters on the windows were painted a neat brown. The shingled roof boasted two gables, and a chimney rose at one end of the house.

Roni stood on the cobbled sidewalk and drank it all in, taking in the details in giant gulps, her eyes brimming with tears of joy, a smile transfixed on her face. It was exactly the way she had pictured it —only better! Lighthearted as a child, every other thought obliterated, she ran lightly up the steps with the key to the front door in her hand. But as she touched the door it opened slightly.

Wondering why no one had bothered to lock the place after her grandfather's death, Roni let herself in and stood in the small neat parlor with the yellowed lace curtains at the windows. A graceful Victorian sofa with curved legs and back and a sturdy wooden rocking chair were positioned in front of the brick and stone hearth. A table bearing an old-fashioned lamp with a fringed shade stood next to the sofa; an oval hooked rug stretched across the floor. A collection of painted china plates adorned one stuccoed wall, and a collection of pewter mugs stood atop the mantel. There was no fire in the fireplace, of course, but three logs were carefully set, so one would only have to light the crumpled newspaper beneath them to have a crackling fire in minutes. It's wonderful! Roni breathed silently. Nothing could be more perfect.

An aroma wafted to her nose, something delicate and spicy emanating from the kitchen beyond. It was then that Roni realized she had obviously been expected; someone was here and kind enough to have prepared some sort of snack.

"Hello?" she called as she walked through the parlor and adjoining dining room and entered the kitchen with its old-fashioned gas stove, chipped porcelain sink, and reasonably modern refrigerator. But no one was there; her only response was a delicious-sounding sizzle inside the oven.

She had turned to go and try the other rooms when the back door opened and a woman walked in. She was older than Roni—somewhere in her late forties, Roni guessed. Her large, plump body was clad in a faded housedress, and her graying hair was pulled back from her face and covered with a yellow kerchief. She had a ruddy complexion and bright blue eyes that fastened themselves on Roni with lively interest.

"Oh, I didn't hear you drive up. It's Ms. Stephens, isn't it?"

Roni smiled. "Yes. Who are you?"

The woman rested the mop she'd been carrying, on the floor. "I'm Lily Bujold. I looked after this place for your grandfather."

"Oh, of course!" She should have realized a widower would have had help with the house. "How kind of you to prepare it for my arrival."

"Well, M. St. Pierre said you'd be coming along sometime this evening. I took a chance and put a rabbit in the oven, but I was beginning to think I was going to have to take it home and give it to my Albert."

Rabbit. So that was what smelled so good! Still, the mention of "M. St. Pierre" was of the most interest to Roni just now. "M. St. Pierre engaged you to come over here today?"

Lily nodded and smiled broadly. "I'm talking about the young M. St. Pierre, of course. A nice man, that. Very thoughtful."

"When . . . when did he talk to you?"

"Yesterday morning, it was. He said you'd be driving up from Nice and it wouldn't be nice for you to find a lot of cobwebs all over the place. The rabbit was my idea, though. I suspected you might not remember to do your grocery shopping first."

"You were certainly right about that. I hadn't even thought of grocery shopping." She laughed. "I guess I'm not very well organized."

Lily shrugged. "There's a lot of things to think about when you're traveling. Especially when you've come all the way from America." She reached out and flicked on the kitchen light. "You know," she said, her eyes steadfastly on Roni's face, "I can see the resemblance."

"To my grandfather, you mean?"

"No. Your mother. Madeleine."

Roni caught her breath. "You knew my mother?"

"Knew her all her life. We grew up together."

Suddenly it dawned on Roni. "You're *that* Lily! My mother's childhood friend!"

"More than childhood. We were friends till she went off to the Sorbonne. Then after she married

70

your father we lost touch. And your grandfather didn't want to talk about her, more's the pity."

"No. He could never accept her marrying an American." Roni stared at her, incredulous. "But I've heard so much about you! My mother talked about you often. She was full of stories about the scrapes you two used to get into."

Lily grinned. "We were wild ones, all right."

"I hope you'll tell me *your* version of the stories. Oh, Lily, I'm so glad to meet you!" Roni couldn't get over the fact that this totally unfamiliar place seemed so very comfortable.

"Well, I'm glad M. St. Pierre's idea was agreeable to you. Shall I fix you a cup of coffee or tea before I go?"

"Do you have to go so soon?"

"Oh, yes, I'm afraid I do. My Albert'll be wanting his dinner." She laughed. "And now that I can't take him the rabbit . . ."

"You will come back, won't you? Often?"

Lily looked pleased. "Any time at all. We live just down the lane there. Number forty-nine. You can pop over if you need anything."

Roni hugged her impulsively as she started to leave. "Thank you for making my arrival so nice. I feel like it's a homecoming, not a first visit."

The older woman nodded understandingly. "Funny . . . it seems like that to me, too. Well," she went on as she passed into the parlor, "there are soup and crackers in the cupboard. And some eggs and milk and a little cheese in the refrigerator. That ought to tide you over till you can get to the market."

"Oh, yes, I'm sure it will. Thank you so much for your thoughtfulness."

Again the wide, self-effacing grin. "You just save your thanks for M. St. Pierre. He deserves most of the credit. Oh, by the way," she said, turning back, "I took the liberty of putting your grandfather's clothes in his old trunk. Thought you'd want the closet for your own things. I didn't touch his desk, though, except to dust a little. Might be some papers there you want to look at."

"Yes. I'll check. Thank you again." Roni waved from the window as the woman made her way down the lane.

Alone, she decided to explore the rest of the cottage. A door from the parlor led to a back room that she decided her grandfather must have used as his bedroom. Probably, she surmised, he hadn't wanted to go up and down the stairs often in the final months of his life. The room was simple to the point of being austere. In addition to the single bed, which was covered with a quilted comforter, it held a sturdy wooden chest of drawers and a hard-backed chair. Atop the chest of drawers stood a framed photograph of a lovely young woman dressed in a loose-fitting dress with a sash tied around her slender waist. Roni had seen other photographs of the same woman. She was her grandmother, old François's beloved wife who had died before her daughter's "disreputable" marriage.

Behind the bedroom was what was obviously an addition to the original cottage. It was a reasonably modern bathroom with a large tub on brass feet and a simple, functional sink. Upstairs, there were two more rooms. The largest had obviously been used at one time as a master bedroom and was dominated by a big old four-poster bed. Blue ruffled curtains hung at the windows, while a worn Turkey carpet covered most of the hardwood floor. The other room, which was much smaller, had apparently been her grandfather's study. An old-fashioned rolltop desk stood against one wall, and the other walls were lined with bookcases. Although the books that filled the shelves were written in French, Roni surveyed them eagerly. No need to worry about long summer nights with so much to keep her occupied!

She chose the room with the four-poster bed as her own, and after making several trips to the car to bring in all her belongings, she unpacked and hung her clothes in the clean-smelling closet. She had brought along a small framed photograph of her parents, which she now placed atop the graceful carved bureau that stood next to one of the gabled windows. Amazing how that one small touch lent her own personality to the place.

It was completely dark outside now, and when she became aware of the hunger pains gnawing in her stomach Roni remembered she'd had very little to eat all day. She changed into her favorite old jeans and shirt and went back downstairs. Humming a little French song her mother had taught her as a child, she took the aromatic rabbit out of the oven and fixed herself a tray to be taken into the parlor. Although the evening was not really cold, she decided she would be justified in lighting the fire, and she settled down to eat, basking in its cheery glow. In addition to the food Lily had told her about, she found a loaf of crusty French bread and a pot of sweet homemade butter. Never had a meal tasted so delicious to her!

She had devoured everything on her plate and was on her way back to the kitchen to put water on for tea when she heard a knock at the front door. Thinking it was Lily come back to see how she was doing, she threw open the door and smiled exuberantly into the night.

"Oh, I've had the most wonderful dinner—" But her breathless exclamation came to a sudden halt when she realized her visitor was not her mother's childhood friend but her impossible next-door neighbor, Philippe St. Pierre.

He was leaning casually on one leg, his right hip thrust out, which gave him the appearance of swaggering, though he was standing perfectly still. He, too, was wearing jeans, but his were of the designer variety and so form-fitting she could see every line of his lower body from his slim, tight hips to his powerful thighs to his rounded, obviously muscular calves. A velour sweater of a brilliant blue covered the upper part of his body, the color providing an interesting contrast to his deeply tanned face and ebony eyes.

When Roni broke off in midsentence, he smiled and held up a bottle of wine. "I forgot to give this to Lily. I hope I'm not too late."

"That," Roni retorted suspiciously, "depends on what you mean by 'too late.' "

"I meant you to have this with your dinner. It's an excellent cabernet."

Roni did not move from where she stood in the middle of the doorway. "I've had my dinner."

"Perhaps it would be a pleasant after-dinner drink, then. If you'll let me in, I'll be happy to open it for you."

Roni frowned at him, but she was aware of a tightening in her chest. Steady, she admonished herself. Don't let this sudden burst of charm fool you. You saw the real Philippe St. Pierre this afternoon, and the less you see of him in the future, the better off you'll be. What was he up to now? she wondered. Had he come to insult her again? Or, worse, to try to dupe her in some new way? "Monsieur St. Pierre—"

"Philippe," he corrected.

She sighed. "All right . . . Philippe. I don't know what you're trying to accomplish, but I'm not in the mood for wine tonight. And if I were, I assure you I'm capable of opening the bottle."

He smiled at her. "I'm just trying to be neighborly, that's all. I wanted to make sure you were settling in all right."

"Thank you." She had no intention of allowing herself to be moved by this unexpected maneuver. Still, she realized she'd be ungracious if she didn't acknowledge his thoughtfulness in engaging Lily to prepare the cottage for her arrival. Stiffly, and still unsmiling, she stepped aside and allowed him to enter the parlor. "Lily told me what you did. I appreciate that."

His black eyes twinkled. "My, how formal! You

75

certainly aren't anything like the woman I walked in the gardens with last night."

Her face flamed red. "I'd rather forget about that, if you don't mind."

"Why? Was it so terrible?"

Her nostrils were assailed by his tangy aftershave, and the smell brought the memory of last night returning with such power that she felt weak throughout her body. Even now, when she was furious and mistrustful, she felt his pull as if he were a magnet drawing her to him. She forced herself to remain rigidly erect. "Last night was a farce," she said acidly, "built, if not on lies, then on certainly pertinent omissions."

"Last night was a misunderstanding." He strode to the fireplace and turned back to face her. "As was this afternoon."

"Oh?" The sight of him standing there in front of the fireplace—*her* fireplace—was incredible. He was Philippe St. Pierre, rich, spoiled playboy heir to a fabulous French dynasty, but he seemed to belong here in this simple country cottage.

"I embarrassed you at the meeting. I'm sorry. It's just that I was so surprised—"

"Humiliated me is a more accurate description," she interrupted, the reminder of the stockholders meeting making her even more uncomfortable than his reference to last night. "You acted as if I were a bug you wanted to step on."

He looked as if he'd been slapped. "I was trying," he said indignantly, "to find out who you were."

They stared at each other for a moment, each

certain that they alone had the right to be offended.

"You could have asked me a little more politely," Roni reproached.

"And you could have answered me without making me drag it out of you," he retorted. "After all, I had every right—"

"And *I* had every right!" Roni shouted. The sound of her voice ringing through the cottage caused her to stop and compose herself. "Anyway, your insults weren't confined to the meeting," she said more quietly.

He stood perfectly still. The scar at his temple pulsed steadily. "You're referring to what I said in the parking lot."

"You accused me of trying to seduce you," Roni reminded him. The pain of that insult came rushing back, and she suddenly found she had to fight back tears burning behind her eyes.

Philippe heaved a heavy sigh. "I don't know why I said that," he admitted. "I knew it wasn't true. It was just that I'd had such a rotten morning, what with my father's illness and the counterfeiting—"

"I beg your pardon?" Roni frowned. "Your father's ill?"

Philippe nodded. "That's why I was late for the meeting. He had a stroke last night. I received the phone call shortly after I left you, and I immediately returned to Grasse. It was his second stroke in two years. Needless to say, I was very worried."

Roni was stunned. He'd been so composed earlier this afternoon and all the while he'd had this terrible thing on his mind. "How . . . how is he now?"

"Better, thank you. Fortunately, it wasn't too bad, and he's not expected to be much worse off than he was before."

"I'm so sorry," Roni murmured. "I had no idea."

"I didn't want to mention it at the meeting. A lot of the stockholders still prefer to think my father takes an active part in the business, and with the current trouble, I didn't want to alarm them more than was necessary."

"I remember the question of counterfeiting coming up at the meeting," Roni mused thoughtfully.

Philippe nodded. "Someone is stealing the formulas for our new scents and reproducing them synthetically. Of course they're not the same as the genuine articles, but they've also got hold of the packaging plans, so they *look* the same and they're half the price and selling like crazy." He stopped and gave her a wry look. "This whole fiasco has reduced our snob appeal somewhat."

A glimmer of a smile found its way to the corners of Roni's mouth. "Touché," she said with equal irony.

Their eyes locked. The tension had lessened, but the electricity between them seemed more charged than ever. It was Philippe who finally broke the silence.

"I can see I have met my match," he declared, seemingly impressed. He moved toward her and put his hands squarely on her shoulders. "Look, what do you say we start out fresh? Why don't we forget about last night and this afternoon and pretend we're meeting right now for the first time?"

She opened her mouth to answer, then realized she didn't know what to say. The look he was giving her seemed sincere, and when he'd spoken of his father's illness he'd seemed so miserable she'd wanted to put her arms around him and hold him. But she couldn't forget the game he'd played with her last night nor that flash of temper he'd displayed only a few hours ago. Philippe St. Pierre was obviously a man of many moods, a mercurial personality who could change in the wink of an eye. Exactly the kind of man Gil was. If she hadn't had the experience of her ex-husband to draw on, perhaps she wouldn't be so wary. But, looking up at Philippe, she knew that she must be on her guard. If she let it slip, even for an instant, she could get lost in the inky depths of those great black eyes.

"Well," he demanded when she continued to remain silent, "aren't you going to give me an answer?"

"I'm sorry. It's just that . . . I don't think it's possible. How can we pretend we haven't met?"

His smile disarmed her. "Easy." He stepped back and offered a low, sweeping bow. "Mademoiselle Stephens? I am Philippe St. Pierre. It is delightful to make your acquaintance. Did you have a pleasant trip from America? I'm so sorry my business made it impossible for me to meet you at the airport."

Roni laughed in spite of herself.

"Do you agree?" Philippe asked. "Can we pretend we have only just met?"

Unable to resist his charm, she gave him a teasing frown. "Does that mean I have to go back to calling you M. St. Pierre?"

He didn't smile. Rather, he fixed her with a look so serious and probing that it seemed almost hypnotic. She could not take her eyes from his, and a little thrill shot through her body. "Not if you join me in a glass of wine, Veronique." He pronounced her name the French way. Suddenly it seemed like the most beautiful name in the world.

She followed him to the kitchen where he found two wine glasses and a corkscrew. Then they took the bottle and the glasses back to the parlor and sat down, Philippe on the old-fashioned sofa, Roni in her grandfather's rocking chair.

"To new friends," Philippe said as he held up his glass. They both drank. "Now," he said, dismissing the toasting, "what do you think of Grasse?"

Roni's eyes grew soft. "I think it may be the most beautiful place on earth."

Philippe nodded. "One of them, certainly. I'm surprised you've never been here before, though. With your mother's being French."

"I'm afraid that's rather a sad situation. When my mother married my father, my grandfather Du Priex didn't approve. He was furious that she'd married a foreigner."

Philippe smiled understandingly. "We French can be pretty chauvinistic at times. You are going to find that out, if you haven't already."

"My grandfather must have been more chauvinistic than most. I can't believe a man would so completely wash his hands of his own daughter. His only child."

"I don't imagine he was proud of the fact. But from what I knew of François, he could be a stubborn old fellow. Once he took a stand, he'd rather die than change his mind."

Roni sighed and sipped her wine. "All those years when they could have been close, visiting back and forth. My mother never stopped writing to him. He never answered even one letter, but she kept writing till the day she died."

Philippe regarded her sympathetically. "How did she die?" he ventured gently. "Or is it too difficult to discuss?"

Roni shook her head. "I've finally come to terms with it. It was two years ago. My father was head of the Foreign Language Department at a college in New Orleans. He and Mother were going to a football game in a town about two hundred miles away, and a friend offered to fly them in his private plane. On the way home the weather turned bad and the plane went down. There were no survivors."

"I'm sorry."

"Naturally, my grandfather was informed, and he wrote to me, inviting me to come and live with him. Obviously, his anti-American feelings didn't extend to his granddaughter."

"Or perhaps once your mother was gone he realized how foolish he'd been."

"Perhaps," Roni agreed. She held her glass as he

refilled it with the deep red wine. She was beginning to feel quite mellow.

"But you didn't accept his invitation."

"No. I got married instead." She was aware of the curious look he gave her. It was the same look she'd seen on his face when she'd told him earlier that she was a divorcée, not an old maid. "My marriage," she added a little tightly, "lasted about six months."

"Care to talk about it?"

"Not really." She would like, she thought to herself, to forget it ever happened. That, she knew, would be the most sensible thing. After all, six months wasn't so very long in a person's lifetime. But those particular six months were etched on her heart, and the scars they left still showed no sign of healing. For a woman who'd been known for her level head and good solid judgment to have made such a colossal mistake was unforgivable. And unforgettable.

"Well, then," Philippe's voice took on a brighter note, "suppose we make some plans."

"What kind of plans?"

"For your summer vacation. You weren't planning to just spend a quiet time at the cottage, were you?"

She grinned. "As a matter of fact, I was."

"Well, I won't allow it. Grasse may be provincial, but there's plenty to do. Picnics and swimming and drives to the outlying countryside. And there are people to meet and occasionally a dance for which the whole town turns out."

"Sounds like fun."

"It is fun. And since you need a guide, I hereby appoint myself. What are you doing tomorrow?"

"Tomorrow? Why, I don't know. I hadn't thought about it."

He frowned. "Unfortunately, I'm going to be tied up all day. Between the business and visiting my father at the hospital . . ."

"You don't have to apologize. I know you're a busy man. I'll keep myself occupied. I'll take a walk and stock up on the things I'll need while I'm here. I may even settle down with one of the books in my grandfather's study."

His eyes met hers. "A very sensible plan. I'll come by about six to fetch you for dinner."

"Dinner?"

"Nothing fancy, mind you. Just a quiet dinner at home. How does that strike you?"

How did it strike her? It struck her as presumptuous and just a bit arrogant. I'll fetch you at six for dinner. No "Would you like to have dinner?" or "May I take you to dinner?" He had simply taken it for granted that she would jump at the chance to spend an evening with him. And at his home! Of course, he had asked how it struck her; that, at least, was a token deference to her own wishes. And Château St. Pierre was said to be one of the great showplaces of France. Imagine how impressed her friends in New Orleans would be when she told them she'd actually dined there! Why, Darleen would never let her hear the end of it if she turned down such a chance. "That . . . would be very nice," she heard herself answer. It was the prospect of seeing the château that was making her tingle, she assured herself—not the fact that she would be alone there with Philippe St. Pierre.

Philippe put his glass down and stood up. "It's settled then. Tomorrow at six."

Roni smiled and he took her hand and put it to his lips as he had done yesterday when he'd left her outside the factory.

"Enchanté, mademoiselle."

She blushed. What was the appropriate answer to that?

Apparently, one was not needed. He looked at her for a long moment, still holding her hand. Then he released her and strode to the door. She could feel his masculine presence in the room long after he had departed for home.

CHAPTER FIVE

Philippe's first order of business the following day was to visit his father at the hospital. To his immense relief, Claude St. Pierre had been taken out of intensive care, and although he looked pale and fragile in the heavy old hospital bed, he was completely alert and able to carry on a normal conversation. He listened thoughtfully as Philippe told him that the stockholders meeting had gone well and that the one mention of the perfume theft had been quickly nipped in the bud.

"Jeanne is going to begin work in the lab today," Philippe added. "Thank God for her training as a chemist!"

Claude nodded but didn't comment. "What about the other matter?" he asked after a moment.

"What other matter?"

"The American girl. François Du Priex's granddaughter. Has she arrived in Grasse?"

A smile sprang to Philippe's lips. "Yes, indeed. I welcomed her personally last evening."

Claude squinted at him. He had seen that look on his son's face before. "I take it she's not exactly an unpleasant person."

Philippe laughed, remembering the greeting she

had given him when he arrived at the cottage. "She can be managed," he replied with a wink, then added more seriously, "actually, she's quite nice. I'm sure the sale will go through smoothly."

The old man raised an eyebrow. "And you'll have a good time closing it, eh?"

"Could be. We'll have to wait and see about that one."

Claude sank back onto his pillows. "Well, everything seems to be under control at the moment."

"Don't you worry about anything, Father. I'll take care of all the problems. You just concentrate on getting well."

His face wore a dry smile. "You're not going to get rid of me this soon. I still have a few good years ahead of me."

"Good. I'll hold you to that." Philippe leaned over and kissed his father's forehead. "I've got to get to work. You get some sleep."

"Sleep! That's all I've done for the past twenty-four hours." Still, he looked extremely weary, and Philippe knew he was simply too proud to admit the toll this new attack had taken on him.

"I'll stop by to see you later this afternoon. I'll play you a game of cribbage if you're up to it."

"Oh, I'll be up to it. I can beat you at cribbage in or out of a hospital bed."

On his way back to the château, Philippe thought about the questions his father had asked about Veronica Stephens. He had assured Claude that the sale of the Du Priex property would go smoothly, but in fact he was having doubts. Once they had agreed to forget about that dreadful confrontation at the Beach Regency, Roni had seemed quite reasonable. Pliable, even. But he had glimpsed a bit of a fighter in her earlier in the day, and he knew better than to assume it would be smooth sailing from here on in. He wished he could close the deal right away and not take the chance of a change of mood during the course of the summer, but he wasn't sure she could be hurried. Perhaps he could probe a little more deeply into her pretty head when she came for dinner tonight.

In a way, he was sorry Du Priex's granddaughter had turned out to be so attractive. He would much rather do business with a woman in whom he could not possibly have a personal interest. As it was, he was going to have to walk a fine line. He certainly didn't want to tie a personal relationship to a business deal, and yet he didn't want to ignore her simply because he wanted to acquire her property. He realized now that she really hadn't known who he was at their first two meetings, and he could cut his tongue out for having accused her of trying to seduce him for her own personal gain. Well, he would make that up to her if she hadn't already forgiven him, and he would proceed cautiously from now on.

Jeanne Van de Maele was waiting for him in the library when he arrived at the château. In total contrast to her usual ultrachic attire, she was wearing a starched white uniform and sturdy rubber-soled oxfords. Her face was completely devoid of makeup, and her lustrous black hair was pulled back from her face and twisted into a neat bun at the base of her neck. Still, her extraordinary beauty could not be dimmed; her perfect features were all the more arresting in her fully exposed face. Her creamy skin was flawless and startlingly white against the midnight black of her hair. Her lips were full and naturally pink, and her dainty nose tilted upward ever so slightly. Her eyes were huge, the color of hothouse violets, heavily fringed by natural black lashes.

What, Philippe wondered for perhaps the hundredth time since he'd met her, had possessed this incredibly beautiful woman to become a private detective? He'd heard the story of how Jeanne's father, a renowned Belgian scientist working out of the International Institute of Brussels, had been kidnapped several years ago by Russian terrorists who wanted an important formula he had recently perfected. But Van de Maele refused to give them the information, and they killed him, a tragedy that changed Jeanne's entire life. Having just graduated from the university at Ghent, she abruptly dropped her plans to become a chemist and went into law enforcement work. The terrorists who killed her father were never found, but Jeanne became an expert policewoman and detective and now operated her own agency in Brussels. Although her fee was exorbitant, she had been highly recommended to Philippe, who stood to lose millions of dollars if the counterfeiting ring stealing his formulas weren't stopped. So far, she had been in his employ one month, and although she hadn't identified the thieves, she seemed to be closing in on someone.

Philippe's father had been dubious about the hiring of Jeanne the first time he'd seen her. In his opinion she was entirely too good-looking to be a proper detective, and he suspected his son of being swayed more by her attractiveness than by her ability. But Philippe had done a thorough investigation of the woman, and her credentials—and track record—were dazzlingly impressive. As for her beauty, Philippe hoped it would cause others in the company to jump to the conclusion that her appearance was the primary reason for her being hired. If she didn't look like a chemist, she certainly wouldn't be spotted as a detective.

Jeanne was sitting in one of the burgundy leather chairs, her shapely legs crossed beneath her starched white skirt, a book about perfumery resting on her lap as Philippe entered the library.

"Sorry to have kept you waiting," he said by way of greeting. "I was at the hospital longer than I expected."

"Your father is improving, I hope?" The extraordinary violet eyes met his.

"Yes, thank you. He's much improved today." Philippe gestured toward her book. "Learning anything from that?"

She did not smile. "There's something to be learned from everything."

Philippe nodded. Her abrupt businesslike attitude made him slightly uncomfortable. "Well, suppose I take you down and introduce you to Alain."

"Fine." She rose and smoothed her skirt with her hands. He noticed she was not wearing nail polish and her nails were cut short—the hands of a working woman.

To save time, they took his car the short distance to the factory. As he led her through the processing room, he was aware of the eyes that followed them. He could almost hear his employees' thoughts: "There goes the young heir and another of his fortune-hunting women."

Alain Dumont was seated behind a row of test tubes, staring at the liquid in each. He was a relatively young man, in his early thirties, but his heavy black beard made him look older. Like a big black bear, Philippe often thought. He looked up as Philippe and Jeanne entered, his bright blue eyes shifting warily from one to the other.

"Hello, Alain. Finding anything exciting in those test tubes?"

The man shook his head and sighed. "Exciting, maybe—but not new."

Philippe turned to Jeanne. "Alain's in the process of trying to develop a new scent for fall marketing. Something lighter than our other scents. Younger, perhaps. Fresher." Jeanne nodded and Philippe addressed the chemist. "Alain, this is Jeanne Van de Maele. I believe I told you I was planning to get someone to help you out." Actually, there were some twenty chemists employed by St. Pierre Industries, but Alain was the top man and he constantly complained of not having competent help.

"I'm pleased to meet you," he said to Jeanne. "Have you worked in perfume before?"

Jeanne met his eyes evenly. "I worked at Worth in Paris."

Alain's eyebrows went up. "Well, then, you have the groundwork. Welcome aboard."

"If you have any problems or questions, feel free to come to me," Philippe told Jeanne. "In the meantime, I'll leave you in Alain's very capable hands."

"Thank you." Jeanne looked at him and smiled.

Philippe wondered how she could possibly pull off such a subterfuge, but he was willing to bet she could do it if anyone could. He gave her a confident look and left her to begin her work.

Roni spent the day settling into the cottage. Lily had come by to check on her first thing in the morning and had told her about an open-air market within walking distance where she could stock up on provisions.

So after breakfasting on scrambled eggs and toasted French bread, she started off on foot, enjoying every minute of her stroll through the fragrant French countryside. When she got to the market, there were so many delicious-looking foods that she wished she'd brought her car, but she had to be content with buying only what she could carry. Her purchases included three fresh oranges, a good-sized country ham, vegetables of all sorts, and a pound of sugar cookies purchased from a woman who said she'd made them herself.

When she got back to the cottage she put the food away and wandered through the rooms, looking for something that needed to be done. Since

Lily had been in just yesterday, there was not a speck of dust anywhere, so she decided to see if any of the drawers needed tidying in her grandfather's study.

As she sat at François's desk she could almost feel the old man's presence. He must have sat here to go over his accounts and perhaps write reminders to himself about work that needed to be done around the cottage. The first drawer was empty, and in the second drawer, she found a ledger, with her grandfather's income and expenses neatly accounted for.

It was in the third drawer, the deep bottom drawer on the right side of the desk, that she found the letters. They were bound in bunches, some attached with rubber bands, others with pieces of faded ribbon. Roni carefully slipped out one of the folded sheets on the top of a pile and looked curiously at the first line. "My darling papa . . ." The letters were from her mother. A rush of pure joy flooded through Roni, and yet she felt as if she wanted to cry. Here were all the letters her mother had written that had never been acknowledged! He must have kept them all, for there appeared to be more than a hundred of them. The stubborn old man who had disowned his daughter had a heart after all.

Roni wondered if reading another person's letters when both parties were dead would be considered an invasion of privacy. Surely not, when the writer was one's own mother and the receiver one's grandfather. One day soon, she decided, she would sort them out chronologically and settle down for what would undoubtedly be an emotional reading session. For now, though, she carefully put them back in the drawer. The only drawer she hadn't opened, the narrow one stretched across the length of the desk, she found locked. She searched in the cubbyholes on top for the key, but it was nowhere to be found. If it didn't turn up, she would have to break the lock, but for the moment, she would leave things as they were.

Lunch consisted of a delicious salad she concocted from the fresh vegetables she'd bought at the market. Afterward, she pulled the rickety old ironing board out of a wall in the kitchen and set about ironing all the things she had unpacked last evening. As she worked she found her thoughts returning again and again to Philippe St. Pierre. The knowledge that she would be seeing him in just a few hours was exhilarating and yet disturbing. She still hadn't entirely forgiven him for what she considered deliberate subterfuge at their first two meetings, but the charm he had exhibited last night was hard to resist. He seemed so genuinely apologetic, so gracious in suggesting he be her "tour guide" while she was in Grasse. And yet it was this easy charm that continued to make her wary.

Gil Tarleton, her ex-husband, had possessed a similar quality. He could charm the birds off the trees—why else would a sensible young woman of twenty-four have agreed to marry after a courtship of only two weeks? It hadn't been the Tarleton money that had swayed her—Roni was sure of that. Certainly Gil's romancing her in the most expensive restaurants in New Orleans had been exciting and glamorous, but Roni had fallen for the man. The clean-cut, athletically built man with the look of a beachboy about him; straight blond hair worn just a little on the long side; bright blue innocent eyes; a full-lipped mouth that smiled so wide it caused the skin under his eyes to crinkle. Nothing about him, Roni remembered with that dull ache that always accompanied her memories of Gil, indicated the kind of man he was inside—volatile, unpredictable, a man who flew into rages for no reason at all and kept a volume of lies on his ever-glib tongue. She'd found out the truth about him soon enough, but by then, they were married and it was too late to make a graceful escape. Besides, the Pollyannaish side of her kept clinging to the hope that if she loved him enough, he would change.

She shook her head as if to dislodge these thoughts and carefully placed her lacy high-necked blouse on its hanger. She should not be thinking of a life that had been over for more than a year. She had a new life, a life that had led her to France and an exciting summer adventure. And, she told herself firmly, these comparisons of Gil and Philippe had to stop. It was grossly unfair to Philippe, a man she hardly knew, to assume that he possessed Gil's darker qualities simply because he, like Gil, had inherited great wealth. And yet, hadn't Philippe encouraged her belief that he was a mere workman when she'd met him in the St. Pierre hothouse? And the way he had raged at her yesterday outside the Beach Regency! He was clearly capable of both lies and intense anger, the two qualities she had grown to despise most in people.

She began to wish she hadn't accepted his dinner invitation, after all. Exciting as a visit to the château seemed, an evening alone with him would be one more step toward a relationship that could prove devastating. She considered calling it off, but since she had not had her grandfather's telephone connected, she did not know how to reach him. She would simply have to see the evening through and remain as cool and detached as she possibly could.

At five o'clock she ran a bath in her grandfather's old porcelain tub with the brass feet and luxuriated in the warm scented water. She had no idea what the proper attire was for dining at the Château St. Pierre, but she'd brought along three dresses and one of them would have to do. Before leaving New Orleans, she and Darleen had deemed them appropriate for fine restaurants, so why not an elegant château? She settled on an emerald green silk with a draped, sleeveless bodice and a circular skirt that swirled around her legs as she walked. Her mother's pearls were fastened around her neck, and she left her hair loose and flowing around her creamy shoulders.

Philippe arrived promptly at six, dressed in beautifully tailored dark brown trousers and an exquisite shirt of white batiste, which he wore open at the neck. Roni was aware of his appraising look as she opened the door to let him in, and she was sure she must be falling far short of the mark set by the more fashionable women of his acquaintance. Still, the dress she was wearing was purchased while she was still Mrs. Tarleton, and although it might not be ultrachic, it was expensive.

"Well," Philippe inquired as he escorted her out to his sleek silver Ferrari, "how did you spend your day?"

Roni told him about her trip to the market and her afternoon of puttering around the cottage. "Not very exciting," she said, laughing, "but I thoroughly enjoyed every bit of it."

It was only a matter of one or two minutes before they reached the huge iron security gates. Although the tour bus had driven straight through and on toward the flower fields, Philippe's car took the winding road to the left and twisted and turned its way up the drive, which was lined with stately olive trees. The lawns beyond were impeccably manicured; here flowers grew in carefully tended beds, not wild and rampant as they did in the fields.

"Has your family had the estate for a great many years?" Roni asked as she stared in wonder at the expanse of ground and vegetation.

"Several generations. My great-great-grandfather purchased the first bit of land. His children and grandchildren added on to it later."

As you plan to do with my property, Roni thought to herself. She understood perfectly, of course. It was only natural that the St. Pierre family should want *all* the land surrounding the estate.

In no time at all Philippe had pulled up to the towering stone mansion and stopped the car. From the passenger seat, Roni had to crane her neck to see to the top of the turreted roof. The structure was huge, but its simple lines and the slate gray of the stone gave it a graceful, elegant look. All the same, it looked more to her like an embassy than someone's house, and she found herself slightly awestruck when Philippe came around to open her door and say to her with a gracious smile, "Welcome to Château St. Pierre, my home."

CHAPTER SIX

A formally attired butler opened the massive double doors and wished Roni a stilted *"Bon jour"* as Philippe led her into the impressive entrance hall. A sparkling crystal chandelier hung from a frescoed twenty-foot ceiling, throwing its splinters of light on the highly polished wood floor and the carved walnut hat rack that stood against one wall, straight-backed and unbending as the butler himself.

"Your shawl, mademoiselle?" the servant asked.

Roni slipped her wrap off her shoulders and handed it to him, then gave herself up to Philippe, who guided her down the long portrait-lined hallway.

The portraits, encased in heavy ornate gold frames and lighted from the top with soft fluorescent bulbs, intrigued Roni at once, and she asked Philippe to slow down so that she might look at them. The subjects of the portraits were attractive though rather severe-looking men and women wearing clothing dating from what Roni judged to be the nineteen twenties to the present time.

"My honorable ancestors," Philippe told her

with an ironic smile. "No great house worth its salt is complete without them."

"Tell me about them." Roni moved to a portrait of a distinguished-looking older man with steel gray hair, a small bristly-looking mustache, and Philippe's dark eyes. "Is this your father?"

"My grandfather. I suppose you might say he's responsible for St. Pierre Industries being what it is today."

"He created the original perfumes?"

"No, that was my great-grandfather." Philippe gestured to the portrait of a much older man, a man whose skin looked leathery and wrinkled, a man who seemed out of place amid this group of people dressed in finery. Philippe's great-grandfather was not wearing a frock coat or smoking jacket but had been painted in his smock, which had evidently been worn over a simple durable shirt and ill-fitting trousers. "His name was Guy St. Pierre. His father, the original owner of our land, was a farmer, but Guy was interested more in flowers than in chickens and vegetables. He began to experiment with extracting the oils from the blooms and mixing them to create various exotic fragrances. The more he worked at what he considered a hobby, the more intrigued he became, and he finally went into perfume making. Of course, it was on a very small scale at first."

"And your grandfather turned it into a larger scale?"

"Yes. He was the one with the head for business. At that time, there were already several other perfumeries in the area, but my grandfather recognized that his father's formulas and blending methods were far superior to the others. And it was he who decided that St. Pierre perfume should have what you call 'snob appeal.' "

Roni blushed. Apparently, Philippe didn't intend to let her forget her outburst at the stockholders meeting. But she was much too interested in the portraits and the stories about the people to bite the bait. She gazed at the picture of the austere-looking woman hanging next to that of Philippe's grandfather. The woman was wearing a black high-necked dress with a cameo pinned at her neck. Her abundant gray hair was braided and twisted into a crown atop her head. Her eyes were light, almost slate blue, and her chin had a strong set to it, indicating, Roni thought, a certain stubbornness of character. "Your grandmother?" she asked Philippe.

He nodded. "She was almost as active in the business as my grandfather. She kept all the books and oversaw the entire operation. She wouldn't stand for any nonsense and cracked the whip around here a great deal. Without her, I'm sure St. Pierre Industries wouldn't have reached the heights it has attained." He put his hand lightly on her arm. "Why don't we finish this tour a little later? Otherwise, there won't be time for cocktails before dinner."

"Oh, of course! I didn't mean to upset your timetable." Roni allowed him to escort her past the portraits, although she did slow down and turn to look at what was obviously a likeness of Philippe himself hanging at the end of the gallery. He looked to be some ten years younger than he was at the present time, but he was still devastatingly handsome in an exquisitely tailored maroon velvet jacket. Rushed as she was, Roni could only glimpse the painting hanging next to it, the portrait of the thin dark-haired woman with enormous brown eyes.

The room to which Philippe escorted her was the great paneled library with an exquisite stone hearth and floor-to-ceiling shelves holding thousands of books. The oversized chairs were all upholstered in deep burgundy leather, as was the invalid's chair that stood back against one wall. Roni was prompted to ask after the elder St. Pierre's health.

"Oh, he's much better today," Philippe assured her. "As a matter of fact, he asked about you."

"Me?" Roni gave him a puzzled look.

"Well, he knew you were scheduled to arrive at your grandfather's cottage. He wanted to make sure you were properly received."

She smiled. "I hope you told him my initial reception was highly improper?"

Philippe grinned. "I'll let you tell him yourself when you meet him. That is, unless I can manage to blot out those memories before then." He moved to the bar. "Are you sticking to Dubonnet, or can I give you something a little more festive?"

"I'll be adventurous and try something festive."

"You're as brave as you are beautiful," Philippe replied, laughing.

Roni strolled about the room admiring the richly hued Tiffany lamps that sat on ormolu end tables, the beautiful Aubusson carpet, the rows and rows of books bound in red leather imprinted with gold. She stopped as she heard the discreet *pop,* then turned back to Philippe, smiling. "Champagne. So that's your festive drink."

"Can you think of a better one?" Philippe expertly poured the foaming liquid into two frosted tulip-shaped crystal glasses. He handed one to Roni.

The tiny bubbles danced and exploded in the glass. "Champagne always makes me think of New Year's Eve."

"In a way, that's what it is," Philippe responded. "The eve of a new adventure for Ms. Veronique Stephens." The smile he gave her seemed to hold some unknown promise.

The château's dining room was the epitome of elegance. Roni guessed most of the furniture to be of the Louis XV period, the gracefully curving tables and chairs featuring dainty cabriole legs, the massive serving cupboard bulging in the style known as bombé. The walls were hung with watered silk of the palest yellow, and the chairs were upholstered to match. The long formal table was set for two, with silver candelabras at either end and a huge flower arrangement in the center. As Philippe held her chair for her, Roni noticed that the place settings were of the most delicate bone china, pale blue embossed with gold scrollwork.

The butler, whom Philippe called La Roche, served the meal, beginning with a spicy chilled Senegalese soup and an entrée of excellent *côtes de veau aux herbes.* The soup was accompanied by the same fine French champagne Philippe had served in the library, and a delightful dry white burgundy was served with the veal. A crisp, crunchy endive and walnut salad was set before them after the dinner plates were removed.

As they ate, Philippe questioned Roni about her life in America.

She told him about Lockhart, where she toiled as an art instructor, and about her small apartment on Carrollton Avenue, which would probably just fit into the St. Pierre dining room.

"I don't imagine you spend much time in your apartment anyway," Philippe speculated. "Your nights are undoubtedly spent with your many admirers."

Roni didn't tell him she preferred spending her free time alone, that she had turned down all but a very few social invitations since her divorce. The dating world was frightening to her now because she couldn't bear the thought of making another dreadful mistake. Better—far better—not to take the chance. She was pleased by the fact that Philippe seemed to regard her as a femme fatale and simply responded to his observation with a small, rather mysterious smile.

"I'm going to hold you to your promise to tell me about the rest of the portraits in the hall," she said, changing the subject. "You sped me past the one of you so fast I could barely catch a glimpse of it."

"I assure you, my portrait is far inferior to most

of the others," Philippe insisted with a shrug, "both in quality and subject matter."

Roni decided he was being modest and did not argue the point. "There was a portrait of a woman hanging next to yours. Is she your sister?"

Philippe frowned thoughtfully. "A woman?"

"Maybe a *girl* would be a better way of describing her. She appeared to be rather young, with dark hair and a rather frail look about her."

"Ah, that is Nicole." Did Roni imagine the slight darkening in the already inordinately dark eyes?

"Nicole?" she repeated. *"Is* she your sister?"

"No." Philippe touched his lips with his napkin and then looked up at her with an intensity that seemed almost defiant. "She was my wife."

His wife. Why this information should have affected her so strongly, Roni couldn't imagine. All she knew was she suddenly felt tiny shock waves darting through her body.

"She's dead now," Philippe went on crisply. He rang the bell summoning La Roche to clear the salad plates.

"I didn't know. I'm sorry." Roni felt awkward, at blame, as if she'd stumbled upon something totally unmentionable. She was glad when La Roche entered with profiteroles in chocolate sauce and a silver coffee server. But when the salad plates had been cleared and the rich dessert set before them, the butler left and the uncomfortable silence continued.

"It's something I don't like to talk about," Philippe said after a moment. "It is . . . difficult."

He must have loved her very much, Roni thought, to be so affected by the mere mention of her. For a fleeting moment, she wondered what it would be like to be loved that much by this very complicated man. Probably, she decided, no one would ever know the answer to that again. From the way he had spoken, it seemed to her that his loving again was out of the question. "I understand," she assured him, wishing only to end the conversation. "I didn't mean to intrude on such a private matter." She turned her attention toward the profiteroles. "These look delicious."

"Yes. We are fortunate in having an excellent cook."

Polite small talk accompanied the remainder of the meal, and by the time they had finished their coffee Roni felt on more comfortable ground.

"Why don't we have our after-dinner drinks in the drawing room?" Philippe suggested, his earlier genial manner having returned. "I can have La Roche bring the coffee there, too, if you like. I suspect I have plied you with a little too much wine tonight."

"You're very perceptive," Roni replied with a slightly embarrassed smile. "Champagne always goes to my head, and I'm afraid I feel a bit fuzzy."

Philippe laughed. "We'd better sober you up before you accuse me of trying to make you drunk so I can take advantage of you." He held her chair as she rose. "Can you walk to the drawing room—or would you prefer me to carry you?"

Roni didn't mind being teased; in fact, she

rather enjoyed it. "I can walk," she assured him. "Just promise to pick me up if I fall."

Actually, she was only moderately light-headed, and she found the feeling rather pleasant. Philippe took her hand as he escorted her to the huge drawing room, again decorated in Louis XV style. Here the walls were covered with pale blue silk, and the darker blue damask curtains at the high narrow windows were drawn back with heavy gold rope. The fireplace was of pure white marble, and as in the library, several logs were burning cheerily.

"What will you have?" Philippe asked her, moving to a glass and gold cart on which stood many bottles of spirits. "Cognac? Amaretto? Tia Maria?"

"I think I'll stick with coffee for the moment," Roni told him. "And I would appreciate your directing me to the powder room first."

"By all means." Philippe led her to an elegant marbled half bath a short way down the hall. As Roni freshened her makeup and combed her hair she stared at her reflection, marveling at the fact that she was here in this fabulous château spending an evening with the famous Philippe St. Pierre! She was enjoying herself thoroughly—probably a little too much. She had promised herself to remain aloof to Philippe's undeniable charms, but he had been so easy to talk to and so genuinely friendly that she had found herself being drawn to him more and more during the course of the evening. And her heart had gone out to him when he had told her about his wife. He had seemed so bereft for a moment, so desperately unhappy. She wondered how many of the glamorous women he dated really knew the *real* Philippe, the sad, vulnerable man inside the magnetic, self-possessed exterior.

She was in the hall, preparing to reenter the drawing room, when she heard the angry, unfamiliar voice. It was a woman, and apparently she and Philippe were engaged in a rather heated argument.

"You didn't even try to find me!" the woman was shouting. "I could have died on the streets of Nice for all you cared!"

"Marie-Catherine, it was your decision to leave me and go to the casino," Philippe responded. His voice was low, but Roni could detect the underlying anger. "If you had come back to the hotel with me, you would have known I had been called back to Grasse."

"Coming back to Grasse was more important than finding me?" The voice was shrill and accusing.

Roni thought she could hear a certain sarcasm in his answer. "Yes, my dear, hard as it might be for you to believe, it was more important than finding you."

"Another woman, no doubt."

"My father had a stroke."

At once the woman's voice changed. She was all apology and concern now. "Oh, Philippe, darling, why didn't you tell me that in the first place? A stroke! How dreadful. Is he going to live? Oh, darling, I'm so sorry!"

Philippe's voice continued to be cool. "Yes,

Marie-Catherine, he's going to live. And your concern is very . . . uh . . . touching."

Apparently, the woman was aware of Philippe's distant attitude. She continued to appear the soul of sympathy. "You see, I simply had no idea. I had become ill myself, and naturally, I was rather upset that you hadn't come to check on me."

"Your illness must have been rather sudden."

"Oh, very! I had scarcely reached the casino before I felt all hot and flushed. I very nearly fainted right in front of the roulette wheels. Fortunately, Henri Petite was nearby and happened to spot me. He took me to the home of his friends, the Balfours, and they put me up for the night."

Roni wondered whether she should return to the powder room or make her presence known. She couldn't possibly continue to stand here eavesdropping; she was ashamed of herself for having remained this long. She didn't see why she should hide in the powder room, however, when she was an invited guest in this house, so she straightened her shoulders and walked into the drawing room with a fixed smile on her face.

The woman with Philippe was no older than herself, an incredible beauty with a tousled mass of red gold hair and eyes a shade of green Roni had never seen before. The black mini she wore displayed most of her long, slim legs, and her halter top dipped low in the back and offered side glimpses of her creamy breasts. With a shock, Roni realized she was the model in the St. Pierre perfume ads.

"Ah! Veronique, I wondered what had happened

108

to you." Philippe's manner was easy. He did not seem in the least perturbed that Roni might have overheard some of his conversation with the woman. "We have an unexpected guest. Mademoiselle Stephens, may I present Mlle. Fontaine."

The model turned and looked at Roni in disbelief. It was as if she were seeing an apparition.

"How do you do?" Roni asked politely. Whoever the woman was, she had not expected to find *another* woman with Philippe tonight. She appeared almost speechless.

"Mlle. Stephens is an American," Philippe went on smoothly. He turned to Roni. "Or should I use the word *madame?*"

Roni shook her head. "You see, I took back my maiden name after I was divorced." She could feel the woman Philippe had called Marie-Catherine giving her a hard, appraising look. "Perhaps you should just introduce me as Veron—Veronique."

"Veronique speaks French well, does she not?" Philippe asked Marie-Catherine. "Almost like a native."

Marie-Catherine stared at Roni for another moment. Then she turned to Philippe and gave him a dazzling smile. "Philippe, the reason I'm here is I have to pick up my car. Henri drove me this far, but he was in a hurry to get back to Paris, so he didn't come in."

Philippe nodded. "Your car's in the side portico where you left it."

"Yes, but my keys . . ." She stopped and darted a look at Roni. "Well, I'm afraid my keys are in your bedroom, darling." Roni saw Philippe's jaw tighten, but he said nothing. "I didn't realize you had a guest, of course, so I'll just pop upstairs . . ." She moved toward the door, but Philippe quickly stopped her.

"I'll go get them for you," he said firmly. "You wait here."

"They're on the night table next to the bed," Marie-Catherine called after him as he walked quickly from the room. She turned to Roni with an apologetic smile. "I'm sorry," she said sheepishly, "I'm afraid it's rather embarrassing."

Roni forced herself to smile back. "No. Not at all."

"You see," Marie-Catherine continued, "Philippe is my fiancé. And, well, since we're getting married so soon . . ."

Roni felt her whole body stiffen. "I—I didn't know," she said, her mouth suddenly dry.

Marie-Catherine was all girlish sweetness now. Her beautiful face was glowing as she spoke. "It's supposed to be a secret. Philippe wants to avoid the press, you know. Once they find out, it could turn into a regular circus. But it's so exciting, really. Philippe is such a wonderful man, and neither of us can wait to be married." She paused and her delicate forehead worked itself into a frown. "Oh, dear, did I say my keys were on the night table? Actually, I think they're in one of the drawers." She gave Roni a conspiratorial look. "I keep some of my things here, of course. Perhaps I'd better go up and find them myself."

She twinkled her incredible green eyes at Roni and floated from the room, her flowery perfume wafting behind her. Roni watched her go with a feeling of dull acceptance. So much for her theory that Philippe was incapable of loving again. She knew she shouldn't be surprised. Marie-Catherine Fontaine was extraordinarily beautiful as well as glossily sophisticated, the perfect kind of wife for someone as rich and prominent as the perfume heir. The fact that he hadn't mentioned he was engaged was not really so surprising, either. His private life was hardly any of Roni's business.

And yet he had kissed her that night in the gardens . . . Roni pushed the memory from her mind. Obviously, all that meant was that he was every bit the playboy the press made him out to be. He may have a beautiful fiancée, but he was the type of man who would take his pleasure where he pleased.

There was no sound from upstairs. Apparently, Philippe and Marie-Catherine had a lovers' quarrel and were probably in the process of making up this very minute. Roni's face flamed at the thought. The thought of facing them when they came down was unbearable. She did the only thing possible under the circumstances. She walked quickly to the front door and let herself out, not even noticing that the night had turned chilly and that she'd left her shawl behind.

She was halfway between the château and the cottage when she heard the roar of his Ferrari. Philippe raced the car up beside her and skidded to a stop. She could sense his anger even before he spoke.

111

"What the hell is this all about?" he demanded. "Couldn't you have waited another five minutes?"

"I'm sorry. It was getting late." Roni kept up her brisk pace.

Philippe cruised along beside her. "At least let me drive you the rest of the way."

Roni turned and looked at him then. His face looked very dark and intense; his black eyes seemed to glitter in the moonlight. "I'm really fine, Philippe," she insisted coolly. "And I'm practically home."

Suddenly the Ferrari stopped and Roni heard the engine grind to a halt. Philippe opened his door and strode purposefully to her side. "All right, if you won't ride, then I'll *walk* you to your door."

Roni steeled herself against his domineering presence. "Philippe, I'm perfectly safe. You have another guest. Go back to her."

She felt, rather than saw, the scowl. "So that's it!" He hesitated, then went on. "For your information, Marie-Catherine is gone." His voice sounded grim. "After a thorough search of my room, it turned out that her keys were in her purse all along."

Roni almost stopped then. Was he telling the truth? But even if he was, she reminded herself, it made no real difference. Whether her keys were in his room or not, Marie-Catherine was still Philippe's future wife. She kept walking.

"Veronique, what's the matter with you?" he demanded sternly. "I thought we were having a pleasant evening."

We were, until she showed up, Roni's heart cried. But of course she couldn't say that to him. How could she admit she was jealous when nothing the slightest bit intimate had passed between them tonight? And how could she *be* jealous, anyway? Philippe was her neighbor, a man she might be doing business with—nothing more. Unfortunately, the feeling whooshing around her body was more real than that last determined thought.

"Dammit, Veronique, look at me!"

She stopped then; the command was too strong to disobey. They were almost to the cottage, the stone walkway only steps away. She looked at him. His face was rigid with controlled anger, and his jaw trembled as if ready to explode.

"I don't know what's gotten into that gorgeous blond head of yours, but I want you to know I consider your behavior absolutely unacceptable. Possibly in America it's considered good manners for a guest to walk out on her host without so much as a parting word, but here in France, it is an insult!"

"Fine!" Roni snapped back hotly. "Then you would do well not to be my host again in the future, wouldn't you?" Bravo! her inner self applauded. Make it a clean break. Don't give him another chance to break down that wall of ice you've built around your heart.

She could feel the tension between them, crackling as surely as if it were a live wire being shorted out. But then suddenly, incredibly, she was in his arms, being crushed against him in a wild embrace. His lips crashed down on hers; his tongue assaulted her mouth, leaving her breathless, weak —and powerless to quell the fire raging inside her. Her arms were pinned down at her sides, her body so close to his she could feel his heart pounding beneath the thin material of his shirt. His hot breath threatened to smother her, and his mouth bruised her lips. Resistance was impossible. His actions had ignited the spark that had been smoldering inside her since he had first kissed her in Nice. She parted her lips, accepting his greedy tongue. Her arms encircled his body, molding it to hers. Still, it wasn't close enough; she wanted more . . . more . . .

One of his hands traveled down her back until it reached her buttocks. She felt the gentle squeezing, felt her lower body being pushed into contact with the throbbing proof of his desire. His other hand was threaded through her hair, pulling at it roughly. She loved the roughness; it made her feel alive, aware of every sensation in her burning body.

His mouth left hers and hovered at her ear. She felt his tongue at her lobe and gasped as it darted in and out of her ear, warm, wet, incredibly sensual. She nipped at his neck, intoxicated by his smell, feeling as if she could devour him then and there.

Pulling at her hair, he raised her head so that her mouth was once again molded to his. Then he let go of her hair and used his free hand to seek her breasts. She uttered a tiny choked cry as he cupped one of them through her dress; she willed him to find his way beneath the neckline to her bare flesh.

And then it was over. His hands no longer possessed her body. He jerked himself away from her so abruptly that she was almost knocked off balance. He steadied her with hands like steel, then looked at her for a long, hypnotic moment. Then he spoke in a voice so hoarse it was almost unrecognizable. "Go inside, Veronique. You are right. You didn't need me to see you to your home."

As she stared at him breathlessly, openmouthed, wanting to protest, wanting only to move back into his arms, he spun around and disappeared into the night.

CHAPTER SEVEN

After a haunted, sleepless night, Roni arose to another picture-perfect day. The late spring sun casting its pale light through her open bedroom window lifted her spirits and momentarily erased last evening's confusion and despair. Still, as she poured her coffee and settled into her grandfather's rocking chair to drink it Roni's thoughts returned to Philippe and the events leading to her hasty departure from Château St. Pierre.

The memory of the beautiful Marie-Catherine was infinitely depressing. The model seemed so at home in the château, so comfortable with Philippe even when she was arguing with him. That kind of familiarity was obviously the result of a relationship of long standing. For the umpteenth time, Roni berated herself for her silly fantasies regarding her own relationship with Philippe. Why on earth hadn't she stuck to her original determination to remain businesslike yet neighborly.

And yet that wild, almost brutal kiss outside the cottage . . . She could feel the fire inside him as he'd pulled her to him in an almost desperate way. *Why?* Why had he even bothered to follow her home, feeling as he did about Marie-Catherine?

For a moment, she allowed herself the luxury of a happy supposition: suppose Marie-Catherine had lied to her? Suppose they weren't engaged at all? Suppose Philippe really did feel the same emotional connection with Roni that she now had to admit she felt for him?

Fool! she chided herself, putting down the coffee cup and hurrying back upstairs to get out of her robe and into jeans and an oversized shirt. You're letting it happen again! You know what kind of man Philippe is—the signs are all too clear. Whether he's engaged or not, he is an infamous playboy, and kisses mean no more to him than a handshake. He will take what he can get from a woman; feelings have nothing to do with it. If you let him, he will take what he can get from you and then toss you aside like the weeds in his flower beds. You must fortify yourself against him while you still can.

The lecture to herself completed, Roni took her sketch pad and went out to her grandfather's garden to make a sketch of the cottage. It would be a nice memory, even after she sold the place. As was often the case, she became absorbed in her work as soon as she made her first mark, and thoughts of Philippe St. Pierre vanished from her mind. She was determined to capture the cottage as best she could; it was the only real link she had to her grandfather.

She had been at work for some time when she was distracted by the sound of twigs snapping, as if someone were approaching the garden. Her first quick glance around revealed no one, but as she pinpointed the direction of the noise, she soon discovered the perpetrator. A small hand was sticking through an opening in the hedge that divided her property from St. Pierre land. As Roni watched, the hand was followed by a head covered with a tangled mass of glossy black hair. When the rest of the body came into view, it proved to be that of a little girl, a very beautiful but very sober little girl. She had a charming, heart-shaped face and pale, almost white skin, and she was observing Roni with somber coal black eyes.

"Well!" Roni exclaimed, putting down her sketch pad and smiling at the child. "What have we here?"

The little girl looked at her for a long moment—and with an intensity Roni found disconcerting. She felt as if she were being carefully measured, and she wasn't at all sure she was passing muster. Perhaps if she addressed the child in French.

But before she could form the words, the little girl spoke. "Are you the granddaughter of M. François?" she asked in charmingly accented English.

"Why, yes," Roni answered, surprised at the question. "As a matter of fact, I am." As the child continued to study her she ventured to ask, "Who are you?"

"I am Nicolette. Didn't M. François tell you about me?"

The question had a wounded ring to it, and in order to avoid hurt feelings, Roni pretended to frown thoughtfully. "Yes, of course he mentioned a Nicolette. But I had no way of knowing it was you. Perhaps you had better tell me your last name."

The child gave her a disdainful look as if she, Roni, were not very bright. "St. Pierre," she replied, the tone of her voice seeming to ask, "Is there any other?"

The name gave Roni a start. She hadn't known there was a child in the St. Pierre family. But then, she reminded herself, she knew very little about the family in general. Perhaps this child was a visiting niece or cousin of Philippe's.

"Then you are a member of a very important family," Roni responded, somewhat intrigued by this new development. "Do you also live in Grasse?"

The dear little face clouded. "M. François did not tell you about me." She was clearly disappointed.

Roni gave her a sympathetic smile. "Well, Nicolette, my grandfather didn't write many letters. He was old, you see, and also very busy."

"Oh, I know!" Nicolette agreed. "He worked for my father."

Roni nodded. "For the whole St. Pierre family. Now tell me"—she patted the ground beside her and the child immediately came over and plopped down—"how did you get to know my grandfather?"

"He was my friend. I visited him every day."

"Oh?" Roni was amused. "You mean you crawled through the hedge every day just to see him?"

The child nodded eagerly. "It was our secret.

I'm not supposed to leave our own grounds. You won't tell my father, will you?"

"Well, of course not! Anyway," Roni added, "I don't know your father."

"Oh, but you do! I saw you with him last night."

The mention of last night drew Roni up short. What on earth was she talking about?

"You had dinner with him at the château," Nicolette went on. "I peeked at you from the top of the stairs."

Roni gasped and swallowed hard. It couldn't be! "You mean," she asked carefully, "your father is Philippe St. Pierre?"

"But of course." Then the child added with a touch of irony in her voice, "He didn't tell you about me, either."

Roni sighed and shook her head. This was yet another clue as to the kind of man Philippe was. Not only did he fail to mention he was engaged, but he also neglected to tell her about his daughter. "The thing is," she said to Nicolette with false brightness, "I found I had to leave the château early. I'm sure if I'd stayed, your father would have told me all about you."

"Perhaps," Nicolette replied without much conviction in her voice. Then, suddenly, she changed the subject. "You have the same eyes as M. François," she declared, looking up at Roni.

"Do I? What a nice thing to say." Roni was enjoying this somber child more and more. "Tell me more about him. What was he like? I never met him, you know."

"Oh, he was very nice. I used to call him *grand-père* when no one else was around."

Roni was touched. Obviously there was a special bond between the two.

"He even made a perfume for me," Nicolette went on, her dark eyes shining at the memory.

"A perfume? My grandfather?"

"Well, he didn't really make it for me. But he gave me a little bit in a vial. It was much nicer than my father's perfumes."

Roni frowned. "Nicolette, you must be mistaken. My grandfather worked for your father, but he didn't actually make the perfumes."

Nicolette smiled. "Oh, I know, mademoiselle. He made only this one perfume. But it was very, very special."

Roni was intrigued. Perhaps there was something to what she said, after all. "Do you still have it? I'd love to see it."

The child shook her head. "I don't know where it is. I had it in my room, sitting on my dressing table. My father says I'm too young to wear perfume, but I like to smell it. But one day I looked for it and it was gone." She sighed. "I think one of the maids took it."

Roni was disappointed. How nice it would have been to have sampled a perfume made by her own grandfather. Oh, well, she told herself. It was undoubtedly just an experiment. François Du Priex was a laborer, not a chemist. Despite Nicolette's testimonial, his efforts must have been amateurish at best.

She was showing her sketch of the cottage to the

child and smiling at the enthusiasm this also elicited when the garden gate swung open and Philippe came striding toward them. He was carrying the shawl Roni had neglected to retrieve when she'd left the château last night.

"Philippe!" Roni jumped up and dusted off her jeans. "You're up bright and early." She willed her voice to remain steady, although the sight of him caused tiny quivers of excitement to race through her body.

Philippe was formally polite. "La Roche told me you left this when you departed last night. I thought you would want it back." He handed her the shawl.

"Thank you." Roni was thrown by the businesslike tone of voice. She cast around for something to say. "As you can see," she finally managed, "I have another visitor." She put an arm around Nicolette, who had also scrambled to her feet.

Philippe did not smile at his daughter. "Nicolette, you do not have permission to be here," he said brusquely. "You will please return to your own home."

"Oh, but she wasn't bothering me," Roni began. But, seeing the purposeful look on Philippe's face, she decided to go no further. He was the child's father, after all. She bent down and planted a kiss on the little girl's cheek. "Run along, *ma petite,*" she said kindly. "We will have another visit soon."

Nicolette smiled faintly. Then she darted a cautious look at her father and scampered through the hole in the hedge.

"That child," Philippe said, shaking his head when she'd gone, "she is incorrigible."

"Oh, but she's charming!" Roni protested. "I hope you won't stop her from visiting me."

Philippe shrugged. "She thinks I don't know how often she came here to visit François. I suppose I should have punished her for leaving the grounds without permission, but I knew how fond she was of him."

"And he of her, apparently."

Philippe nodded abstractly, then faced her, looking deeply into her clear blue eyes, his own earnest and troubled. "Veronique," he began almost passionately, "I must apologize to you."

His intensity took Roni aback. Although he had behaved badly last night, his presence here now wiped all that away. Although she had recounted his shortcomings to herself not two hours ago, all she could think of was how it had felt to be in his arms. "Please," she said softly, "you don't have to—"

But he was determined to have his say. "My behavior toward you last night was unforgivable. I should never have lost my temper like that. I accused you of bad manners when, in fact, it was I who was behaving abominably."

"But I did leave the château without saying good-bye," Roni protested. "I didn't even thank you for the lovely meal."

"It doesn't matter." Philippe put his hands out as if to ward her off. "I know why you left. You were wrong, but it makes no difference. What is important is that you know *I* was wrong."

Roni looked at him, puzzled. This was the second time he'd apologized to her for his flare of temper. But the first apology had been charming and easygoing. What was causing him to be so intense now?

"When I came after you in the car," he went on, "it was to make sure you got home safely. I had no intention of yelling at you or accusing you of anything. And," he finished flatly, "I certainly had no intention of kissing you."

"Oh, but I—" Flustered, Roni didn't know what to say. She felt as if he'd slapped her. Acute disappointment enveloped her. The last thing she wanted him to apologize for was the kiss that had been haunting her through the night and morning. Still, her pride would not allow her to let her feelings show. Why give him the satisfaction of knowing that something so meaningless to him had disturbed her to the point of sleeplessness? "Forget it," she finally managed, pleased at the nonchalant tone she was able to keep in her voice. "It was nothing." Philippe looked at her. Was it her imagination, or did his eyes darken the tiniest bit?

"You are right," he said slowly, his eyes never leaving hers, "it was nothing." For a moment a heavy silence hung between them. Then he straightened his shoulders and once again addressed her in a businesslike manner. "Before I go, there's just one more thing."

"Yes?" Roni smiled at him, wishing desperately that they could get back on the easy terms they'd found before Marie-Catherine had appeared and changed everything.

124

"It has to do with the offer I made about being your tour guide while you are here in Grasse. I'm afraid I must renege. What with my father's illness and the problems with the company, I simply won't have the time. I'm sorry."

The words landed on Roni like physical blows. Damn him, she thought to herself. How dare he have the power to make her feel like this! Three days ago she didn't even know him, and now he had her emotions tied up in knots. Knowing she wouldn't be seeing him again left her feeling an empty ache inside. How eager he had sounded when he'd told her about the picnics and swims and dances they would have in Grasse! What a beautiful picture he'd painted of their summer together! But then, she supposed she'd put too much into those promises in the first place. She should have known from his behavior at the stockholders meeting that he was a man capable of making dreams disappear into thin air.

Well, perhaps it was better this way. She had come to Grasse to do business with Philippe St. Pierre, not to become another one of his romantic entanglements. Now her plans were getting back on course. The fact that Philippe, and not Roni herself, had put them there was a little galling. But even so, it was time to face reality, and she was grateful she was finally being made to realize it.

"I understand perfectly," she said brightly. "Please don't give it another thought."

Philippe studied her. "It is only the timing, I assure you."

"Oh, of course!" She smiled at him. "But to tell

you the truth, I don't really need a guide. I can find my way around perfectly well. Actually, I prefer being alone." She laughed. "The artistic side of me, I suppose."

"Yes." Philippe smiled faintly. "Well, now that that is settled, I'll leave you to your artistic endeavors."

Was there a note of sarcasm in that last statement? Roni suspected there was, but it didn't matter. Nothing mattered but that this impossibly magnetic man get out of her life—and out of her thoughts. She held out a hand to him. "Good-bye, then, Philippe. Thank you for returning my shawl."

He took her hand, and as his own hand closed over it a warmth surged through her body. But too soon he let it drop and with a murmured *"Au revoir"* disappeared through the garden gate.

Roni filled the days that followed by doing her best to prove she was the completely self-sufficient person she had assured Philippe she was. She wrote long letters to her friends in America, describing in detail her grandfather's cottage and the fabulous flower fields surrounding it. In her letter to Darleen Edwards she also described Philippe, painting him as the devastatingly handsome man Darleen suspected he was but minimizing her own relationship with him. She did tell her friend about her dinner at the château, but she made it appear strictly as a business dinner with no mention of Marie-Catherine.

She also spent a good deal of time sketching and

taking long walks around the countryside in search of new subjects. One day she chanced upon a secluded mountain lake. Its beauty was boundless. The water was crystal clear, and wildflowers sprang from crevices in the craggy hills surrounding it. This became one of her favorite spots. Sometimes she even packed a picnic lunch and spent most of the day there sketching and basking in the clean fresh air and the beauty of the surroundings.

And then there was Nicolette. After that first visit, the child had come to see her often, which pleased Roni very much. Always sensitive to children, she sensed a sadness in Nicolette that she suspected was born of loneliness. Although as a St. Pierre the child had everything money could buy, she was obviously lacking in the essentials of companionship and affection.

"It's not that they don't love her," Lily Bujold told Roni one day when the two were having coffee and sharing one of Lily's extraordinary cinnamon nut coffee cakes. "They just don't have time for her. Her father has his hands full running St. Pierre Industries, and her grandfather hasn't been well."

"But has she no friends of her own?" Roni asked, thinking how much Nicolette would enjoy this coffee klatch in which she and Lily were now indulging. "No chums from school she could be spending time with?"

Lily shook her head. "She doesn't go to school. She's being educated by private tutors. As a matter of fact, she's rarely allowed to leave the St. Pierre grounds."

"But why? That's such a cruel thing to do to an eight-year-old."

"Ah, yes. But what they fear is worse. You see, as heiress to one of the richest companies in the world, little Nicolette is a prime target of kidnappers. The only way the family can be sure of her safety is to make sure she's constantly under surveillance. All the servants at the château are expected to watch out for Nicolette, and she has bodyguards that look after her as well."

Roni sighed. "What a dreadful life for such a lively little girl. Like being a captive princess in a huge castle."

"Oh, she's not completely captive," Lily assured her, pushing another slice of coffee cake toward Roni. "M. Philippe takes her out on occasion—picnics and such. And she's allowed to go into town in the company of one of the trusted employees."

But still, Roni thought, it was hardly the normal life for a child.

After that conversation with Lily, she took even more interest in Nicolette, with the result that the child became as close to her as she had been to Roni's grandfather.

During this period, Roni saw nothing at all of Philippe. Occasionally she would hear a car roaring past the cottage, and she would wonder whether it was the perfume magnate in his silver Ferrari, zipping down to Nice or Monte Carlo for an evening with the ravishing Marie-Catherine.

She was well aware that Philippe's absence from her life had not made her any less aware of his

128

existence. She often found herself remembering the moments she had spent with him. The evening they had walked in the hotel gardens in Nice . . . the way he had looked the night he brought the wine to the cottage—so elegant despite his casual attire, so relaxed and happy as he stood in front of the fire . . . and the way he had kissed her . . .

Roni began to consider turning her property over to him right away and returning home to New Orleans. Surely if she were back in her own apartment, surrounded by her own friends, she would finally forget this disturbing man who had made such an impression on her life in so short a time. Surely it was his proximity that made it impossible for her to put him out of her thoughts. Once she had put an ocean between them, she could confine her thoughts to art and teaching—and perhaps finding a man who would be right for her.

She was still wrestling with the matter when the stranger arrived. She was in the kitchen preparing one of her picnic lunches when she heard the sharp rapping on her front door. She opened it to find a well-dressed, middle-aged gentleman standing on her porch. He apologized profusely for having arrived unannounced, explaining that since she did not have a telephone, he had no choice but to simply appear.

"My business is too important to be concerned with ceremony," he told her, speaking in heavily accented English. "I'm sure you will think so, too, when I have explained it to you."

"Oh?" Roni took quick stock of him. He was on

the short side and balding, but he had a pleasant face and she felt sure that whatever business he had with her was legitimate. Furthermore, he quickly handed her a card that bore the name of a real estate company in Grasse and the man's own name, André Lanphere.

"Perhaps you should come in, Monsieur Lanphere," she said, standing aside to allow him to pass. "I can't imagine what business you have with me, but I don't think my doorstep is the proper place to discuss it."

The man smiled and entered the cottage. "It has to do with this piece of property," he explained as he took the seat Roni offered him. "I understand you are planning to sell."

"Well, yes. But I have an offer." She explained the circumstances under which she had acquired the property and included the information that St. Pierre Industries was the prospective buyer.

"But St. Pierre is not your only possibility," M. Lanphere told her when she had finished. "I, too, have an offer for you. One I'm sure you will want to consider."

Roni expressed her surprise. The possibility that someone else might be interested hadn't occurred to her.

"My client is a widow from Paris. With her husband gone, the city life is too much for her and she is looking for some simple place with pleasant surroundings. She has visited Grasse on many occasions and believes she could be happy here."

"Yes, I believe anyone could be happy here," Roni responded with a smile. "But my arrangement with St. Pierre Industries is more or less a fait accompli."

M. Lanphere frowned. "But you haven't actually signed the papers?"

"Oh, no. Nothing like that. I intend to spend the summer here and then turn it over to them." She decided against telling him she was considering cutting her vacation short and leaving right away.

The realtor looked relieved. "Then perhaps my offer will change your mind. My client is prepared to make a cash deal. You see, she happened to pass the cottage shortly after your grandfather passed away, inquired about it, and learned that it might be for sale. Since she has set her heart on it, she is prepared to be quite generous in what she is willing to pay."

When he named the amount, Roni was stunned. It was a good deal more than the offer made by Philippe St. Pierre. Still, her good sense told her she should not reveal the details of the St. Pierre negotiations, nor should she jump at the widow's offer simply because it was larger. Her decision would have to be made after careful consideration. There were other things, purely personal things, that would enter in.

"That is very generous," she agreed when M. Lanphere had finished outlining his proposal. "But of course I can't possibly give you an answer right now."

"No, of course not. You will have to weigh the two." But the realtor had a confident look on his face. He rose from his chair. "Suppose I give you

. . . shall we say, a week? Perhaps you will be able to make up your mind by then."

Roni smiled. "A week will be fine." She walked him to the door and held out her hand to him. "Thank you very much for coming."

He took her hand and bowed over it. "My pleasure, mademoiselle."

After he'd gone, Roni sank into the old-fashioned sofa and heaved a heavy sigh. A new complication. Now she not only had to decide whether to sell or not—although of course she knew she would—but whom to sell to. She was sure any businessperson would tell her she should take the larger offer. But what of the sentimental aspect? She already doubted that her grandfather would approve of her selling at all, but if she did sell she was sure he would want her to turn over the property to the St. Pierres. After all, he had worked for them all his life. He would undoubtedly see it as a matter of loyalty.

Tell Philippe about the new offer and ask him to match it? Roni still remembered the day in Nice when he had accused her of trying to seduce him in order to get him to raise the price. She was sure he would think she was lying about the widow, and the last thing she wanted was another angry scene.

In any case, money was not everything. She had seen firsthand how the desire for it could destroy people's lives. Between her job at Lockhart, the small inheritance her parents had left her, and the settlement she had received from Gil, she was able to live a comfortable life. And the money she would receive from the sale of the cottage—even supposing she accepted the St. Pierre offer—would give her security for a long, long time.

Obviously, she would have to make a decision based on . . . What? Loyalty to her grandfather's memory? The wishes of a widow living out her final years alone? Her own feelings toward Philippe St. Pierre?

And if it were the latter, just what were those feelings? Passion? Distrust? Longing? Hurt?

CHAPTER EIGHT

"Next Saturday is my birthday," Nicolette announced as they sat in the garden, munching on tuna fish sandwiches washed down with strawberry pop. "Papa is giving me a party."

"Why, that's wonderful!" Roni leaned over and kissed the soft white cheek. "Tell me about it. Who's going to be there?"

"Lots of people. Papa invited circus performers to entertain—and a magician and lots of animals." The child gave Roni one of her rare full smiles.

"How exciting!" Roni responded. And how like the rich, she thought privately. Too busy to spend time with their children, but they try to make up for it by giving them lavish birthday parties.

"I want you to come, too. Will you?" Nicolette asked eagerly. Her black eyes begged for a yes.

"Oh, Nicolette, I don't know. I imagine it's up to your father to do the inviting."

"But he said I could invite anyone I want. And I told him I was going to ask you."

Roni's heart gave a small lurch. "Did you, now? And what did he say?" She wondered what Philippe thought about her deepening relationship with his daughter.

"He said it was a good idea. That it would be good for you to be in the company of grown-up people for a change."

"He said that?" Roni tried to hide her irritation. Obviously, the insufferable man assumed that without him to escort her she was forced to live a life of solitude, with only a child for occasional company. The fact that this had pretty much been the case was beside the point.

"He said he would be glad to see you," Nicolette added matter-of-factly. She reached for one of Roni's homemade chocolate chip cookies.

Roni looked at her. "He did?" Her curiosity was definitely piqued. Just how extensive had this conversation been? "What else did he say?"

The child nibbled thoughtfully. "I'm not sure," she said slowly. "I can't remember."

"I suppose you told him about our picnics," Roni prompted, hoping to gain some real insight into Philippe's feelings toward her. "He doesn't mind your coming here now, does he?"

"Oh, no. He's glad we're friends. He likes you."

Roni was careful to sound nonchalant. "So he told you that, too, hmm?" She smiled at the child.

Nicolette shook her black curls. "Not in words. He didn't have to."

"No? Why not?"

"I can tell. He asks me about you sometimes. About if you seem happy . . . and what you do when I'm not around."

"And?" Roni offered her another cookie. "What do you tell him?"

The little girl shrugged. "I don't know what you

135

do. But you *are* happy, aren't you? You do like Grasse?"

I'd like it a lot better if you told me your father was wild with desire for me, Roni thought dryly, knowing, of course, that—even if it were true—Philippe would never admit such a thing to his soon-to-be-nine-years-old daughter. She suppressed a sigh. All this questioning of Nicolette was not going to produce anything substantial. The only person who knew what Philippe felt for her was Philippe himself.

"Yes," she said in answer to the child's question, "I like Grasse. And," she added with real conviction, "I would be delighted to come to your birthday party."

The invitation, she decided later, was a godsend. Whether or not Philippe had any real interest in her, she hoped that when she saw him again, even in the company of others, she would be able to put her feelings about *him* into perspective. The time that had passed since he had returned her shawl had brought no relief as far as her thoughts of him were concerned. In idle moments, she still found herself conjuring up his face, that marvelous sculptured face with the squared-off jaw and the dark, probing eyes. She could still remember the scent of his cologne, musk mingled with spices like cinnamon and thyme.

Once, she had picked up a French fashion magazine and had seen a picture of him with Marie-Catherine Fontaine. They were attending a charity ball in Paris. Dressed in a tuxedo, Philippe looked more handsome than any movie star, and Marie-

Catherine was unbelievably lovely in a cream-colored ball gown with a voluminous skirt and a low-cut, form-fitting bodice. Philippe's arm was around her, and the smile she was smiling was radiant and assured. They are perfect for each other, Roni had had to admit as she'd gazed at the photo. That the admission produced a dull ache in her heart was something she was unable to do anything about.

She found a store in Grasse that sold art supplies and bought a sketch pad and a set of pastels for Nicolette's birthday present. The little girl had shown an interest in Roni's sketching, and it occurred to Roni that the child might take pleasure in learning to draw herself.

On the morning of the party she washed her pale blond hair and let it dry naturally, so that it hung perfectly straight, just past her shoulders. Thanks to the excellent cut she had received in New Orleans before her departure, it fell in an even line and moved when she walked like a solid silken curtain. She wore a minimum amount of makeup, emphasizing only her eyes, and put on a multicolored sundress that in her more fanciful moments made her feel as if she were wearing a rainbow. Satisfied that she looked her very best, she took Nicolette's wrapped present and walked the short distance between the cottage and the château.

Philippe's butler, La Roche, answered the door and directed her through the house to the "park" behind. The party was already in full swing. Huge bunches of balloons mingled with the colors of the flowers in the park's cultivated beds. A hurdy-gurdy filled the air with old, familiar tunes, and a man wearing a clown costume dispensed pink cotton candy from a brightly painted vending cart. Men wearing sports attire and women in sundresses or minis or well-fitting pants stood in groups, holding glasses filled with champagne. Nicolette, the only child Roni could see, was standing alone, nibbling on a cone of cotton candy when she spotted Roni and came running to greet her.

"You came!" she exclaimed, her dark eyes lightening in her excitement. She gestured with her free hand. "Isn't it wonderful? Do you like cotton candy?"

Roni had no wish to begin by having something as sweet as cotton candy, but it was obvious that the little girl was hoping she would join her. Not wanting to hurt her feelings, Roni gave the hoped-for answer.

"I love it! And I haven't had any for a very long time."

"We have lots," Nicolette told her, taking her hand and leading her to the vending cart. "You can have as much as you want."

Roni accepted a cone from the clown, who was clearly pleased to have another taker for his product. Obviously, he was not going to dispense a great deal in this particular crowd.

"I have a present for you," she told Nicolette, holding out the colorfully wrapped package. "Shall I put it with the others?" A huge pile of presents was spread over one of the lawn tables.

"Oh, no, please!" the child insisted. "I would

138

like to open it right now!" She took the package and tried to slip off the giant bow, but because one hand still held the cotton candy, she found the chore difficult.

"Perhaps you'd better wait until you've finished eating," Roni suggested, smiling. "Otherwise, you'll get everything all sticky."

It was then that she spotted Philippe out of the corner of her eye. He had left the group with whom he had been conversing and was walking toward her. As always, she was struck by the grace of his body when he moved, by the proud way he held his head, and by the intense look in his wonderful dark eyes.

"Veronique, what a pleasure to see you." His voice was exactly as she had remembered it. Rich, warm, his speech seductively accented.

"Thank you, Philippe. I'm delighted Nicolette invited me."

Philippe smiled at his daughter. "Away with you, *ma petite,*" he said lightly. "Mlle. Veronique is not your only guest. You have many more to greet."

"Yes, Papa," the child responded. Obediently, she set off in the direction of some new arrivals.

Philippe turned back to Roni. "And how have you been? Are you enjoying yourself here in Grasse?"

"Oh, yes, very much." Roni wished she could elaborate on the ways in which she'd been spending her time, but she was sure he would find solitary picnics at the mountain lake and shopping excursions in the village very dull indeed. Of course, she could tell him about her visit from André Lanphere, but she had no intention of discussing that with him just yet. "And how have you been?" she asked him airily. "I hope your father is better?"

"Yes, thank you. Much better. As a matter of fact, he will be putting in an appearance here today."

"That's wonderful. I look forward to meeting him." Roni smiled up at him and was disconcerted by the look she saw in his eyes. He seemed to be studying her, probing her thoughts, as if he had some question about her. They looked at each other for a long moment, neither of them speaking. As in previous, similar moments, Roni felt a great warmth surge through her.

"Veronique," he began, his voice gentle and yet filled with undertones that seemed almost urgent. "Veronique, I—" But the sentence was never completed. It was interrupted by the arrival of a uniformed maid who told him in rapid French that there was some problem with the circus performers who had just arrived. Philippe gave Roni an apologetic smile. "I'm sorry. I had better tend to this. Please make yourself at home." He made a sweeping gesture with his right arm. "I assure you everyone here is very friendly."

As he hurried away with the maid at his side, Roni sighed. He had seemed on the verge of saying something important. Now she would have to wait to find out what it was. She looked around, wondering if she should try to mingle with the other guests. She was aware that she was still holding the uneaten cone of cotton candy and wondered if it would be possible to get rid of it without Nicolette's seeing her. She was looking around in the hope of finding a trash bin when she heard a voice from behind.

"Why don't you give it to one of the waiters and take some champagne instead?"

She turned to see a man sitting in a wheelchair observing her with a wry smile. He was very distinguished looking, with a full head of snow white hair and a wonderful craggy face from which peered a pair of lively brown eyes. "Daniel," he called as a waiter passed bearing a tray of filled champagne glasses, "kindly relieve this young lady of my granddaughter's favorite food and give her something more useful."

"Of course, Monsieur St. Pierre," the waiter replied politely. He took the paper cone from Roni's hand and held up the tray in front of her. Roni thanked him and picked up one of the chilled glasses.

"Better, eh?" the old man asked as the waiter moved away. His eyes were twinkling, as if Roni amused him.

"Yes, much. Thank you." Roni smiled at him. "You must be Philippe's father."

"You are right. And you, my dear young lady, are François Du Priex's delightful granddaughter."

Roni laughed. "I don't know about the 'delightful' part, but, yes, François was my grandfather."

The old man shook his head slowly. "A terrible loss, his passing. He was a remarkable man. I knew him all my life."

"Yes, I know. My mother told me that you and her father were friends as young men."

He smiled reminiscently. "It's not easy to be friends when one is the *heir*"—he used the word ironically—"to a great company and the other is one of the laborers. But we managed to bridge the gaps, whatever they were. I miss him very much."

Roni was so touched that a small lump began to form in her throat. What a kind man Philippe's father was. "I just wish I had known him," she said quietly. "From what I can tell, he seemed to have a great many facets to his makeup. I only just found out that he even made his own perfume."

Claude St. Pierre frowned. "A perfume? I think you must be mistaken there, my dear. François did not actually work in the laboratory."

"Oh, I realize that. But apparently he did some experimenting on his own. He gave a sample of his creation to your granddaughter." She grinned. "Nicolette thought it was better than all the St. Pierre perfumes put together."

Claude nodded wryly. "Nicolette was very devoted to François. I'll ask her to show me the perfume."

"Oh, but that's the unfortunate part," Roni explained, sighing. "She told me it was stolen from her room. She thinks one of the maids took it."

The old man's eyes narrowed. "That could very well be the case. We screen our help as best we can, but some of them are not above a little petty theft." He paused. "Perhaps François left a formula?"

142

Roni brightened. "I hadn't thought of that. Perhaps he did."

"Have you gone over all his papers? I know he kept a great many records and account books."

"Actually, I've only glanced at them," Roni admitted. "I've been meaning to go through them more thoroughly."

"If you come up with anything, let me know," Claude told her. "If there is a formula, perhaps we can re-create the scent for you."

Roni was about to express her gratitude when a perfumed presence swept in front of her and threw a pair of silky bare arms around the old man. "Claude!" Marie-Catherine Fontaine exclaimed. "How wonderful to see you up and about." She kissed him on both cheeks, causing the old man to chuckle and pinch her cheek affectionately.

"Ah, my dear Marie-Catherine," he enthused, "you are just the tonic I need for getting completely well."

The model laughed with delight. "Then what do you say we run away together? I can share your chair and we can be gone before anyone notices."

Roni didn't hear Philippe's father's reply. She had begun to walk away when it became obvious that Marie-Catherine intended to usurp her place with the old man. And, too, once Philippe's fiancée had made an appearance, Claude had ceased to notice Roni. However, before she could decide what to do next, Nicolette came running toward her, her arms outstretched.

"Come with me, Mademoiselle Roni!" the child

shouted eagerly. "I want you to meet one of my friends. He is like a big, black bear!"

Indeed, the man the child led her to was a big bear of a man with a full dark beard. He scooped Nicolette up in his arms as she introduced "M. Alain" to "Mlle. Roni."

"Ah, you are the paragon of virtue Nicolette reports on daily," Alain said to Roni with a friendly grin. "The American who lives next door."

"Well," Roni responded, amused, "I am the American who lives next door. But a paragon of virtue?" She shook her head wryly.

"In Nikki's eyes, all her friends are faultless," Alain declared. He gently ruffled the child's hair.

"Are you a friend of the family?" Roni asked him.

"In a manner of speaking, I am a *part* of the family," he told her. "My full name is Alain Dumont. I am chief chemist for St. Pierre Industries."

"Then it's you who creates those marvelous scents. How talented you must be!"

Alain inclined his head in humble acknowledgment. "I have a lot of help," he assured her. "It's not easy coming up with a new scent every season."

"Look, the acrobats!" Nicolette pointed to the three men and three women dressed in spangled leotards who were cartwheeling and somersaulting across the lawn. "The circus is beginning!"

At that moment, the hurdy-gurdy struck up a rowdy circus tune. The acrobats were followed by jugglers and clowns, all of them performing at once to the delight of the audience, who had

144

formed a circle around them. Alain, still holding Nicolette, and Roni hurried over to laugh and cheer their antics. Later a trained dog act appeared, followed by a magician who made wondrous things appear out of thin air. Nicolette was clearly beside herself with glee, and Roni's heart was warmed knowing the child was so happy, even if only for the day.

She did, however, experience a wistful moment when she spotted Philippe and Marie-Catherine watching the performance from the other side of the circle, Marie-Catherine's arm locked in Philippe's, their smiling faces reflecting the joy all engaged couples feel at simply being together. But realizing the sight disturbed her made Roni angry at herself. Why shouldn't the two look happy? They were in love and very soon they would be married. Roni, she told herself severely, you have got to come to terms with the fact that Philippe St. Pierre has nothing to do with you.

After the performance, Philippe beckoned to Nicolette, and the child slid out of Alain's arms and rushed to her father. Philippe led her to the center of the circle and asked for silence so that he might speak.

"My friends," he began, holding out his arms as if to embrace everyone in the crowd, "my daughter and I want to thank you for joining us today. As you know, this is a very special day for Nicolette. Today she has turned nine years old." The guests applauded and Nicolette beamed. "Very shortly," he went on, "we will be serving a buffet meal. But first I think we should give my daughter the

chance to name the game she would like to play."
He turned to the child. "Well, *ma petite,* what shall
it be?"

"Hide-and-seek!" Nicolette declared without a
moment's hesitation. "I'll be *it.*"

"Hide-and-seek it is," Philippe agreed. He addressed the guests. "I think we all know how to
play. My daughter will count to one hundred, during which time we must all hide. As Nicolette dis-
covers your hiding places you may come out and
take part in finding the others. The person or per-
sons who remain hidden the longest win the
game."

"What do we win, Philippe?" Marie-Catherine
asked with a flirtatious smile. "A favor from Nikki's father?"

"That depends on who wins," Philippe answered, looking directly into Marie-Catherine's
wide green eyes. Roni could sense the unspoken
meaning. *"Bon,"* Philippe concluded. "Everyone
knows the rules. Let the game begin!"

He stood aside as the magician drew a multicolored scarf from the air and tied it around Nicolette's eyes. Then, as the little girl began to
count, the guests darted around the grounds looking for places to hide.

"Shall we try our luck together?" Alain asked
Roni with an amused smile. "I assure you I know
all the best hiding places."

"I'm sure you do," Roni answered. "But if you
don't mind, I think I'll risk it on my own."

Alain nodded. "As you wish, fair lady. *Bonne
chance."* The heavyset man ambled off in the direc-

146

tion of the gazebo while Roni cast around for her own bit of shelter. She settled on the rose garden just beyond the swimming pool. From what she could tell, no one had ventured quite that far. The other guests had ducked behind the lawn furniture or taken refuge behind hedges or trees.

"Vingt-sept, vingt-huit . . ." Nicolette was counting. There was plenty of time before she reached one hundred.

Roni reached the rose garden and sank down behind a bush fairly bursting with yellow roses. The aroma was magnificent. She was sure she couldn't have picked a better spot to conceal herself.

Nicolette had reached seventy when Roni heard footsteps behind her. With a small twinge of disappointment, she realized someone else had come up with the same idea. Perhaps the rose garden wasn't such an original spot after all.

"Ah! Two minds with a single thought!" Roni turned, startled, as she recognized Philippe's voice. He was smiling down at her, his hair ruffled by the slight wind, his eyes soft and warm. "I should have known you'd head for the flowers, too."

He dropped down beside her, his nearness causing Roni to flush with both pleasure and nervousness. However, she managed to keep the conflicting emotions he aroused in her from showing. "I hope this isn't considered out of bounds," she said lightly.

"No, of course not. Every hiding place is fair in this game." He paused, looking at her. "Are you enjoying the party?"

147

"Oh, yes. It's wonderful. And so exciting for Nicolette.

"She does seem happy, doesn't she?" Philippe shook his head. "I'm afraid the child doesn't have much opportunity for fun. I wish I could do something about it, but with the circumstances the way they are . . ."

"You mean the threat of kidnapping?"

"That, and my busy schedule. There are so few people I can trust with her."

The conversation halted as they heard shouts from the other side of the pool. Nicolette had stopped counting and had found the first hiding place. A woman and two men stepped from behind a chaise lounge, laughing.

"Ah! The little one is alert. Now she and these guests will look for the others." Roni had never seen Philippe looking so relaxed. He seemed to be enjoying himself thoroughly. "Look, she has found Alain! And Marie-Catherine, also."

Roni peeped over the rose bush and saw the model and the chemist strolling out of the white latticed gazebo. "I'm glad he didn't persuade me to go with him," she mused aloud. "Apparently, he doesn't know the best hiding places, after all."

"Quick! Get down!" She felt Philippe's hands on her shoulders, pushing her gently down onto the thick grass. "Someone is coming this way!" He carefully nudged her as close to the rose bush as was safely possible and stretched his own body out next to hers. Roni lay quietly, thrilled by the exquisite feeling of such intimacy. But her heart was

148

pounding so loudly she was sure it would bring Nicolette directly to their side.

She looked at Philippe. His face was only inches from hers; she could feel his warm breath on her cheek. His lips formed a half smile, and his eyes were studying her intently. "Has anyone ever told you roses become you?" he asked softly. "You look as if you belong here in this garden. But the flowers aren't half as lovely as you are."

Roni's heart stopped. Her mouth felt dry. It would be so easy to move in to him, to melt into his embrace, to blend her body with his. But remembering those other kisses—and the pain that followed them—she willed herself to remain where she was. "Maybe we should get up and show ourselves," she suggested. "I think all the others have been found."

"No, Veronique," Philippe whispered. "Not yet."

Slowly, ever so gently, his lips found hers. The sweetness of his kiss overwhelmed her. His lips were so soft, creating just the slightest pressure against hers, and then retreating, only to return with steadily increasing urgency. She found herself responding. Each time his lips left hers she lifted her head upward, straining toward him, relaxing only when he lowered his head and their mouths met once more.

At last, frustrated by his teasing, she flung her arms around him and pulled him to her, her own mouth taking the lead now, pressing itself against his with delicious determination. He met her fire with a raging fire of his own. His hands, which until now had been content to cradle her head, found the sensuous curves of her body, crept inside the bare top of her sundress to caress her bare back, then gently but persistently attempted to work their way forward until they skimmed the flesh of her breasts.

"Oh, God, Philippe, stop!" Roni gasped, aghast at herself for permitting such intimacy. She pulled at his wrists until his hands freed her, then lay back on the grass and stared up at him, tears of longing and frustration welling up in her eyes. "Why are you torturing me like this?" she asked brokenly when she had recovered enough to speak.

Philippe studied her. "I'm sorry," he said quietly. "I did not think of kissing you as torture." He looked wounded, genuinely hurt.

"But it's so meaningless to you. You and Marie-Catherine, you're—" She broke off, the word *engaged* too bitter to be said.

"We're what?" Philippe seemed perplexed. "Veronique, it's true that Marie-Catherine and I were once lovers. Surely you don't begrudge me my past?"

"Your past, no," Roni told him, "but the present . . ." Her words trailed off. How she hated having to discuss Marie-Catherine with him!

Philippe seemed to understand her doubts. "I have no present with Marie-Catherine," he assured her. "The fire has long since burned out."

"But the way she acts toward you. So . . . intimate. And"—an accusing note crept into her voice —"you aren't exactly cool toward her."

"My dear Veronique, I can't help it if Marie-

Catherine still feels something for *me*. As for my behavior toward her, well, one does not act 'cool' toward someone who once meant something to him. And," he added carefully, "Marie-Catherine is still the model for all the St. Pierre ads."

Roni absorbed this information thoughtfully. Could she believe him? When Marie-Catherine had specifically said they were engaged? She wanted to believe him—oh, how she wanted to! But it was all so confusing. She needed time to think.

"Veronique . . ." Philippe was looking down on her, his hand gently stroking her cheek. "Please believe I wouldn't do anything to hurt you."

Her eyes met his. Desire stirred again in her outstretched body. "I want to believe you," she replied huskily. "Oh, Philippe, I—"

"Ha! I have discovered your secret!"

They both jumped as Claude's voice broke into their private world. The old man was seated in his wheelchair, looking down on them, his eyes twinkling merrily. Roni blushed as she realized he could have been watching them for some time. "They are found!" he called to the party guests. "Nikki! Your father and your charming friend have discovered the same hiding place!"

Roni and Philippe rose quickly and brushed themselves off as Nicolette and the others came running over, shouting congratulations to the two who had so successfully managed to outwit the others. Marie-Catherine rushed to Philippe's side and scolded him delightfully for having had them all so confused.

"Really, darling, fun is fun, but we've been looking for you for *ages!* I was beginning to think we were going to have to call the police."

She cast Roni a sour look as she led Philippe back toward the pool area where a huge buffet was being set up. Philippe did not look back at Roni as he let the lovely model take charge, and the soft tears of desire that had begun to form in Roni's eyes suddenly grew hot and threatened to spill over in tears of humiliation. No matter what he had told her, it was obvious that Marie-Catherine was capable of making him forget her in the wink of an eye. Damn, damn, *damn!* Was she never going to learn? She tried to pull herself together and hide her bitter disappointment while she joined the others at the buffet.

Philippe seemed totally occupied with Marie-Catherine. Together, they filled their plates and took them to a picnic table, where they sat with some of the other guests. Roni found a seat next to Alain Dumont, but when he commented on how little she was eating she pleaded a headache and said she thought she'd better go home.

"But there's going to be dancing later," Alain protested. "You can't leave at this hour."

Roni forced a smile. "Perhaps I'll come back. I only live next door. For now, though, I think I should lie down."

Alain nodded understandingly. "Champagne and sunshine don't always mix," he told her. "Would you like me to escort you home?"

"Oh, no, thank you. I'll just sneak off while everyone's enjoying their food. I'll explain to Nico-lette tomorrow."

"Don't forget to come back later, if you're up to it," the chemist urged. "I'd love to have a dance with you."

"Thank you." Roni looked at him, really seeing him for the first time. He was too off-beat looking for her taste, but he had nice eyes and he seemed to be a genuinely nice man.

Why can't I get interested in someone like that? she asked herself as she made her way back to the cottage. She was sure he wasn't the sort of man who would toy with a woman as mercilessly as a cat with a mouse. But of course Roni knew that was the unfortunate quirk in her character: she always fell for the wrong man.

Marie-Catherine saw Philippe's eyes follow Roni as she left the party. "How rude the Ameri-cans are," she commented as she sipped her cham-pagne. "She didn't even say good-bye to you."

"Perhaps there's something wrong. I should go and see."

Philippe began to rise, but Marie-Catherine put a restraining hand on his arm. "Don't be an idiot, Philippe. Didn't you see her talking to Alain? She's probably going to meet him later and is rush-ing home to change."

"Somehow, I doubt that." Philippe frowned.

"You think she prefers you, eh?" The model gave him a rueful look. "What were you two doing over there in the bushes, anyway, darling?"

He chortled. "None of your business . . . *darling.*"

Marie-Catherine did not miss the irony in his voice. She gave him a charming smile. "Really, Philippe, I'm quite prepared to forgive you your meaningless little flings. But when the lady is someone as colorless as the little American—"

"That's enough!" Philippe snapped. "I'm not interested in your opinion of Veronique." He faced her squarely. "And I will decide what is meaningful and what is not in my life."

Marie-Catherine's eyes widened momentarily. Then she moved in closer to him and ran a carefully manicured fingernail lightly up his arm. "Philippe, darling, don't let's fight. I know how much you want the Du Priex property. I won't stand in the way of your getting it."

He cocked his head toward her. "And just what is *that* supposed to mean?"

"Just that if getting it means—er—negotiating with old François's granddaughter, well . . ." She smiled. "You have my permission to negotiate to your heart's content."

"Your permission? Just who the hell do you think you are, Marie-Catherine? My wife?"

His voice was forceful but low. The other party guests had left the picnic table, so their conversation was relatively private.

"Ah, Philippe, you know the answer to that," Marie-Catherine purred, undeterred by the outrage in his tone. "I'm the woman who loves you madly. Who would do anything for you. The woman who—"

"Please don't go on," Philippe told her firmly. "You know as well as I do our affair ended some time ago."

The small heart-shaped face lifted itself to his. "You mean because I left you that night in Nice? I thought I apologized for that, darling."

"It has nothing to do with that night. I never meant to take you to Nice in the first place. It was only because you were so insistent—"

"That you decided to humor me?" Marie-Catherine demanded. "You make it sound as if I were some poor orphan you took pity on!"

"Of course I didn't mean that. I only meant that whatever was between us doesn't exist any longer. As a couple, we simply aren't suited. Our goals are different. Our ideals—"

A slow, sensuous smile crept across Marie-Catherine's face. "But we are suited in one very important way, *mon cher,*" she told him languidly. "You know that very well."

"Sex is not enough to build a relationship on," Philippe replied. His jaw was set in a rigid line. Clearly, her cajoling was having no effect on him.

"But it's so good between us," she persisted. Her green eyes sparkled mischievously. "Let's go inside. Now. In the middle of the party. I'll show you how wrong you are." She rose from her chair and tugged at his arm. Her eyes shining, her tawny hair ruffled from the gentle breeze, she had never looked more enticing.

"No," Philippe said firmly. "It's over between us, Marie-Catherine. Whatever you may think, it's over." He looked at her levelly as her smile faded and the sparkle in her eyes was replaced by a look of bitter disappointment. Then, as if some inner core suddenly gave her new strength, she straightened her shoulders and met his gaze.

"Thank you for your honesty," she said in a dry, brittle voice. "Now, if you don't mind, I'd like another glass of champagne."

Lily was just finishing up the cleaning when Roni reached the cottage. Although Roni had told the Frenchwoman she was capable of keeping the place herself, Lily wouldn't hear of being displaced. She had kept house for old François for the last fifteen years, she had told Roni firmly. And she would keep it for his granddaughter for as long as she was in residence.

When Lily saw Roni, she fixed them each a cup of strong coffee and insisted on hearing all about the party. Who was there? she wanted to know. What did they have to eat? Did Nicolette seem happy? How about M. Philippe? Roni told her about the balloons and the cotton candy and the circus performers and the magician. She rattled off the guest list as near as she could remember, finishing with the name Marie-Catherine Fontaine.

"Oh, that one!" Lily exclaimed with a shake of her kerchief-bound head. "They'd have a hard time keeping her away."

"Do you know her?" Roni asked. As painful as the subject was, she had a perverse desire to know more about the gorgeous model.

"Not to speak to," Lily admitted. "Although I've seen her around here so much that I feel like I know her as well as anybody. Wild, she is. Comes tearing down the road in that red sports car of hers. I don't know how she keeps from being killed."

"I understand she's going to marry Philippe," Roni said, wondering if perhaps the housekeeper could put the picture in its true perspective.

"I've heard that," replied Lily, "but I can't see it myself."

Roni leaned toward her, intrigued. She hoped her own feelings about the matter didn't show on her face. "Why not?" she asked. "She's beautiful and famous. She seems a perfect choice for someone like Philippe."

"Well," Lily said with a frown, "I don't know what you mean by 'someone like Philippe,' but I don't think people give him enough credit. Oh, I know he's depicted in the papers as being quite a playboy, but the truth is, he's a good, hard-working man and I don't think he'd ever be happy with a woman like Mlle. Fontaine."

"No?" Roni shifted in her chair. "What makes you say that?"

"Because even though I've never met the woman, I can tell you there's no substance to her. She's after the St. Pierre fortune—it's as plain as the nose on your face. And M. Philippe's too smart for that. Oh, he may amuse himself with women like her. And why not? It's not easy to turn down something that's so freely offered. But when it comes to getting married, he'll look for a less flighty type." She sipped her coffee. "You ask me, I think he needs someone like you."

Roni blushed, but before she could reply, Lily was pouring more coffee and off on a new tact. "I hope you won't think I'm being too personal," she began boldly, "but as long as we're on the subject, why is it that a girl like you isn't already married?"

Roni took a deep breath. Ordinarily, she felt such questions *were* too personal, but Lily was such a warm, giving person that it seemed natural to open up to her. In fact, she felt she wanted to confide in her. "I was married, once," she said quietly. "I'm divorced."

Lily looked shocked. "Oh, my, I didn't know. I guess you think I'm an old busybody for asking such a thing. I'm sorry, I—"

"It's all right," Roni broke in. "I want to tell you. You were my mother's girlhood confidante, and I could use a confidante right now." She paused. "My husband's name was Gil Tarleton. He was from a very wealthy family in Denver."

"Denver?" Lily repeated thoughtfully. "That's some distance from New Orleans, isn't it?"

"Yes. Over a thousand miles. But when we met he was living in New Orleans. He left Denver because he wanted to start a life of his own, away from the family business. Or so he said." Lily seemed to miss the irony of this last remark, so she continued. "I met him at a Christmas party given by a mutual friend. Gil was very good-looking. Tall, blond, athletic. And he seemed to take an interest in me from the moment we met. The day after the party, he must have sent me a dozen different bouquets of flowers. And the next thing I knew, he was wining and dining me in all the most expensive clubs and restaurants in New Orleans."

"Well, that makes sense," Lily said stolidly. "Shows he had good taste."

Roni smiled and reached out to touch the older woman's plump hand. "Thank you," she said softly. "Anyway, he asked me to marry him after knowing me for only two weeks." She shook her head at the memory. "It was craziness on my part. I was twenty-four years old—not exactly a child. I'd graduated college, had a job—I'd always considered myself someone with her feet on the ground."

"But you accepted his proposal."

Roni nodded. "I knew it was crazy. But Gil was such an exciting man. I'd never known anyone like him. He opened up a whole new world for me. At least," she added, "I had the brains to suggest we wait a few months before we were married. Even though I was sure I was in love, I didn't think we should rush into it."

"And did you wait? Or did this impulsive man of yours sweep you off on a white horse?"

"Nothing nearly so romantic. You see, it was the next day that I got word that my parents . . . that the plane they were riding in . . . had crashed."

"Ah, *ma chérie,*" Lily clucked sympathetically, "that was so sad. I remember when the news came to your grandfather. Such a terrible shock for him. He was never the same afterward."

"I don't know how I got through it," Roni confessed. "I'd always been very close to my parents. I was completely devastated. But," she added softly, "I had Gil."

"And he helped you." Lily's response was a statement, not a question.

Roni nodded. "He was at my side the whole time. He helped me with the arrangements, kept me going during the funeral." She swallowed hard. "Whatever happened afterward, I'll always be grateful to Gil for what he did then."

Lily caught the note of bitterness in her voice. "If," she said understandingly, "you don't want to talk about the rest . . ." Her voice trailed off.

"No, it's okay, really." Roni straightened her shoulders and managed a small smile. "It's just that . . . well, we were married a week after I buried Mom and Dad. After the plane crash, I decided I didn't want to wait. I needed Gil, or at least I thought I did. We had a small, very private ceremony at my Aunt Gwen's home, and then we left for Paradise Island."

Lily's eyes widened. "Paradise Island? This sounds very romantic."

"It's an island in the Caribbean. It's very beautiful, but for me, it turned out to be anything but romantic." Seeing Lily's frown, she hurried on. "There was a casino on the island. I'd never even been in a casino before, but it turned out Gil was an old hand. He was a compulsive gambler."

"He lost a lot of money?"

Roni shrugged. "He lost sometimes. Sometimes he won. That wasn't the point. From the time we got to Paradise Island, I hardly ever saw him. He'd been so attentive before we got married, and then

160

suddenly he began ignoring me completely. And if he wasn't gambling, he was in the bar, drinking." She sighed. "I finally told him—in a very subtle way, of course—that he seemed to be overdoing it, and he flew into a complete rage. I had no idea he had such a temper. He was like a stranger."

"And after you left this island?" Lily inquired. "Did this hot temper continue?"

"It got worse. Not that I had to put up with it a great deal. Gil took a very expensive penthouse for us in New Orleans, but he was hardly ever at home. I knew his business—whatever it was—couldn't be taking all his time, but when I questioned him about it he said it was none of my concern. He also informed me I didn't 'own' him just because I'd managed to 'snag' him."

"Snag him?" Lily snorted. "After the wild courtship he gave you?"

"Ironic, isn't it? I was so completely bewildered by him I didn't know what to do. I kept thinking that if I was patient and loving, he would eventually settle down and we would have the kind of relationship we'd had when we first met."

"But that didn't happen."

"No. And thanks to Gil's sister, Janet, I found out before very long that it wasn't likely to happen. Janet is a terrific lady, and when she came to New Orleans on business, she phoned and asked us to dinner. Gil was out of town at the time, so it ended up being just the two of us. I was a little intimidated by her at first, but she was so friendly and genuine that I finally let my guard down and told her the truth about Gil and me."

"And? Was she surprised?"

"Not at all. She told me Gil had always been a problem. He was the black sheep of the Tarleton family. When he was eighteen he came into a lot of money that had been left to him in trust by his grandfather—and he proceeded to spend it as fast as he could. Janet said a lot of it was spent on women and liquor, but his biggest vice turned out to be gambling. It took him six years to go through the money, but he finally succeeded in going broke."

"I hope his family didn't give him any more," Lily said. "Wealthy people sometimes do crazy things."

"No, they were too smart for that. But there was more money in trust for him—with certain conditions attached. Gil's father had set up this trust so that the only way Gil could get the money was if he proved he was responsible. It was also suggested that it was time he settled down with a wife and family."

"You don't mean he married you as a means to get his money?" Lily was clearly shocked.

Roni nodded. "He'd been spending a lot of time in New Orleans. The French Quarter was one of his favorite haunts. So when he met me, he decided I was the nice, respectable kind of girl he could use to impress his family."

"And you did impress them—I'm sure of that."

"We flew to Denver for a few days right after our honeymoon. And, yes, they did seem to like me. And," she added wearily, "they turned over the rest of the money to him."

"And," Lily finished, "the drinking and gambling began again."

"It had never really stopped," Roni told her. "He was deeply in debt by the time he came into the second trust. Anyway, after Janet told me all this, I confronted Gil. And he admitted it was all true."

"He admitted he married you just so he could get his hands on the money?"

Roni gave an ironic smile. "Quite the gentleman, huh? Of course, the insult was too much for me, and I told him I wanted a divorce. He agreed right away. After all, by this time he had the money."

"Oh, you poor dear," Lily said, sighing. "How painful it must have been for you."

"Yes, it was very painful. And yet in a funny way, I felt relieved to get my freedom back. After all, it was hardly the kind of marriage I'd dreamed of."

"Yes, and I can understand that. But that's the story of your past," Lily said. "You are still very young and very beautiful. There will be another man one day. The *right* man."

"Oh, Lily, I don't know about that. I go out occasionally in New Orleans, but I'm not sure I want to get so deeply involved again. To trust someone and have so much pain . . ." She drifted off as Philippe sprang to her mind. She had suffered pain at his hands despite her attempts to remain uninvolved. She was beginning to think she was the kind of woman who attracted insincere men.

But Lily was having none of it. "What's life without a little pain?" she asked, being unexpectedly blunt. "Haven't you ever heard the expression, 'It's better to have loved and lost than never to have loved at all'?"

"Yes, but—"

Lily cut off her protest. "Anyway, not every man is like your ex-husband. You're a fool if you harden your heart because of one bad apple. The right kind of man would fall in love with you if you'd give him half a chance, but you're not going to find him if you keep your feelings locked up inside a safe."

Roni smiled sadly. As much as she trusted her, she couldn't tell Lily about Philippe, about how she had let down her guard with him, only to be besieged with new doubts. "I suppose you're right," she agreed, not knowing what else to say.

But she couldn't help thinking that the right kind of man didn't seem to be in the cards for her.

It was sunset when he came to her. She was sitting in her garden, drinking coffee and listening to the music drifting over from the party next door. He came through the hedge—as Nicolette always did—suddenly, boldly, a man with a mission.

She jumped up when she saw him. He stopped where he was, his tall, powerful frame silhouetted against the red orange sky.

"Are you all right?" The look in his eyes caused her to shiver. He was not smiling. The energy between them was incredible.

"Yes, of course. Why wouldn't I be?" She looked at him questioningly, not understanding.

"You left the party so suddenly. I thought—"

"I had a little too much champagne," she explained quickly. Her heart was in her throat. Why was he here?

"And perhaps a little too much of Marie-Catherine?"

"I don't understand. Marie-Catherine is your business. I—"

"She has nothing to do with me. I set her straight. I wanted you to know that."

Roni swallowed. She didn't know if she could trust her voice to speak. "Philippe . . . I—" She broke off. His arms were outstretched, waiting for her. With a tiny cry of joy, she ran into them.

She was crying as he kissed her, tears of relief and love mingled with the taste of his lips and tongue. She kissed his mouth, inhaling him, breathing in his very essence. His hands, now becoming so very familiar, roamed her body with unrestrained abandon.

"Come inside," she gasped. "Oh, Philippe, come inside." She pulled away and attempted to lead him to the cottage, but he caught at her hand and forced her to stop.

"I want to," he said huskily. "Oh, God, how I want to! But my daughter's party." He gestured toward the château, and once again, Roni was aware of the music. "I am the host. I cannot be absent for very long."

"Of course. I'm sorry." Roni was red-faced. Obviously, she had been too impetuous.

"Will you come back with me?" Philippe asked her. "The dancing is beginning."

Roni shook her head. Somehow, she didn't want to share Philippe with strangers right now. "No, I'd rather not."

"I could come back here, later." He looked at her meaningfully.

But the spell was broken. That inner voice was trying to make itself heard. Slow down, it was saying to Roni. You still aren't sure of him; he hasn't offered you anything you can count on. Wait a little longer. Don't be in such a hurry to sustain a broken heart.

"The party is likely to last for a while," she told him, mustering a smile. "And the champagne made me sleepy. I'll probably turn in early."

He looked at her for a long moment. Then he nodded. "As you wish, my beautiful Veronique." He blew her a kiss as music swelled in the background.

CHAPTER NINE

Two days after Nicolette's party, Roni drove into Grasse. She had not seen or heard from Philippe since he had stepped through the hedge, and she decided a morning of shopping and a light lunch at one of the outdoor cafés might perk up her lagging spirits.

She had no trouble finding a parking place, but as she walked the quaint, picturesque streets her mind was on neither shopping nor lunch. Memories of those moments of nearly uncontrollable passion in the rose garden—and the meeting that followed outside the cottage—had haunted her thoughts continuously since Saturday, and she was filled with both overwhelming desire and fear. Where was he? Logically, she knew something could have happened to prevent his coming to her, and the fact that she didn't have a phone made immediate contact inconvenient, to say the least. But her own actions at that last encounter niggled at her brain. He had offered to come back that night after the party, and she had told him not to bother. Did he see that as a complete rejection?

Why hadn't she wanted him to come back? When he'd kissed her, she'd been half mad with desire for him. But something had made her hold back; something had kept her from taking the final step. Was it because despite what he had told her about Marie-Catherine, she still didn't trust him?

What did she want from him? A passionate declaration of love? A proposal of marriage? She knew it was much too soon for anything like that. And if they were offered, would she really be so pleased? Her first love affair and subsequent marriage were still painful to remember. As much as her body yearned for Philippe, she still wasn't ready to make a total commitment to anyone else.

Well, then, she wondered, why not abandon herself to an affair with Philippe and to hell with such old-fashioned things as love and commitment?

But in her heart, she knew she could never be so calculatingly uninhibited. I guess I'm just a prude deep down, she decided, sighing inwardly. I don't seem to be able to get past my upbringing. And since there was obviously no simple answer to her dilemma, she pushed the thoughts away and forced herself to concentrate on the store windows she was passing.

In the window of *La Belle Helene,* one of the town's better shops for women's clothing, she spied an attractive three-piece sports outfit and decided to go in and try it on. The saleswoman greeted her in French, which made her wonder whether her "Americanness" was becoming less obvious. She was sure, however, that her correct-but-still-too-formal response gave her away.

The sports outfit consisted of shorts, a wrap-around skirt, and a halter top. The shiny cotton material had a wild floral pattern, the primary colors being a true green and a hot fuchsia. Ordinarily, Roni preferred more subtle colors, but somehow the boldness of this particular outfit intrigued her. She slipped into it in the privacy of one of the shop's small dressing cubicles and was surprised at what a change it made in her appearance. The halter top and the skirt, which was worn over the shorts and revealed a good bit of leg, gave her something of a gypsy look. Although she was blond, if she pulled her hair back on one side and wore long, dangling earrings, she was sure she could look sexy enough even for Philippe St. Pierre. But of course she reminded herself that she wasn't buying the outfit for him. If she got it, it would be because it amused her and because it would be fun to have something so very French to take back to New Orleans.

She was still studying herself in the mirror when she heard voices just outside the dressing room. They were low, but the words were easily distinguishable.

"If worse comes to worse," the woman was saying, "we can always bring Nicolette into it."

"That may not be as easy as you think," the man argued. Both voices sounded vaguely familiar, although Roni couldn't actually place them.

"Don't be ridiculous," the woman answered tartly. "I'll invite her to go swimming at the lake. The child will go anywhere with me. And she'll be allowed because I'm such a *close* friend of the family." The last words held a faintly sarcastic note.

The voices drifted away; obviously, the couple

had moved away from the dressing area. Quickly, Roni slipped out of the three-piece outfit and put on her own yellow walking shorts and matching cotton sweater. She wasn't sure that the child they were talking about was *her* Nicolette, but she was curious as to who the speakers were, all the same.

She emerged from the dressing room in time to see a beautiful woman with wild, tawny hair and a heavily bearded man leaving the shop. Marie-Catherine Fontaine and Alain Dumont. The fleeting curiosity Roni felt as to why this unlikely pair was wandering around Grasse together quickly gave way to a feeling she suspected was close to jealousy. Not because of Philippe this time, but because of Nicolette. Marie-Catherine had been talking about the child as if she were already her stepmother. And the realization that the two were so close gave her a perhaps unwarranted but very real feeling of loss.

Although her heart was no longer in it, she made the purchase and quickly walked back to her car. She decided to skip lunch in town. Eating alone in a restaurant had never appealed to her very much, and she was afraid of running into Marie-Catherine and Alain again. She was glad of her decision when she returned to the cottage and found Nicolette waiting for her in the garden. The sight of the child always gave her a warm feeling.

But Nicolette didn't greet her with her customary enthusiastic hug. "You left my party without saying good-bye," she said, her dark eyes fixed on Roni accusingly. "Weren't you having a good time?"

"Oh, honey, of course I was!" Roni exclaimed quickly, pulling the child to her. "It was a wonderful party. But I did the silliest thing. I drank a little too much of that marvelous champagne your papa was offering, and I got the most terrible headache. I didn't want to tell you I was leaving because you were having such a good time and I didn't want to interrupt." She cupped Nicolette's face in her hands. "I'm sorry if you were hurt."

The child's pouty mouth broke into a smile. "It's okay. I just wish you could have been there for the dancing. I got to dance with my papa!"

This was obviously such a treat that Roni couldn't help being caught up in her enthusiasm. "That's wonderful! It must have been a perfect ending to a perfect day."

"It *was* perfect," Nicolette agreed happily. "But," she added, her smile receding, "I don't think I'll get my birthday wish."

"No? Why not? Was it such an impossible wish?"

"I don't think so, but Papa will never let me go to Nice. At least, not without him, and he's always so busy."

"Your wish was to go to Nice?" Roni asked. "Haven't you been there before?"

"Oh, yes, but not for the Battle of Flowers. Papa always says he'll take me, but he never does."

"Well, as you said, he's a very busy man." Roni was thinking hard. "Tell me about the Battle of Flowers. What's so special about it?"

"Oh, it's *so* beautiful!" she squealed. "First there is a parade, with all the floats made of fresh flow-

171

ers. And there's a king and queen and fairy princess . . . People wear costumes—not just people on the floats but the people on the streets, too. And after the parade, the battle begins!"

"But surely not a real battle?" Roni asked, feigning alarm. "I hope no one gets hurt."

"Oh, no. It is a battle of the flowers. People throw them at each other. I have seen it on television. It looks like so much fun!" Her face was positively glowing as she envisioned the event.

She wants so much to go, Roni thought. Maybe I can make it happen for her. "You know," she told Nicolette, "that sounds like something I'd like to see, too. Do you think your papa would let you go with me?"

The child caught her breath. "I don't know. Maybe. Oh, mademoiselle, would you ask him?"

"Yes, of course I will. But, Nicolette, I know how much your papa worries about you. You mustn't be too disappointed if he says no."

"But he can't say no to you. You won't let him, will you?"

Roni couldn't contain a small chuckle. "I'll do everything I can to get him on our side."

"Can we ask him now?" The little girl was bursting with excitement.

Roni prayed she wouldn't end up being hurt. "I imagine your father's busy at the moment. Maybe I can phone him from Lily's tonight." The real truth was: Roni needed time to prepare for the meeting.

"He won't be too busy," Nicolette insisted.

"He's in his office, but he always lets me come in if I want to."

Roni looked at her. The child was obviously so impatient that she didn't see how she could say no. "All right," she reluctantly agreed, "but if he kicks us out, don't go saying it's my fault."

Nicolette grinned up at her. "Don't worry. I won't." She grabbed Roni's hand and pulled her toward the opening in the hedge. Roni would have liked to comb her hair and freshen her makeup, but Nicolette was determined not to wait a moment longer. She fairly ran along, forcing Roni to walk very fast beside her. She led Roni to one of the St. Pierre Industries buildings some distance from the château. Roni had passed the building the day she had come on the tour, but it was closed to tourists and security was tight. The guard at the entrance smiled at Nicolette but asked Roni to identify herself.

"She's my friend," Nicolette told the man when Roni had given her full name and explained her mission. "She's my father's friend, too. He's expecting us."

"Nicolette," Roni cautioned, not wanting to get caught in a lie.

But the guard waved her protest aside. "It's all right, mademoiselle. M. St. Pierre has left orders that his daughter is to be admitted at all times. And," he smiled, "I'm sure that includes her friends."

Well, at least he does that much for the child, Roni thought as she followed Nicolette up a flight of stairs and into a small, antiseptic-looking office

173

where a stolid middle-aged Frenchwoman sat behind a well-worn desk.

"Hello, Simone," Nicolette greeted her. "We've come to see Papa."

The woman smiled at the child and acknowledged Roni with a nod. "Well, then," she replied briskly, "we'll have to see if we can arrange it." She picked up a telephone and pressed a button in its base. *"Pardon,* monsieur," she said after a moment, "but your daughter is here to see you. With a friend." Another moment, and then she nodded. *"Oui,* monsieur, I will send them in." She replaced the receiver in its cradle and turned to Nicolette. "You may go in, *chérie."*

After the small and impersonal office of the secretary, Roni was astonished to find Philippe ensconced in a large, elegantly appointed room that was decorated in the style of a country hunting lodge. The furniture was of highly polished mahogany and consisted of three mammoth bookcases, a well-equipped bar, a sofa and two enormous leather wing-back chairs, and a massive oblong table that served as Philippe's desk. The polished wood floor was partially covered with animal skins, and the stark white walls were filled with excellent paintings of hunters and hunting parties.

Philippe's eyes widened slightly at the sight of Roni, and Roni thought she detected a momentary flash of pleasure in them. But he quickly regained his old inscrutable expression as he rose to greet her.

"Ah, Veronique . . ." he said warmly. "I did

174

not know you were the friend my little Nikki brought with her." He took her hand and raised it to his lips.

Roni concentrated on being poised and unaffected by him, not on the delicious tingle the contact created.

"Mlle. Roni has something to ask you," Nicolette burst out. She turned and fixed her eyes expectantly on her friend.

"I see. Then perhaps we had all better sit down." Philippe gestured toward the sofa, and when Roni and Nicolette were seated he eased himself into one of the wing-back chairs. "It is nothing serious, I hope?" He looked at Roni.

Roni's eyes caught Nicolette's and twinkled mischievously. "Oh, yes, very serious," she replied solemnly. "At least it's serious as far as Nicolette and I are concerned."

"Ah, then you must tell me right away." Philippe leaned toward her, his dark eyes boring into her own clear blue ones.

Roni was silent for a moment, wondering how best to approach him. In the end, she decided to simply blurt it out. "I want to take Nicolette to Nice to see the Battle of Flowers."

At once, Philippe's expression darkened. His heavy brows knitted together in one of his famous frowns. "So she has told you what an ogre I am and won your sympathy," he said angrily.

"Oh, no, Papa!" Nicolette cried out. "We were only talking about my birthday party, and I said I didn't think I would get my birthday wish."

"Which is exactly the same thing," Philippe replied curtly. "You inferred that you have such a mean papa that your dearest desire is denied you."

"But that's not what—"

"Enough, Nicolette!" Philippe snapped. "I think you must go and leave me alone with Veronique. She will tell me what I need to know."

Nicolette's mouth quivered and she looked as if she were on the verge of tears. "I'm sorry, Papa. I didn't think you'd be angry." Her voice was small and unsteady.

Roni reached out and squeezed her hand. "It's all right, Nicolette," she assured her. "I'll see that your papa understands."

Nicolette cast her an uncertain look, but she seemed slightly less dejected as she walked slowly to the door. "May I wait for you outside?" she asked Roni.

"Yes, of course. I won't be long." Roni smiled at her and Nicolette left, closing the door behind her.

When she had gone, Philippe addressed Roni with annoyance. "I'm sure you think I'm a terrible father," he told her.

"Oh, no, not at all," Roni protested. "I understand perfectly why you're so protective of Nicolette. But she wants to see the Battle of Flowers so badly, and I thought that if I went with her, then perhaps—"

"Veronique, it's not a question of not wanting Nikki to see the battle," Philippe interrupted. "It's a wonderful event, one that everyone should see. But you have no idea what Nice is like on that day. The crowds are enormous. And they are not only full of revelers; they are also full of pickpockets, prostitutes, gypsies, drunks—all sorts of unsavory types. One of them could grab Nicolette and be off with her before you knew what was happening."

Roni digested this, then turned to him earnestly. "Philippe, I understand your fears. Believe me, I do. But there is such a thing as overprotection. Nicolette is a bright, normal nine-year-old, but she's denied almost everything other nine-year-olds do. If you'll just make this one exception, I promise to take good care of her. I'll hold on to her hand at all times, and I won't take my eyes off her for a moment."

Philippe rose and strode to one of the elegant, floor-to-ceiling French windows. He stood looking out, his hands behind his back. He seemed to be grappling with something that was very difficult to put into words.

"I know you would do your best," he began slowly, "but I just can't take the chance." He turned back to Roni, his eyes dark and troubled. "I don't know what more I can tell you."

Roni rose from the couch and joined him at the window. She was beginning to lose hope, but she had to try once more. For Nicolette's sake.

"Then I'd like to make another suggestion," she said evenly. "If you're afraid to trust her with me, then why don't *you* come along? Nothing will happen to her if both of us are there."

Again Philippe's face wore a troubled expression. He looked at her for a long time. And then, just when she was sure all was lost, his manner underwent an abrupt change. His face lost its tense look and his mouth turned up into a smile.

"You have succeeded in convincing me," he said, suddenly looking very happy. "The three of us will attend the Battle of Flowers and we will have a day to remember!"

"Oh, Philippe, that's wonderful!" Roni's impulse was to fly into his arms and give him an exuberant hug, but she stifled it, knowing what impression it would give him. Anyway, Philippe's doubts about going along had obviously stemmed from the fact that she, and not Marie-Catherine, would be accompanying him, and she didn't want things to become more complicated than they already were.

So instead of hugging him, she simply smiled up at him, then hurried from the room to relay the news to Nicolette.

CHAPTER TEN

The morning of the festival dawned warm and sunny and promised to grow hotter as the day wore on. Roni, almost as excited as little Nicolette, decided to wear what she still thought of as her "gypsy" outfit: the three-piece set she'd bought on her shopping expedition in Grasse. She had managed to find some long, dangling earrings in a shade of green that matched the green of the print, and when she was dressed she had to admit she liked what she saw. The bold colors and the design of the outfit—which bared her midriff and most of her left leg—made her look exotic and daring, and the deep gold tan she had acquired since her arrival in France further enhanced the effect.

She felt Philippe's eyes roving her body approvingly when he called for her and escorted her out to his sports car. Although the Ferrari was designed for two people, Nicolette, looking adorable in a pink dress, pink bows in her hair, had managed to wedge herself into the small area behind the passenger seats. Philippe was wearing white denim pants and a white sport shirt, an outfit beautifully complementing his tan. He looked extremely handsome, and as always, Roni felt a sense of awe just being near him.

He was obviously in good spirits as he started the car and headed for the road to Nice. "I hope you meant it when you said you liked flowers," he teased Roni. "You are going to get your fill of them today."

"There can't be too many flowers for me," Roni declared, winking at Nicolette. "What's more, I intend to pick up all the ones that are thrown and bring them home with me."

"You'll have a hard time doing that!" Philippe replied, laughing. "You have no idea how many flowers you'll see in Nice."

"Papa arranged for a place for us to watch the parade," Nicolette announced eagerly. "He says we will have the best view in town."

"I happen to have a friend who has an apartment on the Rue de Liberte," Philippe explained. "He has very kindly invited us to share his balcony."

By the time they reached the famed resort town, the streets were teeming with people. Seeing the density of the crowds, Roni could understand why Philippe had been so worried about bringing his daughter. But now that he had made the commitment, he seemed unconcerned and jauntily parked the car on a sidewalk, since that was the only space still available. He helped Roni and then Nicolette out and, taking his daughter by the hand, led them deep into the throng. Roni marveled at the throng's diversity. Old people with worn, creased

180

faces seemed as sprightly and happy as the children who cavorted through the streets.

"How about some candied fruit?" Philippe suggested as they neared a pushcart from which delicious-looking confections virtually spilled over. "Or would you prefer a bag of nuts?"

"No, the fruit sounds divine," Roni replied.

"Me, too!" chirped Nicolette.

Philippe bought a bag for each of them, then led them to another cart, this one displaying bunches of flowers tied with ribbons. The vendor, an old man with a toothless grin, was doing a booming business. People were buying as many flowers as they could hold, stuffing them into baskets, pockets, hats—whatever containers were available.

"Why are they buying so *many?*" Roni asked. Although she knew this was a flower festival, the enthusiastic participation of the crowd was overwhelming.

"You'll see," Philippe promised with a smile. He finally managed to attract the attention of the vendor, then filled Roni and Nicolette's arms with as many flowers as they could hold.

"Oh, Papa, I love it!" Nicolette squealed. Her eyes were shining like stars as she looked from her father to Roni. "Thank you so much for bringing me here."

"Thank *you* for thinking of it," Philippe responded warmly. He bent down and kissed his daughter's cheek.

Suddenly a shout went up through the crowd. "The parade! The parade is beginning!"

"Quick!" Philippe shouted, taking each of his

charges' hands. "This way!" He led them, stumbling and laughing, to a small building off avenue Jean-Médecin and dragged them up two flights of stairs. As Roni and Nicolette stood gasping for breath he pounded on a heavy door and shouted for someone named Roland. "Hurry up!" he commanded loudly. "Let us in!"

The door was promptly opened by a short, beefy man with a friendly face, who greeted them with wry exasperation. "If you were so afraid you'd miss the parade, you shouldn't have come so late!" he chided lightly, leading them quickly through a cluttered living room and out to a large veranda where several other people were already gathered. "You're in luck, though," he added. "It's just beginning."

The other guests made room as Roni, Philippe, and Nicolette squeezed themselves up against the guardrail.

"Look! Here it comes!" Nicolette shouted, jumping up and down and pointing as a troupe of tumblers dressed as clowns came cartwheeling down the street. They were followed by the first float, which was made entirely of flowers. It was shaped like a huge rose, and in the center stood a beautiful girl wearing a long, billowing gown. On her head she wore a tiara that sparkled dazzlingly in the sunlight. "You see?" Nicolette said to Roni. "Didn't I tell you there would be a fairy princess?"

Roni couldn't resist bending down and giving her a warm hug. "Yes, you did," she agreed happily. "You were right about everything."

The rose float was followed by a one-man band

who received cheers from the crowd as he some-how managed to make music out of the half dozen instruments he had strapped to his back, hands, and legs.

Other floats followed, each one elaborately deco-rated with vibrant flowers. Costumed participants on the floats waved to the crowds, and the specta-tors pelted them with the flowers they'd bought from the vendors. The Flower Queen, a young, dark-haired beauty, happened to glance up as her float glided past the balcony where Roni and the two St. Pierres were standing. She waved at Nico-lette, and the little girl got so excited that she re-leased all the flowers her father had bought her. The Flower Queen caught one of the bunches and waved again in Nicolette's direction.

"Did you see!" the little girl gasped. "The queen caught my flowers!"

At some point during the course of the parade, someone put a glass of champagne in Roni's hand, but she barely sipped it. She didn't need cham-pagne to brighten her mood today. Just being in Nice with Philippe and Nicolette for this fabulous festival was enough to make her head spin. As she stood on the balcony with one hand on Nicolette's shoulder she was very aware of Philippe's body pressing into hers. She told herself it was not delib-erate, that it was the natural result of being squashed in among so many people. But she couldn't help being affected by his nearness.

She never wanted the day to end.

Soon, however, the last float passed their van-tage point. Roni turned to Philippe and offered him a wistful smile. "It was wonderful, Philippe," she declared. "I wish it could have gone on a while longer."

"But it's not over yet, mademoiselle," Roland told her. "In fact, the main event of the day is just beginning."

"You mean the parade isn't the main event?" Roni looked at him in surprise.

"Look below," Philippe told her, turning back to the street.

As Roni followed his lead her eyes met with an incredible sight. People who had been watching the parade had stepped from their places on the sidewalks and taken over the entire street. Shouting and laughing, they were bombarding one another with hordes of flowers, more flowers than Roni would have believed existed. Multicolored petals filled the air like confetti, and their fragrance perfumed the entire city.

"It's the battle!" Nicolette announced, laughing at the look of amazement on Roni's face. "I told you about the Battle of Flowers."

"Yes, but I didn't think you meant a *real* battle!" Roni exclaimed. "This is fantastic!"

"Oh, Papa!" Nicolette cried, turning pleading eyes on Philippe. "Can't we go down and join them?"

"But we have the best view right here," Philippe answered, holding his glass as his host replenished it with champagne. "We'd have to fight our way through the mob down there."

"I don't care. I want to join in the battle." The

child turned to Roni for support. "Don't you, Mademoiselle Roni?"

"Oh, I . . ." Roni didn't know how to answer. It was obvious that Philippe was happy where he was. But Nicolette was so charming in her appeal. And, yes, now that she thought about it, Roni wanted to join in the battle, too. "What do you say, Philippe?" she asked, looking almost as eager as Nicolette. "Don't you think we could handle the mob?"

Philippe gave her an exasperated look, then he laughed. "Oh, all right. Obviously, I'm outnumbered." He grasped Roni and Nicolette's hands and led them out of the apartment and down into the street.

Here it seemed to be raining flowers. Roni was almost giddy with delight. She felt the flowers land in her hair and saw that Philippe and Nicolette were covered with them as well. Philippe quickly grabbed a basket of blooms from a passing vendor and tossed a handful at his daughter. Nicolette responded by snatching another handful from the same basket and returning the favor. She was laughing with the kind of abandonment that comes from total joy.

Watching the child and her father made tears rush to Roni's eyes. They were so beautiful together, both dark and intense, both exuding love and happiness. This, Roni thought, was not the Philippe St. Pierre the columnists wrote about. This was not the playboy scion of the fabulous perfume family. This was a loving father, caught up in the exquisite delight of enjoying his daughter. His

185

eyes glowed exactly as Nicolette's did, and when he turned his glance on Roni she was overwhelmed by the emotion behind it.

"Quick! Let's bombard Veronique," he urged Nicolette with a wicked grin. He threw a handful of flowers directly at her.

"Oh, yes, let's!" Nicolette cried in agreement as she began tossing blossoms at her friend.

Roni feigned anger. "So you want to fight, do you?" She scooped up some flowers from the sidewalk and aimed them at her two companions. Nicolette squealed and clapped her hands as Philippe scooped up twice as many and tossed them back at Roni.

Their own personal battle was in full swing. Roni was sure she had never been happier as she felt the feather-light deluge of Philippe's flowers and tossed out as many of her own. The mingled fragrance of so many varieties of flowers was heavenly.

And then everything changed. Suddenly, the breeze, which had been warm but gentle, changed into a hot, dry wind with almost gale force. It swept the flowers up from the streets and sidewalks and swirled them through the air with stunning ferocity.

Roni was nearly knocked off her feet by the sudden blast, but because she was so happy, she could only laugh at her unsteadiness. "No fair! You're getting help from the wind!" she shouted at Philippe, trying her best to keep her skirt from being blown up.

But Philippe wasn't laughing. "Let's go!" he

commanded curtly, snatching up Nicolette's hand and gesturing for Roni to follow. He turned in the direction of his parked car.

"But wait . . . It's nothing—just a little wind," Roni protested, knowing Nicolette would be as disappointed as she if the outing were to end so abruptly.

Philippe did not respond. His face had a grim look as he braced himself against the wind, dragging his daughter along behind him. And for once, Nicolette was not protesting. She held her free hand to her hair, trying valiantly to keep her pink bows from escaping.

Bewildered, Roni hurried along beside them, a dull feeling of dread creeping through her body. Something was very wrong, and she didn't know what it was. Why should a sudden shift in weather spoil their entire day?

When they reached the car, Philippe opened the door and Nicolette scrambled to her place in back. Roni was on the verge of protesting again, but one look at Philippe's tight face told her she must do as she was told. Silently, she slipped into the passenger seat. Philippe slammed her door shut, then raced around to the other side and slid in behind the wheel. The tires squealed as the Ferrari lurched off the curb and down the street. Through her shock, Roni managed to notice that the streets, which only minutes ago had been filled with people, were almost empty now. It was as if an unknown enemy had taken over the city.

They were almost to the outskirts of town when Roni finally dared to speak. "Will you please tell me what's going on?" she demanded of Philippe. "Why did you spirit us away like that? You'd think the city was under nuclear attack."

"It was because of the sirocco," Nicolette said as Philippe, hunched tensely in the driver's seat, continued to concentrate on the road. "We have to get home and see to the flowers."

"The sirocco? What on earth is that?" Roni turned around to face the child.

"It's that wind that suddenly blew up. It can scorch and ruin the flowers. The only way they can be saved is if we can cover them in time."

Roni looked anxiously at Philippe. "It's really that serious?"

He nodded. "I'm sorry it had to spoil your fun. It doesn't blow through here very often, but when it does we need all the help we can get in the fields. The sirocco could ruin us in one day."

"Oh, Philippe, I had no idea." As they reached the countryside, she could see the dust swirling through the air. The force of the wind could be felt even in the car as Philippe fought to keep it steady on the road. She could imagine the threat it would be to the delicate lavender and jasmine now in bloom in Grasse.

"I just wish they'd find some way of predicting it," Philippe said. "If I'd known, I never would have left today."

They drove in silence for a while, and Roni could feel Philippe's tension. If his fields were destroyed, he would have to buy the flowers for his perfumes. And undoubtedly they would cost a fortune. Strange, Roni thought, she hadn't imagined

188

anything could threaten a man like Philippe. And yet something as primitive as a hot wind could destroy everything.

And the sirocco wasn't the only threat to St. Pierre Industries, she remembered with dismay. There was also the counterfeiting situation she had heard about at the stockholders meeting. Philippe hadn't discussed that fully with her, but she knew it was serious.

When they reached Grasse, it was obvious that the situation was critical. All the flower fields, usually so peaceful, were filled with workmen who were feverishly covering the plants with huge sheets of plastic. Roni could see the ends of the sheets flapping furiously as the men struggled against the wind to fasten them to the ground. The St. Pierre fields were the same.

When they reached the St. Pierre property line, Philippe slammed the car to a halt and jumped out without speaking to either Roni or Nicolette. Stripping off his shirt as he ran, he headed for a spot that seemed to be short of workers. His naked torso gleamed bronze in the sun. His pectorals bulged as he grabbed a sheet of billowing plastic and held it fast until one of the workers could drive a stake through the bottom and secure it.

Not sure what was expected of her, Roni got out of the car and helped Nicolette out after her. The impact of the wind was shocking. In addition to being fiercely hot, it carried the dust from the fields with it. As soon as she was out of the car, Roni could feel the dust settling in her hair and on her skin.

What should she do? Make a dash for the cottage and take Nicolette with her? She was sure Philippe expected her to do something like that, and at the moment, the clean peacefulness of the cottage seemed like a haven. But how could she go home when everyone else was working so hard to save Philippe from destruction? "Nicolette," she said to the child, who looked as if she were about to be blown away, "do you think you can make it to the château? I'd take you to the cottage, but I want to stay here and try to help."

Nicolette shook her head. "I will stay here and help you. Papa needs us both."

"But the wind is too strong for you," Roni protested. "I think you must go inside. Your father will be angry with me if I let you stay out here."

"I'm staying," Nicolette said firmly. "Come." She bolted away, heading for the field where her father was working.

Roni ran after her. Although she had no idea whether she could do what seemed like an impossible job, she joined a group of workers who were attempting to secure still another sheet of plastic. No one looked up as she grabbed one of the ends. The plastic was heavier than she had imagined, and it was all she could do to keep the wind from ripping it from her grasp. Her hair was blowing wildly; she could taste the dust in her mouth. Somehow, she managed to hang on until a man with a stake and hammer managed to secure her side of the plastic to the ground. Then, quickly, she rushed to another group and performed the same task.

She saw Philippe, his body glistening with sweat, his dark hair blowing around his face, run toward Nicolette and speak to her. He looked angry, and the little girl began to cry. Then Philippe pointed toward the château, and Nicolette, after giving him a final pleading look, took off running in that direction. I'm glad he sent her home, Roni thought as she struggled to hang on to the plastic. She's too little to be of any help here.

The afternoon wore on. The wind continued to blow as fiercely as ever, and the workers continued their fight to save the flowers. Roni became more and more exhausted as she moved from one bed to the other, from one field to the other. Her back ached badly, her hands were sore from handling the rough plastic, her eyes stung from the blowing dirt, and her skin was scorched from the sun. If only I could have a drink of water, she thought at one point. But she quickly pushed the thought from her mind. There was no time to go for water. She must stay here until the last bed was covered. The flowers—and Philippe—were depending on her.

She didn't know how she managed at the end. Somewhere along the way, her mind stopped working; only her body was moving, like a robot's. She was dimly aware that they were reaching the last of the flower beds, that only one sheet of plastic remained to be put down. She grabbed one of the sides and held fast, as she had been doing all afternoon.

"Alors!" someone shouted. "It is done."

She was aware of the workmen moving away

from her, of excited voices shouting in French. I must go, too, she thought dully. Perhaps they're moving to another field. But her legs would not move. Try as she might, she couldn't put one foot in front of the other. And as she stood there braced against the wind, even the effort of remaining upright became too much for her. She sank to the ground, grateful for the dark covering that seemed to enfold her.

When she opened her eyes Philippe was standing over her. His white pants were filthy, and his face and upper torso were covered with dirt mingled with sweat. But he was regarding her with a tender smile.

"Are you all right, Veronique?" he asked with concern.

She nodded wearily. "Yes. Yes, I'm fine."

Philippe bent down and helped her to sit upright. "Then let me help you up."

Roni's head was spinning, but his arms felt strong and she was able to get to her feet. She stumbled when she tried to walk, but Philippe was beside her and she quickly regained her balance.

"All right now?" Philippe asked her.

She nodded. Slowly, they made their way across the field. The wind was still whipping around them furiously, but Roni could feel only Philippe's arms. "Where are we going?" she asked. It was difficult to talk, her mouth was so dry.

"The guest house is closest," Philippe replied. "We can shower there and get something to drink."

"Water. How wonderful." Roni managed a

small smile. "Nicolette," she murmured. She had almost forgotten the child. "What happened to her?"

"I ordered her back to the château. She had no business in the fields."

"I'm sorry. It was my fault. I should have taken her in—"

"Shh . . ." Philippe's hand tightened on her arm. "You did the right thing. Everything's going to be fine."

Roni could see the guest house ahead. It was built of the same gray stone as the château and even resembled it in architecture. It looked cool and inviting. Gratefully, Roni let Philippe lead her inside. As the door closed behind them she felt a tremendous sense of relief. Here there was quiet and blissful cleanliness, a million miles away from the storm.

A staircase leading to the second floor stood to the right of the entryway. "Think you can make it?" Philippe asked as he guided her toward it. "Or shall I carry you up?"

"First, a glass of water, then I can make it, thank you." She was feeling much stronger now. After a drink, the promise of a shower was most attractive.

"Here's your water and the bathroom is there," Philippe said, pointing down the hall as they stood on the second-story landing. "I think you'll find everything you need."

"Thank you." Roni's eyes met his. "Will you be . . ."

"There's another bathroom downstairs," he answered, anticipating her question. "I'll shower there and open some cold wine."

"That sounds wonderful." Reluctantly pulling her hand from his, Roni moved toward the door he had pointed out. The first room she entered was a bedroom, which was furnished in Regency antiques. Its dominant feature was a huge four-poster bed covered with an elaborate brocade spread. Roni was tempted to collapse on it and take her shower later, but she continued on to the adjoining bathroom, where she found an abundant supply of towels, soap, and shampoo and even a terrycloth bathrobe hanging on the back of the door.

The heavy stream of water from the shower felt wonderful. She was instantly refreshed as she soaped her skin and shampooed her hair. The soap had a light, fresh scent to it that clung to her body. She made a mental note to find out the name of it.

When she finally felt thoroughly clean, she stepped from the shower and wrapped herself in the robe. It was far too big for her, and she had to loop the belt around her waist twice in order to keep the front from gaping open. In addition, the robe hung just below her knees. Not a very flattering length, she noted as she surveyed herself in the full-length mirror, which covered one entire wall. Still, she was free of that awful dust, and she felt immeasurably cleaner.

She came out of the bathroom barefoot and toweling her still damp hair. Philippe had already returned with the wine. He was standing next to a lovely Regency French writing desk on which rested a silver tray and two crystal tulip glasses.

"Find everything all right?" he asked, offering a concerned smile.

"Yes. Thank you."

He was wearing an old pair of faded jeans, but his chest was bare, his olive skin glowing from his own recent shower. As in the fields, Roni could see every line of the taut, powerful torso; the hard, solid muscles on his shoulders and forearms; the mass of curling dark hair that fanned across his chest, diminishing in width as it traveled downward until a thin line disappeared beneath the low-slung jeans. Beautifully proportioned, he was the perfect figure of a man. Almost, Roni reflected briefly, like an exquisite piece of sculpture. Suddenly, she realized she'd been staring at him and dropped her gaze to the floor, embarrassed.

"I suppose I must look very disreputable," he said, misreading her appraisal of him. "I'm sorry. These jeans were the only clean clothes I could find."

"No. You're fine. Really." Roni smiled at him uncertainly. She wished she'd at least combed her hair and put on a little lipstick. She felt disheveled. A mess. And appearing before him in nothing but a robe made her feel extremely uncomfortable.

Philippe poured the wine and offered her a glass. "This should make us feel better," he said brightly. "There's no champagne downstairs, but this is a nice, dry chablis."

"Anything would taste delicious right now." Roni sipped eagerly. "Mmm. Perfect." She was aware that Philippe had not tasted his. He was watching her with an unreadable expression in his

195

eyes, studying her. It made her uneasy. She took another sip of wine and walked quickly over to the window that looked out over the flower fields. "The wind's still going strong," she remarked, gazing at the swirling dirt and the wildly blowing plastic coverings.

"Yes. It could last well into the night." Philippe had moved up behind her and was looking out over her shoulder. As he spoke, his warm breath touched the back of her neck. She shivered slightly. "Cold?" he asked her.

"Oh, no. Not at all. I guess I'm still just a little . . . shaken." The events of the day had left her not only physically exhausted but emotionally drained as well. The Battle of Flowers had been exhilarating, but the new perception she had gained of Philippe had been far more meaningful. The clear, shining love he had shown toward his daughter, the carefree way he had taken part in the festivities, and the marked attention he had paid to Roni had all but torn down the last of her defenses toward the man. And then the sudden blast of hot wind, the tense drive back to Grasse, the fierce, seemingly endless struggle to protect the precious flowers . . . In this one day she had seen a dozen new sides to Philippe—she had seen, she was sure, the total multifaceted man.

And now he was standing inches away from her, his breath warm on her neck, the fresh smell of bath soap mingling with his natural masculine scent. It all seemed too much for Roni. She didn't want to think about him anymore. She didn't want to have to fight yet again the demons that always accompanied her thoughts of him. If just this once she could relax, let her mind go, let him take charge.

"If you'd like to lie down and rest for a while, I can leave you alone," she heard him say gently. "I promise you won't be disturbed."

The words alarmed her. She didn't want to be alone; she didn't want to put an end to the hours they had spent together. Don't break the spell, she willed him. Don't leave me just when I'm starting to feel so very comfortable with you. "Oh, no, please," she said aloud. "There's no need for that. The wine's already making me feel better."

She felt his hands on her shoulders. Slowly his strong fingers descended to probe the muscles on her lower back. "Maybe this will help relax you." She closed her eyes and gave herself up to the delicious warmth that was flooding her body as he massaged her. But all too soon it stopped. He released her and reached for one of her hands. "Come," he said.

"What . . . ? Where are we going?" She had no desire to move. Between the wine and the brief massage, she was beginning to feel quite euphoric.

"If I'm going to get rid of those tense muscles of yours, I need a proper place to work." He led her back a few steps to the side of the ornately carved four-poster and deftly pulled back the spread. "Lie down. *Lie down,*" he repeated when she merely remained where she was. "I promise you the best massage you've ever had." He took her glass from her and set it on the bedside table.

Roni stared at the bed. She was bone tired, and

the ice blue sheets looked cool and inviting. And yet . . . A tug of doubt brought her out of her fuzzy haze. How could she lie down before Philippe wearing nothing but this loose-fitting bathrobe? It wasn't proper. It wasn't . . .

Words sprang to her mind and disappeared again, illusive as fireflies. Deliberation was useless, argument impossible. She hadn't the strength for it. And a massage . . . a massage would be wonderful. Gratefully, she climbed onto the bed and lay down on her stomach.

"Bon." Philippe sat down next to her and gently smoothed the damp hair away from her neck. She felt his hands move just inside the neck of her robe. "How's that?" he asked. "Feel better?"

"Umm." She was letting go again, drifting off to that heavenly oasis of peace. She could, she realized, easily fall asleep, but sleep was the last thing she wanted right now. She wanted to stay awake, to savor the glorious feeling of Philippe's hands on her body. "Tell me about the sirocco," she suggested, thinking conversation would keep her mind working. "Do you have them often?"

"Once every hundred years would be too often for the flower growers," Philippe answered. "But, unfortunately, we have them more often than that, though not always as severe as you saw today. The sirocco comes in from the Libyan deserts; that's why it is so damaging to the crops."

"I've heard of the mistral," Roni murmured drowsily. "How is that different from the sirocco?"

"The mistral is cold; it comes in off the water. We dread it, too, of course. You see, Veronique,

198

any sort of severity in the elements can cause damage, not only to the flowers but to all vegetation. In Egypt, farmers fear the dusty khamsin; in Africa it is the harmattan. And the monsoons of India are accompanied by torrential rain." As he spoke his fingers skillfully plied her neck and shoulder muscles. The massage he gave her was firm and vigorous yet undeniably sensuous.

"It must be dreadful to live under such threat when you have such a precious crop," she responded, forcing herself to concentrate on the conversation.

"Indeed," he agreed, "but crops aren't the only things affected by these winds."

"No?"

"People are affected, too. It is a known fact that human behavior can change during a wind. People have been known to go crazy during these times. They do and say things they would never dream of under ordinary circumstances. Criminals have been known to be acquitted because their crimes were committed during a mistral or sirocco."

"How fascinating. I'd never heard that."

"So far, no one has been able to explain the effect of the wind on human beings," Philippe declared. "Perhaps no one ever will, but many strange things have occurred during a wind."

His hands traveled slightly downward now, kneading the muscles under her shoulder blades. "I hope," Roni said, feeling like a kitten being determinedly stroked, "your crop will be all right."

"I think we managed to save most of it. The workers got started as soon as they realized what was happening. And your help counted for a great deal as well."

"Mine? I felt totally ineffectual out there. It was all I could do to hang on to the plastic long enough for someone to fasten it down."

"But you *did* hang on. That's the important thing." He removed his hands from her back and gripped her shoulders, gently turning her over to face him. His eyes were warm, glowing with a sort of inner light, as they met hers. "You're quite a woman, Veronique."

She hadn't expected to find his face so close to hers, nor to hear the deep, husky note in his voice. The combined effect caused her to tremble. She was drowning in the dark velvet depths of his eyes, and she was powerless to avert her gaze from his. She felt breathless.

Slowly, carefully, his fingertips began to trace the contours of her face, the gentle touch of a blind man savoring a precious work of art. "You're perfect, even when scrubbed clean of makeup," he mused wonderingly. "A faultless pearl that has no need of enhancement." His voice caught as if choked with emotion. "To think a woman so beautiful would be willing to—"

The rest of the sentence was left unsaid as his head lowered and his mouth met hers. His kiss was soft. His lips clung to hers, pulled away, returned, as a hummingbird returns for a sweet, rich nectar. His hands traveled to her shoulders, gently slipping the robe back. He was still sitting beside her. Her own hands reached for him as if they had a

200

mind of their own; her fingertips caressed the soft hair at the nape of his neck.

"Oh, Veronique," he murmured, covering the area around her mouth with a hundred brief kisses. "My sweet, sweet Veronique." She was dreamily aware of his hand at the belt of her robe, untying the knot and gently parting the terrycloth. Philippe touched one of her breasts, covered it, gently caressed it again and again as if he couldn't get enough of the softness, the white, delicately veined skin.

An incredible sense of well-being surged through her body. She felt as if she were floating. His lips traveled upward from her lips now, dropping butterfly kisses on eyes closed in ecstasy. "Philippe . . ." She ran her hands across his broad chest, feeling the pounding of his heart, stroking the powerful lines of his upper body.

"Don't say anything," he whispered. "Lie still. Let me worship your exquisite body."

She lay back, a small smile on her lips as once again his mouth roamed across her face. He kissed her temples, her ears, the tiny dimple in the hollow of her cheek. His tongue, warm and wet, gently flicked its way down the contours of her throat, stopping in the hollow of her neck to lick her sensuously. Then down across her breastbone, finally reaching her nipples, which stood erect and quivering. He took one full into his mouth and teased it with his tongue, causing her to writhe and moan softly. One of his hands slid down her hips, rubbing provocatively. Her lower body throbbed with a need so strong it was all she could do to keep from crying out.

"No. Don't say it," he murmured, mistaking the low moans in her throat for the instinctive protest that had plagued his last amorous advance. "It's all right. I promise you."

His hand was on her inner thigh now, tickling gently . . . tantalizing . . . making her excruciatingly aware of the one place he still had not touched. His mouth left her breasts and traveled to her navel, his tongue blazing a hot, moist trail as it flicked at skin that felt as if it were on fire.

Her hands, as if they suddenly had a mind of their own, reached out for him. Her fingertips touched the waistband of his jeans, fumbling for the snap that held it closed and ripping at the zipper that contained that part of him she now knew she could not do without.

He helped her by pushing the jeans from his hips and freeing his legs, then caught her off guard as he plunged his head downward and tasted the most exquisite spot of all. She arched her hips upward, opening herself to him . . . defenseless . . . trusting . . . powerless to resist what she had fought so long.

Every nerve in her body was focused on one electrifying point. She felt the explosion mounting inside her; she didn't know how much longer she could bear its being contained.

A little cry escaped her. She was so close . . . so close . . .

"Not yet, my impatient darling." Philippe's voice sounded far away, somewhere beyond the whirling depths of her passion. "We have waited too long to let this moment pass so quickly."

And then, once again, his mouth was on hers, pushing her head back against the pillow. For the first time, his body covered hers. His brawny chest crushed her breasts, his strong legs pinned her thighs, and she could feel his hardness pushing at the spot he had so exquisitely aroused. But still he continued to tease her. Complete union was not yet a reality.

I will go mad, she thought as she desperately sought some way to envelop him. If he continues to tease me, I will surely go mad.

But at last, not even a lover as strong as Philippe could delay the ultimate intoxicating moment. Just when she was sure she could not stand another minute of his teasing, he suddenly came to her, thrusting purposefully until the resulting explosion made her gasp with pleasure that went so deep it seemed to reverberate through every fiber of her body.

She felt his climax almost immediately thereafter, and his arms tightened around her then as he held her close. And when he finally released her and turned her face to his, he was looking at her as if she were a precious treasure.

"All right?" he asked with a gentle, loving smile.

She nodded happily, contentedly. She wanted only to gaze at him, to feel his arms around her, now and forever. I love him, she thought with quiet joy. I don't know what his true feelings are for me, but I can't deny mine anymore.

He was turned on his side, regarding her tenderly. "A centime," he said.

"A what?"

"Isn't that what you say in America? 'A penny for your thoughts'? In France we say a centime."

She blushed. "They aren't for sale. At least, not right now." She looked at him. "What about yours? Are yours for sale?"

He answered slowly. "You must know what mine are. Oh, Veronique, I never thought—"

"Shh." She lifted her mouth to his. Although she had asked, she suddenly didn't want to hear his answer. In her experience, pillow talk was not something that could be trusted. At this moment all she wanted to do was lie in his arms and bask in the nearness of him. Words were not even important. "I don't have a centime," she said in helpless explanation.

He raised up on one arm and gave her an amused look. "I wasn't planning to present you with a bill. But since you insist on obeying the rules, why don't we have another glass of wine instead?" He reached for the bottle and refilled their glasses.

Roni was embarrassed. "I guess I'm a little disconnected," she confessed. "So much has happened today. The Battle of Flowers and the sirocco and now . . . this . . ."

"And of the three, which did you enjoy most?" Philippe teased. "The Battle of Flowers, *oui?*"

"Let's say I liked that second best." Their eyes met over the tops of their wine glasses. "It was wonderful seeing you with Nicolette," she went

204

on. The look he was giving her was causing a funny tingling in her stomach, and she wasn't prepared to surrender to it again just yet. "You two obviously adore each other."

He nodded. "Nicolette has been my life for the past seven years."

"I can't help wondering why you didn't mention her that night at the château, when you told me about her mother." Roni wondered if she were being too inquisitive, but the question had occurred to her more than once, and now seemed as good a time as any to ask it.

Philippe smiled wryly. "My sweet, we had only just become acquainted. I hardly thought it was the time to spring a nine-year-old child on you." He tilted his wine glass until it clinked with hers. "To you, my lovely Veronique."

They sipped, their eyes still locked together. Roni could no longer deny the desire rising in her again. From the look on Philippe's face, it was obvious he was feeling the same thing. Slowly, without shifting his glance, he removed the glass from her hand. Roni heard the faint sound of both glasses being set on the table. But all her other senses were obliterated in the fresh rush of passion. Philippe's arms were around her again, and his mouth was roaming her body, causing her to gasp in pleasure. Their lovemaking was more leisurely this time but full of deep need, nonetheless. Together, they explored each other's bodies, stopping occasionally to kiss long and lingeringly, then resuming the exploration until they were both breathless with desire. Their second union was as

205

beautiful as their first. They melded together with long, languid strokes, once again climaxing at exactly the same time and clinging together afterward in wild exultation.

"I'd like to keep you here forever," Philippe whispered when they could at last speak. "I never want to let you go."

Ah, if only it could be, Roni thought, pressing against him and kissing the back of his neck. "I suppose that's my cue to get up," she said dreamily, not moving.

Philippe held her close. "Alas, yes. The afternoon is gone and I must check the fields. And my father will expect a full report." He pulled back and looked at her regretfully.

She smiled. "I understand. It's all right." She gently disengaged herself from him and sat up. Then, remembering the shape her clothes were in, she made a face. "Although I don't look forward to getting dressed."

"Well," Philippe replied, grinning, misunderstanding, "I suppose you could go home au naturel. But I don't know what Lily would say if she happened to be at the cottage."

Roni laughed. "Knowing Lily, she'd probably give three cheers." She rose and reached for the bathrobe.

Philippe reached out and took her hand. "If I can possibly get free later . . ."

She shook her head. "No, really. I do understand. The wind could last all night and you'll want to keep watch." She turned to him and kissed his shoulder. "Promise to let me know if you need me."

"I'll let that line pass," Philippe replied. He gave her a lingering look. Then he let her go and gave her a playful swat on her derriere. "Go get dressed. I'll drive you home."

Going back out into the wind was like leaving a beautiful dream, and neither spoke during the short ride to the cottage. But when he had stopped the car in the driveway, Philippe reached for her and kissed her fervently. "*Au revoir,* Roni," he whispered. "Think of me."

CHAPTER ELEVEN

How could she think of anything else? Her whole body still burned from the remembrance of his caresses; all her senses were attuned only to him—his smell, his touch, the wonderful, melodic sound of his voice. She relived their lovemaking, moment by moment, as once again she showered and then laundered her grime-filled clothes.

She was gripped by a feeling of loneliness; she had been away from him for less than an hour and already she missed him desperately. I must get my mind off him, she thought as she slipped into a thin pale blue caftan and tied her hair back with a matching ribbon. I've never let any man dominate my thoughts like this, and I certainly can't let Philippe do it. Only by remaining her own person, she insisted to herself, could she ever hope to make Philippe love her as much as she loved him.

She decided to spend the evening curled up with a book from her grandfather's collection. She knew concentration would be difficult, but perhaps she could find something absorbing enough to hold her attention. Hopefully, she hurried to her grandfather's study. But when she opened the door the scene before her eyes caused her to cry out in shock and dismay.

The study was a total wreck. Drawers had been flung open and their contents emptied onto the floor. Papers were scattered everywhere, and even the books had been torn from their shelves and left wherever they fell. Some of the books that were very old had been broken at their spines, the yellowed pages spilling out in complete disorder. A chair had been overturned and lay sprawled on the floor, its legs pointing at the opposite wall. It was the first thing Roni rushed to set right.

Methodically, almost mindlessly, she began picking up the books and scattered papers. Her brain was numb with shock. Who was responsible for this? And why? For God's sake, *why?* François's desk had been ransacked, and it occurred to her that someone might have been looking for his personal papers. But when she sorted out the mess, she could find nothing missing. Even the letters in the bottom drawer were all accounted for. Then she saw the locked center drawer.

Although the lock was intact, the wood around it was full of deep scratches, as if someone had tried to pry it open. Obviously, they had not succeeded, owing, Roni suspected, to the sound of Philippe's car when it pulled into the driveway. Her return must have frightened the thief off.

Was something of value inside that drawer? Having failed to find the key earlier, Roni knew looking for it now would be hopeless. Obviously, the intruder had searched and failed. There was nothing for her to do but break into the drawer herself. She remembered seeing a toolbox in the closet in her grandfather's bedroom and went to fetch it. She didn't have the slightest idea how to break a lock, but after a great deal of perseverance —and almost complete destruction of the drawer —she finally succeeded.

She saw the envelope right away. It was lying in the center of the drawer, and it was addressed to her in her grandfather's handwriting. Catching her breath, she snatched it up and ripped it open. It contained two sheets of paper, one of which contained odd scribbles and numbers that seemed completely indecipherable. Written on the other page was a letter:

My dear granddaughter,

I know that we will never meet and that by the time you read this I shall be gone. I know, my dear Veronique, that I wronged your beloved mother very deeply, and I will never forgive myself for that. The only way in which I can even begin to atone for my sin is to make life easier for you, whom I have never seen. That is why I have made you my heiress. This house, and the stock I have left you in St. Pierre Industries, is not nearly enough to make up for the pain I caused your mother in her lifetime. Indeed, I can never make up for that. But there is one thing more that I can give you that will perhaps secure the future of my descendants through you. My beloved grandchild, I have left you a formula for my own perfume, with which I have experimented for many years. I believe it is a unique and elegant fragrance and one that St. Pierre Industries should be happy to market for you. I don't say that you must take the formula to M. St. Pierre, but he has been good to me and will treat you fairly in matters of price and royalties.

God bless you, my dear Veronique. Though you may have had reason to doubt it, I am, and have always been, your loving and devoted granpapa.

François Du Priex

Roni stared first at the letter and then at the formula for the perfume. She recalled Nicolette's telling her about the perfume François had made for her, the perfume that had disappeared from the little girl's bedroom. It was all true! A burst of excitement washed over her. Imagine how pleased Philippe would be when he learned of this! Old François had obviously thought he had come up with something very special. This could be the savior of St. Pierre Industries, particularly now, when the counterfeiting scandal loomed so threateningly.

But until she saw Philippe, she must keep the formula absolutely safe. Undoubtedly, it was what her intruder was looking for when he ransacked the office. Somehow, someone else knew about the formula and was determined to get to it first. She considered running over to Lily's and phoning the police but decided it could wait until tomorrow.

The fact that her arrival had frightened the intruder off made her feel certain he would not return again tonight.

She thought hard and finally decided the best place for the formula was among the pile of letters her mother had written to François. Even if the intruder should return, the letters had already been rifled through. Carefully, she hid both the formula and accompanying note. Then she set about straightening up the room. She replaced the contents of the drawers and gingerly returned the books to the shelves.

She had just finished up when the doorbell rang. Philippe! she thought joyously. The threat of the sirocco must be over! She took the stairs two at a time, smoothing her hair as she ran. Her heart was pounding so loudly she was sure it could be heard all the way to the château.

But when she opened the door, it was not Philippe who was waiting there. Marie-Catherine Fontaine, looking as beautiful as ever, stood before her. She was wearing a long emerald green cape, the hood of which she had pulled up over her head to protect her from the wind and blowing dirt. Her face was impeccably made up, and she was regarding Roni with eyes that raged in open fury. In fact, her anger could be felt so acutely that Roni involuntarily took a step back.

"Yes?" she asked warily. "Is there something I can do for you?" She stiffened, prepared for a battle about which she knew nothing.

"I want to talk to you. Please let me come inside. The wind is still very strong."

Roni had no desire to talk to Marie-Catherine, but the model's voice was so authoritative she found herself unlatching the screen and standing aside as she swept in.

"I'm very busy at the moment," she told her, wishing she were not alone in the cottage. "I can't give you much time."

"This won't take much time," Marie-Catherine said coldly. She glared at Roni. "It's about Philippe."

"Philippe St. Pierre? What about him?" Roni's heart was in her throat. Had something happened to Philippe?

"I know what happened between you today. I saw you in Nice. At the Battle of Flowers. And then I followed you back to Grasse."

Roni's eyes narrowed. "So? I can't see that my being with Philippe was any of your concern."

"I saw you go to the fields." Marie-Catherine's voice was full of sarcasm. "How very clever of you to help cover the flowers. Philippe must have been terribly impressed."

Roni railed at the implication. "I didn't do it for Philippe," she retorted hotly. "I did it because the workers needed all the help they could get."

"And you're noble as well," Marie-Catherine sniped. "I suppose going to the guest house afterward didn't have anything to do with Philippe, either?"

"Since you know so much, you undoubtedly know I was exhausted once the flowers were finally covered," Roni replied indignantly. "Philippe took me to the guest house so I could shower and rest a little."

"And was the four-poster comfortable?" the model asked with a bitter smile. "Oh, believe me, I know how inviting the guest house can be. I've spent many an afternoon there with Philippe."

Roni struggled for control. She would not let Marie-Catherine's jealousy ruin the still-fresh memory of her afternoon of love. "If this is what you came to tell me," she said, eyeing her evenly, "I assume you can leave satisfied. Forgive me if I don't see you to the door."

But Marie-Catherine didn't move. "That's only part of it," she said icily.

"Oh? And the other part?" Roni braced herself for more of the bitter accusations.

"I came to remind you that Philippe is *mine.*" Marie-Catherine's eyes flashed with anger. They, like the cape she wore, were the exact color of emeralds—and every bit as hard. "He may not be above dallying with other women now and then," she went on, "but *I'm* the one he's going to marry. And if you don't want to be made a complete fool of, I suggest you leave Grasse as soon as you can get packed."

Roni's eyes widened in amazement. The nerve of this woman, thinking she could order her to leave! "My relationship with Philippe is my business," she shot back. "And I intend to stay in Grasse as long as I please. Now I suggest *you* leave my home!"

As Marie-Catherine continued to face her, Roni couldn't help being exhilarated by the exchange.

Ordinarily, she was the kind of person who hated confrontations, but she suddenly realized she was enjoying this one. I'm actually fighting for my rights, she thought with a kind of awe. The irony of the fact that she considered her relationship with Philippe her right crossed her mind. Only this morning she had been bracing herself against any intimacy with the man at all.

But Marie-Catherine wasn't through with her own argument. "I suppose you think you can make him fall in love with you," she declared snidely. She uttered a brittle laugh. "Believe me, that dream has been shared by women who have far more to offer than you."

"Oh?" Roni felt the stinging insult, but was careful not to show that it had any effect. "I suppose you think he's still in love with you."

Marie-Catherine tossed her magnificent head. "I have no doubt he has told you it is all over between us. Of course he would have to say that in order to get a prim little schoolteacher into bed. But I assure you, now that the challenge is over, Philippe will return to me. As," she added significantly, "he always has in the past."

Roni drew herself up to her full height. "What makes you think the 'challenge' is over?" she asked steadily.

Marie-Catherine smiled. "My dear, it's written all over your face. Only a woman who has also possessed Philippe could not fail to detect that smug look of physical satisfaction. He is a marvelous lover, is he not?"

"Get out!" Roni shouted, her face flaming. "I won't listen to another word!"

But Marie-Catherine stood her ground. With a start, Roni realized the model's expression had taken on an almost demented quality. Her green eyes held a wild, maniacal gleam. "You are the one who must get out," she said in a voice so low-pitched it was almost a hiss. "Whether you know it or not, I am accustomed to getting what I want. And if something stands in my way, I have no qualms whatsoever about getting rid of it—any way I can."

The viciousness of her words caused Roni to flinch in spite of herself. The beautiful French-woman clearly meant to have Philippe. Her final declaration carried an implied threat—and at this moment, Roni had no doubt that she was fully capable of carrying it out. For a brief, dizzying moment, she wondered if Marie-Catherine meant to kill her if she didn't remove herself from Philippe's life. But the absurdity of such a thought quickly replaced her fear. Still, Marie-Catherine's very presence chilled Roni to the bone.

The model seemed to take Roni's lack of verbal response as an indication that her point had hit home. With a satisfied smile, she turned toward the door, her cape billowing behind her. "Now that we understand each other," she shot back at Roni, "I will bid you *au revoir.*" With ballerinalike grace, she strode to the door, opened it, and disappeared into the night.

Roni lost no time in closing the door and bolting it. Her nerves on edge, she sank onto her sofa and hugged a throw pillow against herself to reduce her shaking.

What on earth was she going to do? She couldn't let the rantings of a jealous woman influence her feelings toward Philippe. Could she? What, she allowed herself to wonder, if the rantings had some truth to them? *Had* Philippe been interested only in her conquest? Would he be interested at all now that the challenge was over? She didn't want to believe Philippe was that kind of man. And yet . . . Who was Veronica Stephens, anyway? How could an American art teacher fit into the life of a world-famous perfume magnate?

Roni bit into her lower lip thoughtfully. Marie-Catherine did seem to be more Philippe's type. She was part of his world—elegant, sophisticated, a celebrity in her own right. And she was very beautiful. Roni swallowed back the lump in her throat. Even if Philippe had told her the truth about his relationship with the model, her fight was far from over. Obviously, Marie-Catherine had no intention of giving up on the man, and she had declared herself an adversary.

Roni sighed and tossed the pillow aside. Maybe, she decided finally, the answer is to do nothing. Make no judgments, have no expectations. If and when it became clear that Philippe's advances were the result of real feeling and not the excitement of new conquest, she would welcome him back into her arms.

In the meantime, she would put everything on hold. Having made the decision, she felt slightly less shaky. She got to her feet and went to the kitchen to make some coffee. Coffee always seemed to help her put things into perspective.

She was sitting quietly at the kitchen table finishing her second cup of coffee when the doorbell sounded. The tone filled her with dread. But it was Philippe who stood at the door. Philippe, wearing jeans and an old shirt, a swatch of dark hair falling over his forehead, his eyes regarding her with unabashed eagerness.

"It's over, Veronique!" he exclaimed without giving her time to so much as speak his name. "The sirocco is losing its force. The fields are safe and St. Pierre will have flowers for perfume!" He pulled open the screen door and reached for her, gathering her into his arms.

"Oh, I'm glad the flowers are safe!" she breathed, feeling so very comfortable in his embrace. But then she remembered her previous visitor. She stiffened and pulled away. "Thank you for coming to tell me."

"That's not all I came for," Philippe said with a wicked smile. "We are going to have a celebration that will last all night long." Oblivious to her coolness, he grabbed her once again and smothered her face with kisses. His hands roamed her body familiarly, touching her in places that only hours ago had made her gasp in pleasure.

But although she longed to give herself up to him and revel in the ecstasy only his body could provide, she knew abandon was impossible. There were still too many doubts in her mind, too many indications that she was already in over her head with the man. Remembering her decision to put things on hold, she wrenched herself free.

Philippe reacted to her unexpected response first with surprise, then with disbelief. "Veronique, what's wrong? Has something happened since this afternoon?"

"No. Nothing." She had no intention of telling him about Marie-Catherine. "I'm . . . I'm just not in the mood, that's all."

He grinned. "I tired you out, did I? Well, then, perhaps I'll let you sleep a little first." When this reply did not produce even a small smile, he paused and studied her intently. "Oh, my darling, don't tell me you've started to regret what we did? Veronique, it was fantastic, a perfect union. There is nothing to be ashamed of because we both received so much pleasure."

"Philippe, please." She was close to tears. She had to get rid of him before she broke down completely—or gave in completely. "It was wrong. It shouldn't have happened. It was too fast . . ."

His face was filled with incredulity. "How can you say such a thing?" He cupped her face in his hands and looked at her. "Veronique, you did receive pleasure from me, didn't you? Everything that happened—your reactions—"

"My reactions were beyond my control!" she burst out, her face contorted with pain. "I wasn't responsible for what happened with you in the guest house."

Philippe frowned. "Are you saying," he began slowly, "that I forced myself on you? Because I assure you—"

"No," Roni interrupted, "it wasn't you. It wasn't me, either. It was . . . the wind."

Philippe released her and looked at her in complete amazement.

"You said people do crazy things during a wind like the sirocco," she went on. "The sirocco was to blame for what I did. I am not responsible for my actions."

"I don't believe this!" He was angry now. "You are telling me that what went on between us was just some meaningless thing caused by the wind?" His dark eyes blazed at her.

No! Roni's heart cried. What went on between us was the result of my love for you! But of course she couldn't tell him that. Not while there were still so many unanswered questions.

"Yes," she answered dully, hating herself for taking the cowardly way out. "That's exactly what it was."

For an instant he seemed hesitant, as if he were considering taking her in his arms despite everything. But as he stared at her he saw the stubbornness in her eyes. "Very well, Veronique," he said at last, his voice cold but his eyes looking very, very sad, "we'll leave it at that."

Then he turned and left.

CHAPTER TWELVE

Sleep that night was impossible. Roni had only to close her eyes to see Philippe's face—his thick brows knitted together in an angry frown, his dark eyes filled with surprise and disappointment, his sensuous mouth tight with frustration and incomprehension. She couldn't stop thinking about the way he had turned from her when she'd insisted their lovemaking had been only the result of the wind; about the way his shoulders, usually so strong and proud, had slumped with dejection.

But I can't feel sorry for him, she told herself as she tossed and turned and beat her pillow in helpless agony. He's had so many women. He may be with someone else this very minute. And yet in that brief moment she had been in his arms, it had felt so right. She had been so tempted to forget about Marie-Catherine and her taunts and abandon herself to Philippe once again.

I'm not cut out for this kind of doubt and intrigue, she realized miserably. I must put Philippe and everything that's happened behind me and get back to my old familiar life. Once I'm back in New Orleans where I belong, I'll forget all this.

She wondered what she should do about the cottage. Should she sell to the St. Pierres or call the man who had made the offer on behalf of the widow? And what about her grandfather's perfume formula? If she didn't turn it over to St. Pierre Industries, what would she do with it?

A hazy dawn filled the sky. She looked out the window from her bed. The wind seemed to have stopped blowing, making the morning seem almost eerily quiet. They'll uncover the flowers today, she thought idly. She wondered if Philippe would help as he had helped to cover them. Probably not, she decided. Now that the threat was over, he could go about more gentlemanly pursuits. She wondered if he had gone to Marie-Catherine after he had left her last night. Obviously, the model was staying somewhere in Grasse. Possibly the two of them were together right now.

"I know how inviting the guest house can be," Marie-Catherine had told her. "I've spent many an afternoon there with Philippe."

They could be there together at this very moment. Stop torturing yourself, her good sense admonished her. Forget him. Sell the cottage and go home!

Sometime in the early morning hours she drifted off in an uneasy sleep. The rigors of the previous day—the excitement of the Battle of Flowers, the hard work in the flower fields, the consuming moments of passion, and the agony of her confrontation with Marie-Catherine—had taken their toll. Still, it was not a long rest, and she woke to feel the sun warming her body through the open window. She glanced at the bedside clock. Ten thirty. She felt more tired, if possible, than when she had gone to bed. Every bone in her body ached.

She struggled out of bed, ran a brush through her hair, and put on shorts and a halter. Although she had no appetite, she realized she hadn't eaten a solid meal since yesterday morning; so she fixed herself two soft-boiled eggs and a piece of toast. The food tasted flat, but she felt a little better when she had finished. Even so, she dreaded facing the rest of the day. She knew she would have to come to a decision regarding the cottage, and she had no idea how she was going to make it.

She was washing up the few dishes she had used when she heard a car drive up and stop. It was not, she knew, Philippe's sports car. That had a sound all its own, and her ear could pick it up from some distance away. She went to the window and looked out. A man was getting out of the car and walking toward her door. He was tall and very blond.

She looked again, her mind refusing to believe what her eyes told her. "It can't be!" she breathed aloud. But it was. The man approaching her door was Gilbert Tarleton, her former husband. No! Oh, no! she screamed silently. Her palms began to sweat and her stomach was suddenly full of knots. What in the name of God was he doing here? I won't go to the door. I'll stay here in the kitchen and wait until he goes away. But at the sound of his knock, she found herself walking to the living room. He had known exactly where to find her; she was sure he wouldn't give up after one attempt at a meeting.

When she opened the door, the life she had

shared with him came rushing back. The blue eyes that focused on her in such a friendly way were the same eyes that had swept her into the delicious fantasy that had turned into a horrible nightmare. The smile was the same one that had once wrenched her heart, the smile that had all too soon changed to a habitual angry scowl. But his manner at this moment was cordial and light.

"Roni! You really are here!" His face was joyful, his tone expressing sincere pleasure. "I was so afraid my information was wrong, or that you'd be gone by the time I got here." As Roni stood stock still, her hand on the doorknob, still too much in shock to trust her voice, he went on. "You look wonderful! France obviously agrees with you."

"I—this is a surprise." Why, Roni wondered, did the most dramatic moments of her life seem to take place at this door? She felt at a disadvantage, yet she was wary of inviting him in.

Gil, however, was not one to stand on ceremony. "And what a terrific old place!" he enthused, giving her a gentle nudge and walking past her into the living room. "Who would have thought your grandfather would leave it to you, after all?"

Gil knew about François, of course. At the time of her parents' death, Roni had told him about the estrangement between her mother and the old Frenchman. But the fact that he, too, had died, that he had left her this cottage—those things had happened sometime after their parting.

"How did you know?" she asked. She wondered

if he had hired a private detective to investigate her. It was something she wouldn't put past him.

"Janet, of course," he replied easily. "She keeps me posted on everything you do. She's one of your biggest fans, you know."

Janet. Of course. Despite the bitterness of the divorce, Roni had continued to keep in touch with Gil's sister. She had even written her from Grasse, telling her all about the cottage and the flowers and little Nicolette. Everything, in fact, except Philippe. But she hadn't thought Janet would pass those things on to Gil. She had always had the impression that the two were far from friendly.

"How *is* Janet?" she responded stiffly. She wished he would state his business and leave.

"Oh, you know Sis. She's always in top form. Forging ahead with her job at the store. She's got more energy than the rest of the family put together."

"Gil . . ." Roni couldn't bear the small talk any longer. Better to find out what he wanted and get it over with. "What are you doing here? I can't believe it's a coincidence that you happen to be in Grasse."

Gil eased himself into François's old rocking chair and beamed up at her. "Great place, Grasse," he declared. "Although I'm sure it'll look a lot better once all that plastic's removed from the flowers."

"Yes, there was a strong wind. The sirocco."

"You're telling *me*. I arrived in that wind last night. It's amazing I managed to keep my car on the road. All's quiet today, though."

225

Roni looked at him. "You were going to tell me why you came."

He studied her for a moment, opened his mouth as if to answer, then changed his mind. "I think that should wait," he said finally. "Suppose I tell you over dinner tonight."

She shook her head firmly. "I can't have dinner with you. Please, just tell me now."

He smiled cajolingly. "Roni, my sweet little Roni, don't act so cold toward me . . . please. I come only as a friend. If I'd known you'd be so suspicious, I'd have brought a white flag."

"I just don't know what we have to say to each other. We're a part of each other's pasts."

"Very recent pasts," he corrected her. "And it wasn't *all* bad, was it?" His eyes twinkled at her.

"Gil—"

He stopped her before she could go on. "All right, all right, I know I was a bit of a bastard. But you're free of me now, and there's no reason why we can't at least engage in friendly conversation. Is there?"

"It depends on what the conversation's about." Roni refused to be taken in by the old familiar charm.

He shrugged. "Everything. Nothing. Roni, the truth is, I was traveling through France, and when I got to Nice I remembered you were here in Grasse. So I thought that, for old times' sake, I'd look you up and maybe buy you dinner. Is anything wrong with that?"

"Your wife can answer that better than I can."

A shadow clouded his face. "Roni, so much has

226

happened. I can't tell you everything all at once. Please have dinner with me tonight, and I'll explain then."

"I can't. I told you that."

He brushed her protestation aside. "You won't even have to be alone with me. You can bring your own car. We'll eat at Chez Pierre. I understand it's the best restaurant in town. Correct?"

"So I hear. I haven't been there."

"What? Don't tell me you've buried yourself out here among the flowers? That's all the more reason for you to agree. You must partake of at least a little of what Grasse has to offer."

It was true. She had been burying herself. But until yesterday, life had been so pleasant here at the cottage. With Nicolette's visits and Lily's lively chatter. And her sketching and long walks and picnic lunches in the garden. But she had to admit it would be nice to dine in a fine restaurant for a change. And if she didn't have to be alone with Gil . . .

"I'll meet you there at eight o'clock," Gil said, reading the indecision on her face. "We'll have a nice dinner, and when you've had enough of me, you can leave." He smiled, showing his perfect teeth. "Agreed?"

Roni sighed. She didn't know how she could bear another night alone at the cottage. Maybe the diversion would do her good, take her mind off Philippe, if only for a few hours. "Agreed," she replied finally.

"Fantastic." He jumped up and kissed her cheek. "See you at eight."

* * *

He was waiting at the bar when she arrived and was at her side before Georges, the maître d'hôtel, could ask her name or whether she had a reservation.

"This is the lady I've been expecting," Gil told him, putting a possessive arm around Roni's shoulders.

"Ah, *oui,* monsieur. She is as lovely as you said she would be. Perhaps even lovelier." The maître d' took Roni's hand and raised it to his lips. "Would Monsieur prefer to remain at the bar, or shall I escort you to your table?"

"The table, please," Roni said after Gil had deferred to her preference.

"Very well. Please follow me."

They were led to a quiet corner table, which was set with fine bone china and elegant silver. A bouquet of jasmine and delicate white roses adorned the center. It was a charming room. Beautifully appointed yet unpretentious enough to allow relaxation and comfort.

"May I bring Mademoiselle a cocktail?" Georges asked, still hovering.

Gil's drink was just being brought from the bar. To Roni's surprise, it was a glass of mineral water.

"I'll have the same as M. Tarleton," she answered, a bit curious but relieved in view of his past history with alcohol.

"Are you sure?" Gil asked her. "Don't feel you have to follow my example."

"I think it's a good example." And, as Georges relayed the order to one of the waiters, she added with a wry smile, "But I have to admit I'm surprised."

Gil returned the smile with one of his own. "So is everyone else who knows me. As a matter of fact, I have a hard time believing it myself." He raised his glass and took a sip.

"Any special reason, or did you just lose your taste for anything stronger?" Roni hoped she didn't sound sarcastic, but a nondrinking Gil was too much for her to comprehend.

"They say alcoholics never lose their taste for it," he replied quietly. "It's a daily test of strength."

"I see." She raised the glass that had just been set in front of her. "May you continue to pass the test." She sipped, then asked tentatively, "Does this mean you've admitted you have a problem?"

He raised his eyes heavenward. "Admitted? That's putting it mildly. I've just spent the last three months in a hospital drying out. And I assure you that I don't intend to go through that again."

Roni was impressed. Although she wondered whether his admittance to the hospital was voluntary. "Let's change the subject," she suggested. Gil's personal problems were no concern of hers. "Are you going to tell me what you're doing in Grasse?"

His blue eyes rested lightly on her face. "First, may I tell you how lovely you look tonight?"

She felt her stomach contract. The last thing she wanted was a compliment from Gil. She had heard too many of them before—and they had led her down the path to heartbreak. Still, etiquette called for her to acknowledge his words with a simple "Thank you." And she had to admit she was relieved that she had been able to put herself together reasonably well after an almost sleepless night and a highly troubled day. The problem with Philippe had been difficult enough to deal with, but when the added burden of Gil's appearance had come right on the heels of it, she'd wondered how she would be able to cope with any of it. While it was true that Gil's appearance had largely taken her mind off Philippe, it presented an even more disturbing situation. She didn't trust Gil, and she couldn't believe his motive for seeking her out was a strictly social one. She had to know the *real* reason; she knew she would be in for another sleepless night if the mystery were not solved.

"I came here to see you," he said in answer to her question. "It's as simple as that."

"But the reason you're in France. Is it a vacation?" She supposed their both being in the same country at the same time wasn't really so strange. A great many people traveled to France in the summer.

"No, I"—he shifted uncomfortably—"I wasn't quite truthful with you this morning. I didn't just 'happen' to be in the area. The whole purpose of my trip is you."

Again, the dreadful contraction in her stomach. She tensed and made an involuntary fist with the hand that was resting loosely on her lap. "But why?" she breathed, almost afraid to hear the answer. "There's nothing—"

230

"Roni, I came because I had to apologize." He was leaning toward her across the table, looking at her with an urgent expression on his face. "I know you think there's nothing to talk about. But there is! There's *everything* to talk about. You were my wife and I treated you terribly. Do you think I can forget that?"

She eyed him evenly. "It's a little late to be having regrets now." She wished she could simply get up and go, but her innate good manners made her reluctant to leave the restaurant so abruptly.

"But I didn't know what I was doing at the time," Gil protested, his eyes pleading for understanding. "Roni, whether you know it or not, I was sick. And not just from the alcohol, although I admit I was far from sober most of the time. You see, excessive drinking wasn't the only thing I was treated for in that hospital I told you about. I went through a great deal of psychotherapy. I was suffering from complete schizophrenia. I loved you and wanted to be a good husband to you, but at the same time, I couldn't control my appetites for the, shall we say, 'sleazier' side of life."

"Gil, you forget that I know the truth," Roni said, unmoved by this emotional confession. "You married me because you wanted to get at your trust fund, not because you wanted to settle down to married life."

He looked at her for a long moment. Then his shoulders slumped, as if a heavy weight had fallen on them. "Yes, that's true. I don't like having to admit it, but that *was* the reason I asked you to marry me so soon after we met. But, Roni"—he

231

straightened up again and his voice carried its earlier urgency—"after we were married, I realized what a wonderful woman you really were. In my more rational moments, I knew I had actually fallen in love with you. But the problem was that I had more irrational moments than rational ones."

Roni studied him, a small frown on her face. Could it be true? she wondered. Had he really been mentally ill throughout the nightmare of their marriage? Was it possible he *had* loved her after all? It was an interesting explanation but one with too many inherent doubts to allow her to let down her guard. "I suppose," she said, challenging him, "that's why you married someone else the minute we were divorced."

He looked as if he had been physically attacked. "Roni, don't you know enough about human nature to know we do things out of pain? I married Rita as a defense mechanism. I was so hurt by the fact that you wanted a divorce that I wanted to hurt you back."

"Well, you certainly succeeded with that one," Roni answered dryly. Then, refusing to probe any deeper into this painful subject, she suggested they call the waiter and look at the menu.

"In a minute," Gil said. He put a hand on her arm as if to restrain her. "First, let me say what I came thousands of miles to say." He lowered his voice. His eyes were filled with emotion. "I'm sorry. I'm sorry for everything. For rushing you into marriage and for treating you so badly. I don't know if you can ever forgive me, but at least you know that *I* know how much suffering I caused you."

Unable to meet the intensity in his blue eyes, Roni looked down at the tablecloth. She had expected this evening to be difficult, but she hadn't realized how much emotion Gil was still able to arouse in her. Just sitting across from him brought back so many memories. Their first meeting . . . their first kiss . . . their wedding at Aunt Gwen's . . . the honeymoon in Nassau. And, of course, the horrors. The drinking, the gambling, the abusive language. The pain of knowing he was spending the night with somebody else.

When she finally trusted her voice to speak, she forced herself to look up at him. "All right," she began hoarsely, "you've had your say. And frankly, Gil, the whole thing is something I'd like desperately to forget. If you want me to say I forgive you, then I forgive you. But I don't think I can talk about it anymore."

Fortunately, the waiter rescued them from further conversation. He approached their table bearing elegant oversized menus and, after handing one to each of them, launched into a litany of the evening specialties. When they had ordered, Roni fended off the possibility of resuming the subject by telling Gil about Grasse and how much she was enjoying staying in her grandfather's cottage.

"Will you show me around if I stay a couple of days?" Gil asked. "Now that the air's clear between us, I hope we can be friends."

"Oh, Gil, I—" She broke off, thrown by the request. True, Gil seemed a changed man, and he was offering friendship, not a threat. But she would still feel better if he would simply leave her alone after tonight.

"Please don't say no," he urged before she could start again. "Just give me two days of your time. Show me the flower fields and the perfume factories and the sketches you told Janet about in your letter. And maybe take me on one of your picnics at the mountain lake."

She gasped inwardly at the realization that he knew so much about her life here. But of course she had written a great many details to Janet. Obviously, she had let him see the complete letter.

"You will do it, won't you?" he pleaded as the waiter arrived with their first course, sea scallops with piquant sauce. "I'm returning to Denver on Sunday."

She sighed. How could she refuse such a simple, innocent request? Anyway, she suspected getting through the next couple of days would be easier with Gil in the picture. He would keep her too busy to allow much thought for Philippe. She smiled at him as she picked up her fork. "I'll expect you at the cottage at ten in the morning," she told him, and took her first bite of what turned out to be an exquisite meal.

For the next two days she acted as Gil's escort in and around Grasse. They strolled the country lanes near the cottage, reveling in the perfumed air and the cloudless, perfect days. They bought fruit and cheese and bread at the outdoor market and took them to the lake, where they had their picnic.

Gil was even introduced to Nicolette, who was invited to join them for strawberries and cream in Roni's garden. Roni felt something resembling contentment as she watched the two cavorting on the lawn, Nicolette giggling delightedly.

She was still wary of Gil, of course. She doubted whether she would ever really trust him again. But to her relief, he made no advances toward her other than a friendly peck on the cheek when arriving or departing. During one of their excursions he told her that when he returned to Denver, he would be going to work for his father's mining company, and he was determined to do well there. "I'm starting at the bottom," he said with a wry grimace. "But that's the only way I can really learn the business." He was clearly hoping to follow in his father's footsteps and take his rightful place as head of the company one day.

He really has changed, Roni had marveled. She was genuinely glad for him, although she had no interest in his life other than wishing him well. He had killed the love she'd felt for him while they were married.

On the afternoon of his last day in Grasse, Gil asked if Roni would like to have dinner with him in Nice. "We'll do the town," he told her. "Dinner, the casino . . . the works."

"But it's such a long drive," Roni protested, "and you'll have to drive back tomorrow to catch your plane."

He shrugged. "It's not that far to drive for an evening." He chuckled. "Now that I'm not drinking, I've gotten pretty good at it."

Roni considered the invitation and decided to accept. She had yet to sample the Nice nightlife, and she couldn't begrudge Gil a farewell dinner. After all, this might well be the last time she would ever see him.

They dined at La Pignata, a charming outdoor restaurant in the hills above the city. The warm, balmy night and the stars overhead were conducive to romance, but Roni and Gil kept their conversation light as they sampled the rich and flavorful *pâté de canard*. Soft dance music provided the perfect background.

"You need some wine with your meal," Gil told her, signaling for a waiter. "Nothing this good should be without the proper accompaniment."

"No, really," Roni insisted, "I'm very happy with mineral water. Besides, I'd feel funny drinking alone."

Gil hesitated. "Perhaps I should join you."

"Oh, no. Please don't order anything on my account."

"But tonight calls for something special. My last night in Europe, the beginning of my new job." He looked at her meaningfully. "A new relationship for us."

"But you just went through all that treatment. If you have a drink now—"

"It won't cause any problems, believe me. I've got the thing under control now. And I think," he concluded as the waiter approached, "this calls for more than wine. It's a celebration." He turned to the waiter. "A bottle of your finest champagne, please."

"Oui, monsieur. Right away."

Roni studied him as the waiter hurried off. Was it a mistake to let him order the champagne? She had heard that once an alcoholic had even one small drink, they became addicted all over again. And yet Gil had seemed sure he could handle it. She decided to enjoy the champagne and stop worrying. She would see to it that he didn't drink anything beyond this one bottle.

They had finished their pâté and were waiting for their entrées when Gil suddenly reached over and took her hand. "These days have been wonderful for me, Roni," he said softly.

She smiled. "I've enjoyed them, too."

"I'm sorry it's so late in the game. Our whole marriage should have been like this."

She used her free hand to pick up her glass. "That was another time. The past is past."

His fingers pressed hers. "It's not too late to start again." As she turned to him, startled, he rushed on. "Roni, I told you the other day I loved you during the time we were married. I was so mixed up I didn't know how to handle it then. But things are so different now. The only thing that's the same is the love I still feel for you."

She pulled her hand free. She had to put a stop to this. "No, Gil, please don't talk about us," she said firmly. "I've enjoyed the past few days, too, but anything more between us is impossible."

He eyed her steadily. "Why?" he asked quietly. "Are you in love with someone else?"

"No!" Her answer was too quick, too fervent. Careful, she told herself, calm down. Don't let him

237

get you flustered. "I assure you there's no one," she went on. "It's just that I have a whole new life now. And I like it the way it is."

"Are you planning to stay in France?"

"No. Absolutely not. I'm going to sell the cottage and go home to New Orleans at the end of the summer." Or maybe before the end of the summer, she added silently.

"Roni . . ." He reached for her hand again and turned to her intently.

She pulled forcibly away. "Gil, please. If you don't stop this, I'll leave." She wondered how she'd manage to get back to Grasse, but fortunately, she wasn't put to the test. Gil sighed and turned to the *suprême de volaille à blanc* that had just arrived.

"All right, Roni. If that's the way you want it." He drained his glass and signaled to the waiter to pour out some more.

Roni also turned to her champagne to get through the moment. She felt awkward and uncomfortable. No way would she consider going back to Gil. What on earth had made him think she would? She was so disconcerted that she didn't hear him ask the waiter for a second bottle.

By the time their dessert arrived, the conversation had returned to more general topics and Roni was beginning to feel quite mellow. And then, to her shock, she saw a familiar face entering the dining area. Philippe St. Pierre, looking very dashing and outrageously handsome in a well-cut charcoal gray suit was following the maître d' through the maze of tables. At his side was an extraordinarily beautiful woman—and it was not Marie-Catherine Fontaine!

Philippe's companion was far too physically well endowed to be a model. She wore a white Grecian-style gown that was draped seductively over firm, ample breasts and clung to a curvaceous, womanly body. Her features were so perfect they might have been sculpted. Her deep blue eyes commanded instant attention. Her dark, lustrous hair was pulled back from her face on one side and hung in shining waves past her shoulder on the opposite side. She seemed completely at ease with Philippe as the two were seated, her head bent toward him as she listened to something he had to say.

Roni felt her hands begin to shake. Just seeing him caused such a violent reaction she didn't know how she was going to get through the rest of the evening. She watched as he said something to the waiter, who immediately scurried off. He seemed deeply absorbed in the woman he was with. Whatever they were discussing, it was clearly of great importance.

"You know those people over there?" Gil saw her staring at them and eyed them curiously.

"Yes. Well, that is, I know the man. He's my next door neighbor."

"Oh?" Gil's eyebrows shot up, then he turned his body for a better look. "Don't tell me that's the infamous Philippe St. Pierre!"

Roni forced a smile and tried to appear casual. "Don't believe everything you read. He doesn't live up to his reputation."

"Meaning he hasn't tried to seduce you?" Gil

laughed as Roni blushed. "He's a fool if he hasn't. Although," he added, glancing over to the other table, "it looks as if he's doing okay tonight."

Roni felt her heart constrict, causing actual physical pain. The woman with Philippe was hanging on his every word. One could almost see the electricity between them. Obviously, he's in the process of adding someone else to his list of conquests, she concluded grudgingly. The thought of that afternoon with Philippe blazed into her mind, and she reached for her glass, willing the champagne to dull at least some of the pain.

It was at this moment that Philippe looked up and saw her staring at him. At first his face registered surprise, then his mouth tightened and his eyes narrowed perceptively. Unable to look away, Roni watched as he raised a glass filled with dark red wine and held it toward her in a private ironic toast. When he had drunk, he turned back to his companion and resumed their conversation.

"Hey, are you with me or at that table over there?"

"Huh?" Roni started. She realized Gil had been saying something to her, and she had been too caught up in the exchange with Philippe to hear.

"I said, would you like to dance? The music's nice and easy, and the dance floor's practically empty."

Roni wasn't sure she had the strength to rise from her chair, much less dance, but she managed to nod and let Gil escort her to the floor. Here, in Gil's arms, moving to the slow beat of the music, a gentle breeze ruffling her hair, she felt herself on the verge of tears. It was all so romantic—and all so wrong! If only things had been different, she thought miserably, closing her eyes tight to squeeze back the stinging tears. If only it were Philippe's arms around her. If only . . .

But Philippe was with another woman—undoubtedly one of many. Roni had to face reality once and for all. I can do without him, she vowed fiercely. And I can start by showing him I can!

Deliberately, she moved closer to Gil and put her cheek against his. A small smile played over her lips. Surprised but obviously pleased, he gathered her in and ran a hand down her back, caressing her soft skin beneath the silky material of her dress. Roni closed her eyes and placed her hand on the back of his neck, moving sensuously against him in time to the music. The champagne was making her both relaxed and brave, and she gently maneuvered Gil to Philippe's side of the floor. Let him see that she could attract the opposite sex every bit as well as *he* could!

"Like old times, huh?" Gil said, his breath warm on her neck.

"Umm. I think maybe *better* than old times." Roni looked up at him and smiled into his eyes.

Gil studied her for a moment, then slowly his head moved toward hers and their lips joined. Although she had felt no physical interest in him since his arrival in Grasse, the combined forces of the champagne, the music, and the energy created by Philippe's presence caused her to respond in a way that astonished even Gil. She kissed him back with unrestrained fervor, parting her lips to allow his tongue full entry, and drew his body even closer to her own. Thus encouraged, Gil's hands slipped down to her thighs and pressed them forward, fusing their lower bodies together as they moved provocatively in time to the music.

It wasn't until the music stopped that they moved apart, Gil frankly aroused, Roni feeling a bit like an actress in a play. Philippe was looking at her, and her performance had been for him.

"Ready to go?" Gil asked as he led her back to their table.

Go? How could they leave when Philippe was still so devastatingly close? "But we haven't finished the champagne," Roni protested. She reached for her glass and drained it, signaling the waiter for more.

"We could order another bottle at the hotel in Grasse. Or, better yet, we could check into the Négresco here in Nice."

The words brought Roni up short. Flirting with Gil may have been a game with her, but her ex-husband was taking it seriously. "But what about the casino?" she asked hopefully. She remembered how he liked to gamble. Perhaps if he got caught up in chemin de fer, he would forget about her.

"The casino can wait for another night."

"But you're leaving tomorrow."

"I'll stay on. All summer, if you like. Oh, Roni, sweetheart . . ." Gil grabbed her hand and pressed it hard. "You do still care for me. I could feel it out there on the dance floor. Let's try again, get married again . . ."

"No." Roni shook her head. She had to stop

this; she had to get out of here. Using Gil to make Philippe jealous had been a dreadful mistake. Gil —the new changed Gil—didn't deserve it. And as for Philippe . . . She glanced toward his table. He and the dark-haired woman were having their dinner, still deeply engaged in conversation. "Gil, I'm sorry," she said, looking earnestly at the man to whom she had once been married. "I don't know what's wrong with me. Suddenly, I feel awful. Maybe it's the champagne. We've had almost two bottles." At least part of what she said was true. She *did* feel awful, but not from the champagne.

Gil looked concerned, although Roni thought she saw disappointment in his eyes as well. "Would you like some coffee?" he asked her.

"No, thank you. What I'd really like is to go home. I'm sorry to spoil your evening, but I should have known better than to drink so much." In truth, the effects of the champagne were almost totally gone. The realization of what a childish little game she'd been playing had sobered her up fast.

Now she wanted only to get away. Away from Gil and his mistaken notion about her. And most of all, away from the black-eyed man who, God help her, she still hadn't managed to stop loving.

CHAPTER THIRTEEN

The sick feeling in the pit of her stomach was there when she awoke. Last night . . . Something had happened last night . . . Her body felt cold as she remembered.

Slowly, it all came into perspective. The outdoor restaurant in Nice. Dining with Gil under the stars. The arrival of Philippe with the beautiful dark-haired woman. The deliberate flirtation with Gil to arouse Philippe's jealousy, and Gil's mistaking it for genuine interest.

How could she have behaved in such a way? Dully, she recalled Gil's proposal of marriage, his suggestion that they spend the night together. Fortunately, she had been able to cool his ardor without an angry scene. He had brought her home in gentlemanly fashion, although he had taken her in his arms at the door to the cottage and begged to be allowed to stay the night. When she had staunchly refused, he had looked at her sadly and said he would respect her wishes. But he also said that although he was returning to Denver, he was sure he would never stop loving her, and that if she should change her mind about him—or have any desire simply to see him—she was to call him and he would come to her, wherever she was.

Roni had to admit this new turn of events was flattering, but she didn't like the side of her that had behaved so seductively with one man in order to entice another. Playing games with people was not her usual style, and she hated herself for being so shallow as to have let it happen.

I've got to get away from here, she told herself as she rose from her bed and slipped on a cool cotton peignoir. Philippe has made me unrecognizable even to myself, and I have to go home where I can find me again. She would make the decision on the sale of the cottage today, and then she would arrange for her trip back to New Orleans. She was brushing out her hair when she heard the peal of the doorbell. She fervently hoped her visitor wasn't Gil, come to say a last good-bye. She didn't want to face him again—she didn't want to see the sadness in his eyes that had so disturbed her when he left her last night.

But it was an even worse prospect she had to face when, still in her peignoir, she opened the door. Philippe was standing there, his eyes unsmiling, his mouth a grim, straight line.

"I'm sorry to bother you," he said before she could express surprise at his being there. "I'm looking for Nicolette."

Roni's inner alarm system went on alert. Finding his daughter seemed a thin excuse for coming over like this. There were plenty of servants at the château to fetch her. What did he really want? She tensed, readying herself for some verbal attack, and answered crisply and to the point. "Nicolette's not here."

He frowned, and his eyes seemed more troubled than angry. "You're sure? Has she been here this morning at all?"

What did he think she was doing? Hiding the child from him? "Of course I'm sure," she replied, her voice heavy with annoyance. "And, no, she has not been here this morning."

He looked at her, hard, and then his body seemed to sag.

"Is something wrong?" She began to believe Nicolette *was* his motive in coming, after all.

"She's missing from the château. Her nurse couldn't find her when she went to call her for her piano lesson an hour or so ago. She searched the house and the grounds, but she's nowhere around. And it's not like her to run off without telling someone. Except," he added, "when she comes over here."

His voice sounded faintly accusatory. Was he suggesting she encouraged the child to visit her in secret? "She's not here," she repeated coldly, adding with a touch of sarcasm, "Why not ask your new girlfriend? Maybe she knows where she is."

At first Philippe looked puzzled, but as the meaning of what she had said sank in, his face took on the dark look she had seen so many times in the past. "The subject," he declared, "is Nicolette. But if you have nothing to tell me, I'll go and look elsewhere."

"Wait!" she called out as he turned to leave. Until this moment, she hadn't really taken the child's disappearance seriously. An hour's absence means nothing in the case of most children; they usually turn up in some nook or cranny, absorbed in a book or a puppy or some friend who happened to come along. But Nicolette was different. As heiress to the St. Pierre fortune, she was carefully watched most of the time. And, too, she had been made aware of the need to keep someone informed of her whereabouts, and she was too honest a child to deliberately sneak off and let everyone worry about her. "Come in. Maybe I can help."

Roni held open the screen and Philippe, reluctant but clearly hoping for some clue, however small, turned back and entered the cottage.

"Please sit down." Roni suddenly felt uncomfortable in her thin peignoir. Once again, Philippe's powerful masculine magnetism was affecting her. She willed herself to remain calm, and when he had seated himself on the sofa she sat tentatively on the edge of the chair facing it. "Are you sure she's not anywhere in the château? She told me she likes to explore the attics sometimes. Apparently, there are a lot of old clothes up there and she likes to play 'dress up.'"

Philippe shook his head. "The entire staff scoured the place. And she wouldn't hide if she knew we were looking for her."

"No, I'm sure she wouldn't." Roni thought hard. "Could she have gone over to Lily's? I know it's unusual, but the two do seem to have an affinity for each other. Lily makes her special treats if she's here during one of Nicolette's visits."

"We tried Lily. I stopped there on the way over here."

Silence engulfed them as they each became absorbed in their own thoughts. Where could she be? Roni was beginning to be as worried as Philippe. "Maybe," she said suddenly, struck with a new idea, "this is the day Marie-Catherine took her to the lake."

Philippe's eyebrows lifted. "The lake? Why would Marie-Catherine do that?"

Roni didn't like discussing Marie-Catherine with him, but since she had brought the subject up, she had no choice but to go on with it. She told him about the day she had seen the model and Alain Dumont in Grasse, and about the conversation she'd overheard between them. "She said she might take her to the lake for a swim one day. It sounded like she was planning a special treat for Nicolette."

"Wait a minute." Philippe raised a hand to stop her. "You say you saw Marie-Catherine in Grasse with Alain Dumont?" His eyes were bright with incredulity. "Are you positive it was Alain?"

"Absolutely. I had just met him at Nicolette's birthday party. He seemed," she added for no particular reason, "like a nice man."

Philippe didn't answer. His face was clouded. There was no mistaking the fact that he was deeply troubled. Roni sat watching him, uncertain as to what to say. Then, to her dismay, he suddenly rose and strode to the door. He pushed open the screen without even turning back.

"Philippe?" she called after him. "Are you going to the lake? Do you want me to go with you?"

He paused for an instant only. "No, Veronique, I'll handle this. Thank you for your help."

His abrupt departure left her bewildered. Clearly, it had something to do with Alain Dumont. Was Philippe angry because Alain had been in Grasse with Marie-Catherine? Apparently he was, because the news seemed to make him forget Nicolette entirely. She sighed, and the bitterness she had previously felt toward him came stealing back. Probably he had decided Nicolette *was* with Marie-Catherine. And he was furious because he had just learned that the lady he claimed to have rebuffed was interested in another man.

She renewed her decision to go home as she changed into shorts and a T-shirt and went back downstairs to fix a late breakfast. The situation was becoming worse and worse. She simply couldn't handle it anymore. As she was buttering her toast, the doorbell sounded and she rushed to answer, thinking it might be news of Nicolette's return home. But instead of someone from the château, she found herself facing a skinny teenaged boy who was holding an envelope.

"Mademoiselle Roni Stephens?"

"Oui."

He thrust out the envelope, and when she had taken it from him he ran to his bicycle and pedaled rapidly away. Roni looked after him in astonishment. Who was he? And who had sent him with this note? She tore open the envelope wondering if it could be from Gil, a final good-bye or some such thing. But it only took a glance to realize it was something much more important than that.

The words *Nicolette, alive,* and *formula* jumped out at her. Alarmed, she stepped back inside and sank down on the sofa to give it a thorough reading.

> *Dear Mademoiselle Stephens,*
>
> *If you wish to see your little friend Nicolette St. Pierre alive, you must follow these instructions.*
>
> *You must come to the mountain lake as soon as you receive this letter. You must bring the formula for the perfume created by François Du Priex with you. You will find a canoe tied up at the end of the path leading from your property to the lake. You must cross the lake in the canoe and leave the formula in a bottle you will find on the other side. The bottle, which is watertight when capped, will be immediately recognizable. Do not bring anyone to the lake with you. Do not tell anyone about the formula —or about this letter.*
>
> *If you obey these instructions, the child will be released unharmed.*

There was no signature.

It's a joke, Roni thought, grasping at a thin straw of hope. It's like something out of an old movie. Philippe sent the note just to see what I would do. But her instincts told her it was not a joke. No one would be so cruel as to threaten Nicolette, and certainly not her father.

The formula. Someone knew about the formula her grandfather had left her. The memory of the ransacked study came rushing back. Of course! This letter was sent by the same person who had entered her house and searched the room. Whoever it was was determined to get his hands on it, and he was holding Nicolette as the bait.

A cold chill shot down her back. That darling little girl was in grave danger! I must tell Philippe! she thought, ignoring the warning in the letter. He'll know what to do. But the telephone company had never gotten around to activating the phone in the cottage, and she had no idea where Philippe had gone after he'd left her. Getting in the car and driving to the château would take precious time, and there was no guarantee that he was there. The police! She could drive to Grasse and show the note to them. But, again, the time it would take might be crucial to whether Nicolette lived or died.

I'll have to do as the letter says, she decided, racing up to her grandfather's study to retrieve the formula. She found it where she had left it, in the collection of letters from her mother, and quickly dashed off a copy of it before thrusting it in her pocket and setting off for the lake as fast as her legs could carry her.

The canoe was tied up next to a tree at the end of the path, just as the note had said it would be. Roni untied the rope and pushed off without even considering the possibility that she might not be able to navigate it properly. She had never been in a canoe before, but she picked up the paddle and plunged it into the water. At first the little craft merely spun in a circle, and it took some experimentation before she could get it moving in the right direction.

I should have taken the car to the other side, she berated herself. The bridge spanning the lake was only minutes away. But the letter had specifically said she must take the canoe. Please let me get it there! she prayed as she continued to flounder.

Then, at last, she had it heading across the expanse of water. She was grasping the paddle so tightly that her hands began to cramp, but she paid them no attention. Nothing mattered except Nicolette's safety.

She was halfway across, praying she was traveling in a direct line toward the waiting bottle, when the paddle slipped from her grasp. Alarmed, she looked down to see it floating alongside the canoe. No problem, she told herself as she fell to her knees in an effort to retrieve it. Thank God it's close enough to reach. But as she leaned out of the canoe, her weight caused the light craft to list, and before she could get her hands on the paddle, she found herself being catapulted into the lake. Despite the warmth of the sun, the water was ice-cold, and her whole body underwent a jarring shock as it was immersed.

Keep moving! she commanded herself as she surfaced and frantically tried to orient herself. Don't panic. Just swim the rest of the way. The realization that she was still in control encouraged her, and she struck out for the spot toward which she had been directing the canoe. She desperately hoped the formula would still be decipherable when she got there.

She saw the man dive into the water before she had swum more than a few yards. He had obviously seen her accident from the opposite bank and was heading toward her. Although Roni had only glimpsed him as he left the bank, the thick, heavy body and dark full beard made him instantly recognizable. Alain Dumont. He was clearly a good swimmer; the speed with which he was approaching Roni was alarming. Almost numb now, both from the iciness of the water and the shock of seeing Alain, her brain could register only one thought: Alain was the kidnapper. And Roni's fall into the water had provided him with the perfect way of getting rid of her so she would not be around to identify him later. He's going to kill me, she concluded, panic beginning to envelop her. He's coming out here to drown me.

Frantically, she changed her direction and struck out for the shore from which she had left in the canoe. It would be difficult to outswim Alain; but Roni was strong, and with almost superhuman effort, she began putting distance between them. But the numbing effect the water was having on her body was working against her. Her arms felt more and more like frozen blocks of ice, and lifting them became a nearly impossible chore. Almost before she knew it, Alain was upon her—she could see the top of his head as he streaked to her side. She tried to swim faster, kicking wildly, but it was no use. She screamed as she felt Alain's hand on her leg, pulling her backward toward him.

"Help! Help!" she yelled, trying desperately to kick him away and loosen herself from his grasp. But it was no use. Alain was strong; his arm felt like a vise as it locked itself around her neck.

"Hush!" he commanded. "No one can hear you out here. Just do as I say."

"Let go of me!" She was losing control of her body. Her struggles against Alain only served to make her more exhausted, and she was gulping great quantities of water.

"Be still, I tell you!" His voice was harsh and angry. She saw him raise one arm, as if to strike her.

"Please. Let me *go!*" Roni was hysterical now. Sheer terror engulfed her as she realized what Alain was about to do. With one final burst of strength, she pulled out of his grasp. But she could not avoid the flailing fist; the pain was sharp, though briefly felt. She slipped into the depths of the water as darkness closed around her.

CHAPTER FOURTEEN

Philippe's face was floating in front of hers; huge, distorted, seemingly disconnected from his body. His black eyes were staring at her, the thick black brows knitted in a frown.

"Veronique! Answer me!" His voice was sharp. He sounded angry.

Roni felt herself shiver, and the darkness began to close in again. Why . . . ? she wondered vaguely. Why should her last thoughts be of Philippe?

"Philippe." She murmured his name aloud. The water wasn't cold anymore. It felt good. Like she was floating on a cloud.

"Veronique! I'm here! It's me. Philippe. Open your eyes. We can't lose you now."

His voice seemed to be coming from a long way off. She tried to do as she was told. Your eyes, she commanded herself, echoing Philippe. Open your eyes. They fluttered, opened, then closed again.

"That's it, Veronique. Try again. Try harder."

"Philippe?" He was in focus now.

"Yes, yes, it's me. Are you all right? Can you sit up?" She felt his hands on her shoulders, lifting her upright. She didn't have the strength to remain that way on her own and slumped back, but he squatted down next to her and slipped an arm around her back. "Take some deep breaths. You're going to be fine. Everything's all right."

She did as she was told. Immediately, she felt better. She looked around and realized she was lying on the far bank of the lake. The sun felt warm on her body. "What happened?" she asked. Then, remembering, she murmured, ". . . that man . . . Alain Dumont . . ."

"Don't think about him. Don't think about anything but getting your strength back. We almost lost you out there."

"He tried to kill me." She felt tears coming to her eyes as the panic she had felt in the water came flooding back. She had thought she was drowning. How had she survived?

"No. *No!* I did what I did in order to save her!"

That voice. Alain's voice. Roni began to shake uncontrollably. "Keep him away from me . . ."

"It's all right. You're safe." Philippe sounded firm. Unemotional. "No one's going to hurt you now."

She looked into his eyes and gathered strength. She took another deep breath and sat up straighter. "Tell me what happened," she said steadily. "How did you know I was here?"

"I didn't. I came here looking for Nicolette."

"Nicolette!" Roni gasped. She'd forgotten all about the child. "Is she—"

"We don't know anything yet. I came out here on the off chance that the conversation you overheard between Alain and Marie-Catherine had some significance. Although I found it hard to believe Nicolette and Marie-Catherine would be here together."

"Philippe, listen to me. I know what's happened to Nicolette. She's been kidnapped. Alain is holding her for ransom. He wants the formula for my grandfather's perfume. I was bringing it to him when I fell out of the canoe. He tried to drown me so I wouldn't tell—"

"No!" Alain rushed up and stood before her angrily. "I was trying to save you. I saw you fall into the water, and I didn't know if you could swim. Then when you tried to fight me . . . I hit you. Knocking you unconscious was the only way I could get you back to shore."

Philippe jumped up and faced him squarely. "We'll discuss your intentions toward Mlle. Stephens later. What I want to know is, is what she says true? Were you waiting out here for her? And what the hell is this formula you're talking about?" The last question was addressed to Roni. He glared down at her as he asked it.

Roni stuttered a little, intimidated by his blazing countenance. "My g—grandfather created a p—perfume. He thought it could b—be important. He left it for me in a locked drawer in his d—desk."

Philippe's eyes went back to Alain. "How did *you* know about it? And what have you done with my daughter?" He took a threatening step toward him. "If anything's happened to her, so help me, I'll—"

"No!" The chemist's response was a cry of agony. "She's all right. I swear it! Marie-Catherine took her to Nice."

"So Marie-Catherine's involved in this, too." He turned back to Roni. "You were right. The two of them were hatching a plot. Against me."

"Philippe, listen to me." Alain was speaking in rapid French. "I couldn't help myself. God forgive me, I couldn't help falling in love with Marie-Catherine. I never thought I'd have a chance with someone like her. Someone so beautiful. So exquisite."

"So corrupt," Philippe added grimly.

"Yes, she is corrupt." Alain sighed heavily. "She cares only for herself, and it doesn't matter what she has to do in order to promote her own comfort and happiness." He shook his head and looked down at the ground. "I knew she belonged to you, Philippe, but when she started showing an interest in me, I couldn't resist her. We began to meet in secret. I became obsessed with her—she was like an addiction to me."

Roni shot a glance at Philippe. He was listening intently, his jaw set firmly, his mouth a rigid line. He did not react to the words "I knew she belonged to you" but merely stood quietly and heard Alain out.

"The trouble was," the chemist went on, "I couldn't give her the things you gave her. I'm a working man. I have no money for furs and jewels and fancy cars. But I had to find some way to keep her. I'd have done anything for her."

"Including kidnapping my daughter!"

"But Nicolette wasn't to be hurt. You must be-

258

lieve that, Philippe." He stopped, but from the expression on his face, it was clear he had more to say.

Philippe understood. "There's something else," he prodded. "Tell me everything."

Alain took a deep breath. "The words are hard to say, Philippe."

"Say them. Leave nothing out."

Alain's head drooped. "There's a syndicate. They make synthetic perfume."

Philippe was aghast. His face paled. "Good God, Dumont! Are you saying . . . ?"

Alain nodded. He looked completely miserable. "They wanted the formulas for St. Pierre perfumes. That way, they could produce them synthetically and put them in stores at a reduced price. They paid a great deal of money."

Philippe looked as if a bomb had exploded beneath him. He seemed completely shattered. "So you and Marie-Catherine were the leak," he muttered brokenly.

Alain dabbed at his eyes with the backs of his hands. "I cursed myself every night for betraying you. If it hadn't been for Marie-Catherine . . ." He took a deep breath. "I tried to resist—I swear to you, I tried. But Marie-Catherine, she was desperate for money. The night of Nicolette's birthday party, she told me you had ended things between the two of you. 'Dumped' her was how she put it. I was glad, of course. But she knew it meant giving up her dream of becoming your wife, of having the things the St. Pierre name and fortune could bring. She made one last attempt by paying a visit to Mlle. Stephens." He looked at Roni. "She knew you were the reason for Philippe's defection. But"—he smiled ironically—"she told me you would not let him go."

Philippe turned to Roni, and the two of them exchanged glances. But Roni could read nothing in the dark, troubled eyes.

"She told me," the chemist went on, "if we could get money some other way, perhaps the two of us could—" He broke off and shook his head. "She would never have married me," he said bitterly. "She only said those things to tease me. And I, fool that I am, took the bait."

Roni remained very still, trying to absorb it all. Marie-Catherine said Philippe dumped her . . . the night of Nicolette's party.

Suddenly, Alain turned back to her. "The syndicate contacted you, too, mademoiselle. They were trying to buy your grandfather's property from you."

Roni gasped. "Not the widow?"

"There was no widow. It was a story to make the idea more acceptable to you."

Roni thought of the money she had been offered and of her curiosity at why the widow was willing to pay so much more than the St. Pierres. She thought, too, of the times she had nearly given in and accepted the offer. But it was Philippe who asked the question she was beginning to formulate.

"What possible use could they have had for that? When they had the formulas?"

"The springs," Alain reminded him. "The springs you use to irrigate your fields in emergencies are on that land. They want to control them. They know that the perfume thefts have brought the company close to bankruptcy as it is. If they could also control the springs, they might force you to sell your own property."

"Dear God." Philippe seemed to age twenty years. His whole body slumped in dejection. Roni longed to reach out and touch him, but she remained where she was. She was still too weak and frightened to do more than absorb the series of shocks.

"Tell me," Philippe said wearily, "about Veronique's part in this. How did you know about François's perfume formula, and what made you think Veronique had it?"

"François gave a small vial of the perfume to Nicolette. She showed it to Marie-Catherine, who then stole it from Nikki's room. Then, on the day of Nikki's birthday party, Marie-Catherine overheard Mlle. Stephens discussing the perfume with your father. Claude suggested there might be a formula among François's business records." He paused and swallowed hard. "I went to the cottage myself to find it. It was the day of the sirocco. Unfortunately, Mlle. Stephens returned home before I could complete my task. I went back later, but the locked desk drawer had been broken open, and I knew Mlle. Stephens had opened it and found the formula. At least I was sure enough to help Marie-Catherine stage the kidnapping and send the ransom note."

"You say Marie-Catherine took Nicolette to

Nice," Philippe reiterated. "Is that where they are now?"

"I imagine they're on their way back here by now. Our plan was that if Mlle. Stephens came through with the formula, we would return Nicolette to the château and she would never know the real reason for her little outing. Marie-Catherine told her she had your permission to take her," he added. "That's why she went off without a word to anyone."

Philippe looked at him carefully. "And if Veronique *hadn't* come through with the formula? What were your plans for my daughter then?"

"I felt sure she'd come through," Alain said quickly. "Nikki spoke to me of her 'American friend' many times. I knew they were very close and that Mlle. Stephens would do anything to help the child. I also knew there was no telephone at the cottage. I personally ordered the phone company not to reactivate it, so there was no quick way to get help."

For a long moment Philippe stood completely still. His face was white, and a vein in his neck pulsed visibly. The tension in the air was so thick that Roni felt as if it were weighing her down. Breathlessly, she waited to see what would happen next.

"You bastard!" Suddenly Philippe was flying at Alain. His hands were gripping the chemist's shoulders, shaking him wildly. His face was contorted with rage. Roni was so frightened she cried out. Obviously, Philippe meant to kill the man. But Alain was bigger and more solidly built. Any minute he could strike out at Philippe and deliver heavy punishment of his own.

"Stop it!" she shouted, jumping to her feet and reaching out a restraining hand to Philippe. "This is not helping Nicolette!"

Her words had an instant effect on Philippe. He let go of Alain abruptly, causing the chemist to struggle to regain his balance. "You're right," he said, taking her arm roughly. "We must get to a telephone. The police will handle things from here." He led her to a small outboard motor boat he had tied up a few yards away. "If Alain tries to escape, he won't get far." He threw the chemist a menacing look.

"Papa!" Nicolette's voice filled the air. They looked around to see her running toward them, her dark curls flying, her arms outstretched. Philippe ran to meet her and scooped her up in an almost desperate embrace.

"Thank God," he murmured, nestling his face in her hair. "Thank God."

Roni felt the lump forming in her throat and looked away. The moment was too emotional and private to be shared. In the distance, she saw two policemen approaching. Marie-Catherine, looking frantic, was walking between them. She was not handcuffed, but one of the officers had a firm grip on her arm.

"Is one of you Philippe St. Pierre?" one of the men asked, looking from Philippe to Alain.

Philippe, still holding Nicolette, stepped forward. "I am Philippe St. Pierre."

"I understand you've been looking for your

daughter. I take it this is the little girl?" He nodded toward Nicolette.

"Yes. Thank you. Where did you find her?"

"She was in the car with the woman. They just drove up. The car's parked down there by the bridge."

Marie-Catherine forced a smile. "I took Nikki to Nice this morning, darling," she said to Philippe in a high, unnatural voice. "We had a good time, didn't we, *ma petite?*"

Philippe did not smile back. "This woman . . . and this man"—he gestured toward Alain—"kidnapped my daughter. I want them put under arrest."

The policeman frowned. "That's a very serious charge, monsieur. Do you have proof to back it up?"

"I can give you everything you need. M. Dumont is prepared to make a full confession."

"No!" Marie-Catherine looked at Alain in alarm. "It's not true. I don't know what—"

Alain went to her and took her hand. "I'm afraid it is true, my dear," he said sadly. "I have told Philippe everything, and I am prepared to tell the police, also."

The beautiful model's face tightened as she digested this. For a moment the green eyes registered stark terror. But then, as if she had suddenly taken center stage in one of the St. Pierre commercials, she tossed back her hair, pulled her hand from Alain's, and turned to face Philippe.

"It's *your* fault!" she hissed at him, her emerald eyes flashing. "If you hadn't been such a two-timing bastard, it wouldn't have come to this. We had everything, you and I. Looks, flair, joie de vivre. As lovers, we were the most talked-about couple in Europe. As husband and wife, we would have kept the society world on its ear." Her voice deepened —it was thick with hate. "But you said it was over. That it wouldn't work." Her eyes darted to Roni, who was mesmerized by the spiteful confession. "You had other fish to fry—like the little American. Oh, I knew it wouldn't last, that you would come back to me eventually," she said, addressing Philippe again, "but I was tired of waiting. I had the chance to make my own fortune, and I took it. You *forced* me to take it!"

For a long moment, no one spoke. Then the officer in charge encircled Marie-Catherine's slim wrists with handcuffs and nodded in the direction of his car. "You'll have to come to the station with us," he said to Philippe. "You'll have to file charges."

"Yes." Philippe's voice was cold, distant. With Nicolette still in his arms, he walked after the policeman and Marie-Catherine, Alain trudging along beside him. He did not look back at Roni.

Roni stood staring after him, too drained of energy and emotion to care that they were leaving her behind. Nicolette was safe—that was the only thing that was important. But the tortured look in Philippe's eyes as Marie-Catherine had confessed was something she would remember for a long, long time.

"Mademoiselle? Do you live near here? Would you like me to take you home?"

265

She turned with a start at the sound of the unfamiliar voice. It was the second policeman. He was looking at her anxiously.

She was suddenly aware of how she must look—thoroughly wet, bedraggled, and helpless. She smiled in spite of herself. "Yes, please," she said quietly. "I would appreciate that." She took his arm gratefully as they started for the bridge.

CHAPTER FIFTEEN

It was Lily who got her out of her wet clothes and into a hot bath, and it was Lily who insisted she get some hot broth down even though she said she wasn't hungry.

"Thank God you were here!" Roni told her as, wrapped in a thick terrycloth robe, she sat in front of the fire, sipping the soup and gratefully allowing the Frenchwoman to fuss over her. She had told Lily everything, from the earlier attempted burglary at the cottage to Nicolette's kidnapping to Alain and Marie-Catherine's involvement with the crime syndicate. Although clearly horrified, the kindly housekeeper listened calmly and provided a solid and sympathetic sounding board on which Roni could vent her still highly emotional reactions to the terror she had experienced in the water.

"I always knew Mlle. Fontaine was a bad one," Lily declared, shaking her head in dismay. "Though I must say I never took her for a criminal."

"I guess she was so driven to obtain money and power she didn't care how she got it," Roni responded. She sighed. "I can't help feeling sorry for

Alain, though. If it hadn't been for Marie-Catherine, he'd never have gotten into such serious trouble."

"Shows you what the power of love can do." The housekeeper removed Roni's empty bowl and took it to the kitchen as Roni reflected on these last words. *The power of love.* So far, it seemed to her that the power was mostly destructive. She herself had felt its effect more than once, and Philippe and Alain had both been badly hurt as a result of their involvement with Marie-Catherine.

She was sure it would take Philippe a long time to recover from what had happened. Possibly, he would be mistrustful of all women in the future. In any case, it was obvious there was no hope of a deeper relationship developing between Philippe and herself. He hadn't even glanced back at her when he left for the police station. That was how little she meant to him.

"Oh, dear, I almost forgot." Lily was moving toward her, holding a huge florist's box. "This should perk your spirits up, all right. It got here just before you did." She placed the box on the table along with a letter-sized envelope. "There wasn't much mail. Just that one piece."

Roni glanced at the envelope. The return address was Janet Tarleton's. She put it aside. Although she welcomed letters from her former sister-in-law, the contents of the box were more intriguing.

It contained three dozen long-stemmed yellow roses. The sight of them caused a lump to form in her throat. Philippe? she thought, wondering. He must have ordered them before . . . She snatched up the accompanying card and ripped open the envelope. Instantly, her little balloon of hope deflated. The message, covering both sides of the card, was from Gil.

I realize flowers are redundant in this part of the country, but I remembered you always loved yellow roses. I know this will come as a surprise to you, but I am still in Grasse. You see, my sweet Roni, I found I couldn't leave after all. Last night proved to me that the feelings we once shared are still very much in evidence. I want to see you tonight in order to convince you of that. Eight o'clock at Chez Pierre? I will be waiting.

Yours always,
Gil

Roni dropped the note back into the box and shook her head. She'd thought Gil was finally out of her life. Now she would have to deal with him all over again.

"You obviously have an admirer," Lily teased when she saw the roses. She reached for the box. "Let me put them in water for you."

Roni nodded and reached for the letter from Janet. She would decide what to do about Gil later. His sister's news was of the fashion world and buying trips to New York and Honolulu. She was dating a man she'd met in Denver, but so far, nothing serious had developed. "Family news is not very exciting," she said in conclusion. "Everyone is pretty much the same—including Gil, who's in your part of the world with his wife. I suspect the French wine industry will be depleted of its stock by the time he leaves."

With his wife. Roni stared at the words. *Wine industry will be depleted of its stock.* Suddenly, it all made sense. Gil's unexpected arrival . . . his persistent attentions to her . . . the champagne he drank despite his insistence that he was on the wagon. He hadn't changed at all! What's more, he was after something. Roni was sure of it. Not her —he had never been interested in her for her own self. What, then?

She tapped at the letter thoughtfully. The cottage. It came to her in a burst of understanding. He'd heard she'd become a woman of property, and he wanted to share in the bounty.

The bastard! Her outrage lifted her out of the hopeless lethargy she'd felt since returning from the lake. He was playing her for the fool . . . *again!*

But I'm not a fool, she thought grimly. At least, not anymore. She rose from the table, her face set with determination.

"Can I get you something else?" Lily asked.

Roni looked around, startled. She'd forgotten she wasn't alone. "No, thank you, Lily. In fact, I think I've taken up too much of your time already. You were finished with your work when I came in."

The housekeeper shrugged. "I can stay with you

while you take a nap. Under the circumstances, you might not want to be alone."

"No, honestly, I'm not afraid. Alain and Marie-Catherine are in police custody. Nothing can happen to me now."

Lily looked at her with concern. "Well, if you're sure, then. I'll be getting on home. I could look in on you later."

Roni shook her head. Then she went to the woman and put her arms around her. "You've been so kind to me since I've been here. I don't know how to thank you."

Lily smiled and ruffled her hair. "There's no need for thanks. I'm happy to help. For you . . . and for Madeleine."

Roni kissed her soft, rosy cheek and bade her good-bye, promising she would send for her if the need arose. "I think I'll take your advice and have a nap," she said, more to pacify her than anything else. "I don't want to think about anything for a while."

As soon as she was alone she looked at her watch. How could it be only three fifteen? She had lived a lifetime today. She wished she really could take that nap, but there was still something she had to do. Quickly, she got dressed and hurried to her car. For the second time today she felt an angry frustration over the fact that the telephone had never been activated. But now, of course, she knew the reason. The syndicate must have a lot of power, she reflected, to be able to influence the French telephone company. Oh, well. After today she wouldn't be needing a phone.

In Grasse, she pulled up in front of a travel agency she had noticed on some of her previous visits. The woman in charge was arranging some brochures on a table when she entered.

"Bon jour," she greeted Roni. "May I help you, mademoiselle?"

"Yes, please. I want to book a flight to the United States. New Orleans, Louisiana."

"Of course, mademoiselle. When do you wish to go?" The woman stepped to her desk and reached for a notepad and pencil.

"Tomorrow. As early as possible."

The woman nodded. "There's a flight leaving Nice for Paris at twelve noon, and a connecting flight on to New York. Would that be satisfactory?"

"Yes, fine."

"It will take me a few minutes to get confirmations. Please sit down and make yourself comfortable."

"Thank you. Do you have another phone I could use? I have to make a call. It's local—an office here in Grasse."

"Certainly. Just come this way." The agent led her to a desk at the back of the office and pointed out the telephone. "Please, be my guest."

"Thanks." Roni had the number of Philippe's attorney in her purse. She was relieved to find him in. He recognized her name as soon as she identified herself and apologized for not seeking her out during the time she had been in the area.

"I hope you're enjoying your summer here," he said graciously.

But Roni was not in the mood for pleasantries. She got right to the point. "I want to sell my grandfather's cottage to the St. Pierres. I'd appreciate your getting the papers ready for me to sign today."

"Well, I'm afraid that's a little rushed," the attorney told her. "The office closes in an hour. In any case, there's no hurry. I understand you intend to stay on for the rest of the summer."

"No," Roni replied brusquely. "I'm leaving tomorrow."

"I see." The voice at the other end was thoughtful. "Well, then, suppose I prepare the papers and bring them by first thing in the morning? I can drive you to the airport, too, if you like."

"Thank you, but that won't be necessary. I have a rented car. My plane leaves from Nice at noon."

"Then suppose I come to you at nine. I'll have all the papers ready. All you will have to do is sign."

"Fine. Thank you."

"Thank *you,* mademoiselle. M. St. Pierre will be very pleased."

Yes, I'm sure he will, Roni thought as she hung up. He'll have his land and I'll be out of his hair. She glanced at the travel agent, who was still working on her ticket. Roni hesitated, then reached for the phone again. I might as well wrap it all up, she told herself. She placed a call to the La Reserve du Parc Hôtel.

She could hear music in the background when Gil picked up the phone in his room. "Roni!" he

273

said in surprise. "I didn't expect to hear from you until later."

"I'm in Grasse now," she told him coolly.

A pause. Then, "Well, that's fine. Wonderful. Come right over."

"No." Roni steeled herself. "I'm not coming to your hotel, now or ever. And I don't want you to try and contact me again."

Gil sounded alarmed. "But, honey—"

"I mean it, Gil. I'm on to your tricks now. You haven't changed at all since we split up. I suggest you take your wife to Paris. Maybe you can find some woman there the two of you can dupe."

"Look, I don't know what you're talking about. What's all this about 'duping'? If you think I—"

"Forget it, Gil," Roni snapped. "I'm as tired of your explanations as I am of you." She slammed the receiver down. There! she thought with a stab of satisfaction. At least I've taken *some* positive action. She rose as she saw the travel agent moving toward her.

"So!" the woman said with a smile. "You're all set on the twelve o'clock flight from Nice, with changes of plane in Paris and New York. And you wish to pay by credit card, *oui?*"

Minutes later, Roni was in her car and headed toward home, feeling overwhelmingly saddened. What had started out to be such a promising summer had ended in tragedy and heartbreak. I should be glad it's over, she thought fervently. But common sense didn't mean much in the face of what she was leaving behind.

She spent the evening packing. She would leave

the furniture; the only things she wanted to keep were her mother's letters and a few mementos of her grandfather's. She left a note for Lily, offering her François's clothes to do with as she wished. Knowing the practical Frenchwoman, they would undoubtedly be put to good use.

As she pulled the letters out of the drawer a loose piece of paper fluttered to the floor. Roni bent down and picked it up. It was the copy she had made of the perfume formula. She studied it abstractly. She supposed it might be worth something, but it was such a painful reminder of today's events she could hardly bear to think about it. For her, the perfume industry was a corrupt, back-stabbing business of which she wanted no part. As far as she was concerned, the formula belonged in the garbage.

She had taken her first step toward the waste-basket when she heard the deep voice from the doorway of her grandfather's study.

"How about calling it Veronique?"

Philippe was standing there, a small, hopeful smile on his face. He was wearing white linen trousers and a white full-sleeved peasant shirt. He had never looked so handsome.

Roni let out a small gasp. "I—I didn't hear you come in."

"Obviously. I knocked several times and called out several more. I knew you were here because I saw your car; so I decided to come in and make sure you were all right."

"Oh." Roni wasn't surprised that she hadn't heard him. She'd been so absorbed in her own thoughts she wouldn't have heard another sirocco. She looked at him helplessly. She had no idea what to say.

"The perfume could make you a very rich woman," he went on, seemingly unaware of her discomfort. "I haven't had the opportunity to smell it, of course, but knowing your grandfather, I would be willing to bet on its excellence."

Roni shook her head uncertainly. "I don't know anything about marketing perfume."

"I'm not so sure about that. What about that 'wholesome image' you said you wanted to project? Or have you forgotten the speech you made at the stockholders meeting?" He was regarding her with a wry grin.

Roni tensed. "Philippe, I'm in no mood to be teased."

"Sorry." He took a step toward her. "Actually, I meant what I said. This could be the product you were thinking of."

Roni heaved a sigh. "Maybe. But producing it. Getting it into the stores . . ."

"St. Pierre Industries will do all that. All you have to do is sit back and collect the royalties."

"You make it sound so simple."

"It is simple, Veronique." He looked at her steadily. "That is, if you trust me."

Trust him. That phrase again. It seemed to her he'd been asking her to trust him ever since she'd arrived in Grasse—and once she had actually let down her guard. Once, in a cozy guest house, during a violent wind . . . But they were talking about perfume, not about the mistake that would haunt her for the rest of her life. In any case, the perfume didn't matter to her one way or the other. She held out the formula to him. Whatever happened, so be it.

Philippe took it, folded it carefully, and put it in his pocket. "I'll have the contract drawn up as soon as possible. And now that that's over, can we discuss something far more important?"

Roni shrugged. "Like what?"

"Like your leaving Grasse tomorrow. Louis, my attorney, phoned and said you had agreed to sell this cottage. I came to ask you to change your mind."

"But why? You need the land. The springs—"

"I need you more, Veronique." His eyes were dark and intense. "I want you to stay here until I can convince you I'm not the scoundrel you think I am."

Her stomach turned over. "Philippe . . ."

"No, wait. Don't say anything just yet. Give me the chance to apologize."

"For what? I don't understand." Be careful, her good sense whispered. Don't let him charm you again.

"A thousand things." He sighed. "For my behavior in Nice, at the stockholders meeting, for one thing. For not being totally truthful with you the first time we met. For reneging on my promise to be your guide while you were here in Grasse. *Wait,*" he implored as she opened her mouth to interrupt. "I haven't apologized for the cruelest thing of all. I should have admitted long ago that I am wildly in love with you."

277

Roni thrust out a hand and steadied herself against her grandfather's desk. Her head was spinning. Was it possible that it was true, that Philippe was really in love with her? Oh, *please* let it be true, she prayed silently. But there were still too many unanswered questions to put her complete trust in his declaration.

Philippe saw the doubt in her eyes. "Tell me," he said softly, "what is it that bothers you? Let me answer all your questions."

She looked up and stared at him. He was regarding her tenderly—and anxiously.

"I know why you sent me away that night after the sirocco," he went on, before she could say anything. "Marie-Catherine gave Alain a full account of the conversation she had with you." He took a step toward her. "Veronique, if only you'd told me . . ."

"I couldn't!" she confessed miserably. "Marie-Catherine looked half crazy that night. I was worried about what she would do if I told you. Also" —her voice lowered and her eyes begged for understanding—"she said I was just one of your many conquests. I—I thought it might be true."

"Conquest?" Philippe's echoing cry carried a note of disbelief. "Is that all you thought you were to me? It's true I have known other women, but, Veronique, I thought you recognized the special spark between us. It was there from the beginning." He smiled. "A little contrary at times, but there, all the same." He became serious again. "Veronique, once I got to know you, I knew there could be no other woman for me again."

278

Roni took a deep breath. Her heart wanted to sing for joy. But the answer to her next question could destroy everything. Still, she had to ask it. She had to. "Philippe," she began hesitantly, "what about the woman I saw you with at the restaurant in Nice? You seemed very absorbed in her." She winced at the boldness of the question— but she had to know.

Philippe looked surprised. "But that was Jeanne," he replied, as if the name should mean something to her.

"Jeanne? Who is she?"

"You mean I haven't told you about Jeanne Van de Maele? She's the detective I hired to try and find the link to the perfume thefts. And by the way, she's the one who got the police out to the lake this morning. I stopped in to see her after you told me about that conversation you overheard between Alain and Marie-Catherine."

Roni looked dazed. "A detective . . . ?" she murmured, trying to make sense out of the words.

Philippe chuckled. "I admit she doesn't exactly fit the image. But as it happens, she's a damned good one. She suspected Marie-Catherine almost from the beginning. As our product model, she had advance knowledge of our new perfumes—and the packaging, of course. But until I told her you'd seen Marie-Catherine with Alain, Jeanne couldn't figure out how she got her hands on the formulas."

"Of course. Alain is your chief chemist." Roni looked at him wonderingly. "So your evening with Jeanne was a business dinner?"

"Yes, my darling Veronique, that's all it was.

But while we're on the subject of that dinner
. . ." His eyes narrowed. "Who was that strapping
fellow *you* were with last night? You looked as if
you were ready to let him make love to you right
there on the dance floor."

Roni blushed furiously. "He—he's my ex-husband."

Philippe was silent as he grappled with this. The
scar at his temple began to throb. "So," he said
slowly, "he has come to take you back."

"Yes. I mean *no!*" Roni faced him desperately.
"He wanted to take me back, but I wouldn't hear
of it. I only agreed to go to the restaurant with him
because it was to be his last night in France. Then,
when I saw you there"—she looked at him guiltily
—"I was so jealous that I wanted to make you
jealous, too."

Philippe looked at her for a long moment. His
face had the look of a child who has been unfairly
punished but who has been given a cookie to com-
pensate for the injustice. "Well," he said, half dis-
mayed, half amused, "you certainly did that. I was
seriously considering slugging the guy." He smiled
at her. "I'm willing to forget, if you are. Now, can
we please kiss and make up?"

"There's just one more thing."

"Yes?" He was beginning to look impatient.

She hoped she wasn't pushing him too far. "It's
your . . . uh . . . temperament."

His eyebrows arched upward. "And just what is
wrong with my temperament?"

"I don't know. I find it so bewildering. Since our
first kiss in Nice you've been as changeable as . . .

280

as the sirocco. Warm and gentle one minute, angry and harsh the next."

He stood very still. "My love," he said softly, "don't you know fear when you see it?"

"Fear? What on earth were you afraid of?"

"Of you, my darling Veronique. I've never been so affected by a woman in all my life. From the first moment I met you, I was impossibly drawn to you. As I came to know you better, I realized you were the woman I'd dreamed of but never believed I'd find. Not only beautiful but honest and brave and incredibly strong. You're a miracle, Veronique."

"Then how could you have been afraid of me?" Her voice was a whisper. She was so choked with emotion that she could scarcely breathe.

"Because I knew that if I let my emotions go, I would be consumed by my love for you. And, shallow as it may seem, I'm not the sort of man who wishes to be consumed by anything—unless, perhaps, it's work. All my adult life, I've prided myself on being the kind of man who is in control of everything. But you! You have me at sixes and sevens. All those times I was harsh and angry with you, it was all a facade. To stifle my desire to make love to you. I'm not used to having a woman in my thoughts day and night," he finished simply. "I used to laugh at men who suffered from such a malady."

"And," Roni ventured softly, daring now to actually believe what she was hearing, "you've changed your mind."

"I was ready to change it that afternoon in the

281

guest house. It was so beautiful . . . But then, that night, when you rejected me . . ."

"I'm sorry!" Roni cried. "I'm so sorry."

"I was prepared to end it then and there," Philippe told her. "And when I saw you last night with your ex-husband, I told myself I was well rid of you. But today at the lake, when I realized how close I came to losing you, I knew I had to admit what I felt for you—whether or not my feelings were returned. Not admitting it wouldn't have made it any less real. Veronique"—he reached out and grasped her arms with his hands—"can you possibly understand any of this? And would you think I've gone completely mad if I ask you to marry me?"

"I—I don't know." His hands on her arms were burning her flesh. Tears of joy were forming in her eyes. And yet there was still one cloud hanging over this almost perfect moment. "Nicole," she breathed, afraid to break the spell but knowing she must clear everything up before she could give him an answer. "You say you've never been consumed by a woman before. What about your wife?"

"Ah, yes. Nicole." He dropped his hands and turned slightly away from her. "I suppose I do owe it to you to tell you about her. Let's sit down for a moment."

"Don't tell me if you don't want to. I just thought—"

"No, you're entitled to know. Nicole was a Tournier, a member of the great French publishing empire. She was born to wealth and privilege, just as I was. We knew each other as children, and we

282

were always invited to the same birthday parties, the same sporting and social events. This togetherness continued through our adolescence. We summered at the same resorts; we skied at the same places. For many years," he explained, "Nicole was just someone with whom I shared the same friends, the same privileged sort of life. But then one night we met at a cotillion, and I realized she wasn't just the little Tournier kid anymore. She was a charming and desirable young woman. I asked her to dance, and *she* began to look at *me* with new eyes. The chemistry was definitely there, and we soon became inseparable.

Roni listened quietly, intently. "Did," she asked him when he paused, "you love her very much?"

His eyes took on a faraway look. "Yes," he said after a moment. "She was very important to me. Although I'm not sure she knew *how* important. It was my pigheaded absorption with business that was responsible for her death."

"Philippe, I shouldn't have brought it up. I didn't mean to—"

But he was determined to go on. "Nicole thought I was working too hard and wanted me to take a vacation. I finally agreed to a skiing trip to Mont Blanc, mainly to get her off my back. We'd been there only two or three days when I received a telephone call regarding a business matter. It wasn't anything terribly important; it could have been settled over the telephone. But I blew it all out of proportion and insisted on coming back to Grasse. Nicole begged me not to, but when I couldn't be dissuaded, she insisted on coming with me." He sighed deeply, and the scar on his face seemed to take on a pinkish color. "A rather severe winter storm had kicked up, but of course I chose to ignore it. As we drove, the road became more and more treacherous; the ice was forming in solid patches. We were almost halfway down the mountain when a car coming from the opposite direction skidded out of control and came straight toward us. I reacted instantly and swerved to miss it—which I did. Unfortunately, I crashed my own car into a tree. I came away with only minor injuries, the scar on my face being one of them. Nicole was killed."

"Oh, Philippe, darling . . ." Roni rushed to him and threw her arms around him, wanting only to shut out the pain she knew he was feeling. "I'm so sorry I brought it up. Please don't think about it anymore."

He pulled her closer and kissed the top of her head. "I suppose Nicole's another reason I was afraid of loving you," he said hoarsely. "I know the accident couldn't have been helped, but I've always felt guilty about her death. I never wanted to put another woman in the dangerous position of being my wife. But I see it's no good," he went on before Roni could protest further. "I realized today that real love is so rare that anyone who doesn't grab it when he has the chance is a fool." He pulled back and looked into her clear blue eyes, now soft with tenderness, intently. "Veronique, I know you don't love me. But if you will just stay here the rest of the summer and give me a chance, I'll show you how good I can be for you."

The tears Roni had been holding back came rolling down her cheeks. "Oh, my darling, what makes you think I don't love you? I've loved you practically since the day we met. Only I wouldn't admit it to myself until the day we went to the Battle of Flowers. The day of the sirocco."

His eyes twinkled mischievously. "Then it wasn't the wind that caused you to abandon yourself to me that day?"

Roni smiled through her tears. "No, but it was a good excuse, don't you think?"

"Too good. You had me believing it."

Philippe reached for her again and kissed her deeply. She melted into his arms, knowing she would never feel the pain of his rejection again.

"Oh, Philippe, I love you . . ." she murmured as their lips parted, then met again. Her body was flooded with the joy of knowing that it belonged to him now and forever.

When he spoke again, his lips were at her ear. "There's no sirocco now," he whispered. "You'll have no excuse if you abandon yourself to me this time."

"Maybe," she began, laughing up at him, feeling more lighthearted than she'd felt since leaving home, "maybe we could arrange a honeymoon in India . . . during the monsoons."

"Sorry," Philippe said, scooping her up in his arms and starting determinedly toward the stairs. "You and I will just have to create our own turbulence. Beginning right now!"